For Bobbi:

I hope you will fin[d] sort of stuff I usually [a]m unable to recommend for ... positions at the Archives of Traditional Music. They insisted that the individual to be appointed have professional experience, experience as a graduate assistant was not sufficient. Finally, they appointed Marilyn Graf to the position and she has done very well. In any case, I think you fared better living in New York City. Eve has been gone for over seven long years. I am now ninety-seven.

With my hearty best wishes,

Unfortunately, I was not able to fully proofread this volume before it went to press. I therefore apologize in advance for any error you may encounter. GL.

AN *AFFAIR* WITH A *LADYBUG*

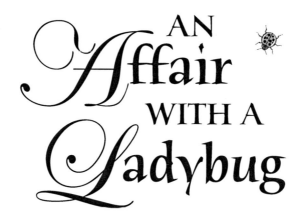

AN
Affair
WITH A
Ladybug

And Other Fiction

George List

AUTHOR HOUSE

AuthorHouse™
1663 Liberty Drive, Suite 200
Bloomington, IN 47403
www.authorhouse.com
Phone: 1-800-839-8640

First published by AuthorHouse 5/28/2008

ISBN: 978-1-4343-8826-1 (sc)

Printed in the United States of America
Bloomington, Indiana

This book is printed on acid-free paper.

In loving memory of

Eve Ehrlichman List,

WIFE,

COMRADE,

MUSICIAN,

MOTHER

AND

LIGHT OF MY LIFE

FOR SIXTY SEVEN YEARS.

CONTENTS

Acknowledgements

I acknowledge with much appreciation the contributions of Mary Blizzard to this book. She not only designed the front cover but the entire book as well. I am grateful to my regular reader, Victoria Witte, for her patience and reading some of the material presented in this book over and over again until I was satisfied with my rewriting of it. Thanks are also due to Christopher Hotard who prepared a preliminary version of this book, to Pauline Caldwell for taking the two photographs included in this book and to Patricia Burner who read some of the material in the book to me.

NOVELLA

An AFFAIR with a LADYBUG

It was 1961, a warm day in early June. A fitful breeze blew up from the valley below and caressed Laurie's bare legs. Luxuriating in its coolness, she lay back on her frayed blue blanket and looked up at the mist of green leaves that screened her from the hot June sun. The leaves were swirling, but even as she watched they stilled, and she both saw and felt that the tantalizing breeze had gone away.

Well, she thought, it would come back. It always had. She had discovered it on her first trip to the hilltop. A stubborn burr had stuck to the seat of her slacks and she had to take them off to remove it. It was then that she and the breeze became acquainted. No one else seemed to come up here but there was always the chance of a visitor. As she wasn't particularly anxious to be seen lying around in panties, since then she had brought a skirt and changed. She wondered why one could lie around in a bathing suit but not in panties. Just custom, she decided, but no more. The same reason you didn't wear a bathing suit to the prom.

It was so peaceful up here. No one ever bothered her. She often came up here mornings, particularly—though she never told him that—when she could no longer stand being under the same roof as her father. Oh, why did she have to have a distinguished English professor for a father? She admired him but she could hardly talk in front of him. Whatever she said, he thought it should be said differently.

"Laurie," he would say, "you have an excellent mind but you don't use it properly. You let your thoughts spill out at random, not in a meaningful sequence. Perhaps it would help if you considered yourself to be a journalist writing a news story." Then the old formula: "Give all the salient points in the first paragraph, and then elaborate each point in sequence."

Damn! He treated her as though she were still a Freshman in high school. He had forgotten that she had written for four years on the high school paper and, of course, he didn't know that she was writing like mad now. Not his kind of stuff, more in the line of stream of consciousness. Dr. Dupree liked her stuff, but she wouldn't dare show it to Daddy.

A bird shrilled above her and caught her attention. Like other birds, it repeated its call several times, but this one seemed to have several different calls. The first was a melodic arc, ascending and then descending. The second went from mid to low to high, like a check mark in the air. The third was a sort of buzzing noise, and the fourth a glorious cascade of various notes. This, Laurie knew, was a mockingbird. She listened to it sing for quite a while. As far as she could tell a particular sequence of calls was never repeated. Nice and random, she thought. No journalist, this bird. It was probably the way she would have done it had she been a mockingbird.

The cool breeze again blew up the hill. A slight gust raised Laurie's skirt and explored her thigh. It was very nice, she thought, having the breeze make love to her. It wouldn't try to make her; almost every man she had dated had wanted to. Actually, she liked the preliminaries but wasn't too sure about the main act.

"What you need," her friend Millicent had said, "is to find the right guy to break you in." Millie had been broken in when she was sixteen. She had been curious and had gone to a friend of the family, a bachelor in his thirties, and had asked him to show her how it was done. He had obliged, but had warned her that she wouldn't get much out of it the first time.

"Was he right?" Laurie had asked.

"Not really. I didn't get an orgasm or anything like that, but I sure enjoyed feeling him inside me and his bare body against me."

Laurie had thought that Josiah would be the right guy but what a disaster that had turned out to be. Jo had fought in Korea and after several years had come back to school. He wouldn't talk about the war, but there were lots of things that they did talk about, like the movie Ben Hur—which they both liked—and Uris' novel Exodus, which Jo liked immensely and she felt was overdone. Jo was really civilized. He played a reasonably good Chopin—but nothing like her mother's—and an equally good game of tennis. They took long walks together, visited museums, played Scrabble at the Union, and had drinks at his apartment. And, of course, there were the preliminaries.

She had really liked Jo, but she had waited too long to take the plunge. The day it was supposed to happen—it was Saturday and she didn't have to be back at the dorm until midnight—she woke to find that her period had come on several days early. There was nothing to do but to call Jo and explain why she couldn't come.

"I don't believe you," he had said. "It's an excuse, you're chicken."

"You expect me to come over and prove it to you?"

"Yes, I'll be waiting for you."

He was still waiting but it had taken her quite a while to get over that. But now there was Rod Dunham. She had met him last night at the Bartons' and it had been immediate, she wasn't quite sure why. Was it because his face was so interesting or because he talked with such ease and confidence? So had Josiah. Damn him! But Jo was twenty-seven and Rod couldn't be more than twenty-one. When Rod had asked her to go swimming this afternoon, she had been more than willing to agree.

Laurie suddenly felt a tickling sensation on her right thigh just above the knee. She sat up, pulled up her skirt, and crooked her leg to see what was there. It was a ladybug. She watched, fascinated, while the gaily colored, polka-dotted little hump slowly crawled up her thigh. At first she didn't know whether she liked the tickling sensation it produced or not. Finally she decided that she didn't and addressed it out loud according to tradition:

> "*Ladybug, ladybug, fly away home.*
> *Your house is on fire, your children are alone.*"

The polka dots paid her no heed but continued to move forward. By this time the tiny creature was reaching the edge of her panties. Far enough, she decided. She reached down and carefully picked up the ladybug between thumb and forefinger and, with equal care, placed it upon a leaf of a nearby bush.

"Fly away home," she repeated. But the tiny insect did not move. Perhaps it was a gentleman bug and felt no responsibility for its children. But it hadn't acted like a gentleman. If you're a male, she thought, I could almost say that I had an affair. He bug or she bug, she thought, it certainly didn't intend to go home. Perhaps it was time for her to go home. She checked her watch; it sure was. She had promised Mom to help with lunch and Rod was picking her up afterwards. She quickly changed back from skirt to slacks, shook out the blanket, and packed both in her knapsack. Shouldering the knapsack, she rapidly picked her way down the hill.

2

Margaret stirred a dollop of mayonnaise into the mixture in the bowl and said, "That's it, I think. Your father likes just a hint of mayonnaise. He really doesn't want to taste it."

"I don't like too much mayonnaise myself," Laurie said.

"I'm glad there's one thing the two of you do agree upon," Margaret said as she carried the bowl of salad to the kitchen table. "You must've had a nice morning on your hilltop; you seem to have had trouble carrying yourself away."

"Yes, I had an unusually interesting morning. A mockingbird gave a special concert just for me."

"Mockingbirds do sing beautifully, " her mother said as she returned to the kitchen counter.

"And," Laurie added, "I was nearly ravished by a ladybug."

"My, my! What un-ladylike behavior."

Laurie laughed, "Mom, you're a hard one to kid."

"Well, what did happen?"

"Not much. Somehow a ladybug began to crawl up my thigh. I caught it just before it went under my panties."

"You have the same sense of humor as your father. Why don't you share this with him? I'm sure he'd enjoy it."

Laurie hesitated before replying. "I don't know; he doesn't seem to like anything I say."

"That's because the two of you are so serious about disagreeing. Things would be a lot better around here if both of you would show a little good humor."

Then the teakettle began to sing and almost immediately Meryl Crowley appeared in the doorway. "Did I hear lunch music?"

"Your ears do not deceive you," answered his wife. She filled the mugs with hot tea while Laurie buttered the toast and placed the slices on a plate. They carried these to the table and joined Meryl.

"In this God-forsaken place the Times comes two days late," Meryl grumbled, placing his folded newspaper next to his plate.

"You really can't expect the same mail service at a country cottage as you do at a city apartment," Margaret commented.

"I suppose, but there's nothing left worth reading except the reviews and editorials."

"I thought you liked the Times' book reviews."

"I usually do, but today I find them rather dull and I don't know why."

"Mental indigestion," proposed his wife. "You've been working too hard on your book."

"Possibly."

While they were talking Laurie had been covertly examining her parents. She knew that everybody considered her father to be very handsome, and she supposed he was, but she thought of him as the 'tan man.' He had a tanned face, wore a tan shirt, and she knew he would be wearing tan trousers and shoes to match. Of course, his hair and eyes were brown, so it was really the 'brown and tan man.'

What a lovely contrast her mother made with her dark hair and dark blue eyes and the green slacks over which she wore a mannish shirt with pink and white stripes. And just like her to add a white, frilly apron to such an outfit. Suddenly Laurie realized that her father was addressing her.

"What's new on the hilltop?"

"Not too much. But I did hear my first mockingbird of the season."

"I would have enjoyed that. Any encounters with other local fauna?"

Laurie wavered, then made up her mind. "Why, yes, I had an affair with a ladybug."

Meryl raised his eyebrows. "So you engaged in a bit of bestiality?"

"Meryl!" "Daddy!" the women exclaimed simultaneously.

"Don't be so shocked, ladies," Meryl said, enjoying himself. "Bestiality is just the common term for sexual intercourse between humans and animals."

"Whatever it means," his wife said indignantly, "it's a horrid term to apply to your own daughter."

Damn! Laurie said to herself. So that's good humor? "I'm going swimming with Rod at his place. I've got to get my things together." She placed her napkin on the table and left the room.

Margaret watched her go and then turned to Meryl, "Did you have to do that? You hurt her."

"I don't see how. I was just expanding on Laurie's own idea. If she can joke about sex, why can't I? She ought to be amused, not hurt."

"If you two had better relations, she might have been amused but not with your criticizing almost everything she says."

"I don't think I'm being unnecessarily critical. I'm just trying to help the girl."

"Professors can be so stupid! But I don't want to discuss it further until she's gone."

Laurie appeared in the doorway. "Rod will be here in a moment. I'll wait outside." And she was gone.

Margaret called after her, "But you haven't finished your lunch."

Laurie's voice was heard from the distance, "I've had enough."

"You see," Margaret said to her husband, "she doesn't want to come back to the table."

"Perhaps engaging in bestiality impairs the appetite."

Margaret's voice rose, "For God's sake! Will you get off that track?"

For a few moments neither spoke. Meryl returned to his lunch. Margaret picked up Laurie's discarded napkin, smoothed it out, and folded it into smaller and smaller squares. For a time they ate in silence. Then Meryl spoke. "It was just a joking reference."

"I know it was meant that way, but you've been so critical of Laurie that she's hyper-sensitive to anything you say."

"Margaret, you may not realize it, but I'm very proud of our daughter; she's a very talented young woman. Rather than knocking her down, as you seem to think I'm doing, I'm trying to help her make maximum use of her potential. She's capable of expressing herself much better than she does. So I am endeavoring to assist her in organizing her thoughts so that her communication will be more lucid. I intend to help her in any way I can."

"Hell is paved with good intentions!" Margaret's voice was sharp with anger. "What you are accomplishing is nothing like what you intend." She shoved the little fat square of napkin she was holding underneath the edge of her plate and nearly overturned it. "Have you any idea how intimidating it is to have a distinguished professor as a father?"

"You don't seem to find me intimidating."

"I'm your wife, not your daughter. Laurie feels she's no match for you in argument and she'd rather be silent or leave. After all, you're her father. It's sort of a love-hate relationship."

"If she hates me, I certainly don't hate her."

"You really don't understand. Take, for example, that 'never, never' business you're always pulling on her."

"Why should such a capable girl continually say that she can never do this or never do that? Of course she'll be able to do it. She said that she'd never be accepted at Radcliffe. With her grade average there was never any question about her being admitted to Radcliffe. I knew she would be admitted, you must have known it, why didn't she?"

"When Laurie said that she wouldn't be accepted by Radcliffe, she didn't mean that she never would be admitted to Radcliffe."

"You mean that she didn't mean what she said?"

"Not exactly. Look at it this way: saying never is like taking out insurance.

Laurie was almost one hundred percent sure that she would be accepted. But if by some chance she wasn't, she had saved face and softened the pain of refusal by having said in advance that she wouldn't be. When she was accepted she could just forget what she had said before."

"That's pretty juvenile psychology."

"In your eyes, perhaps, but not in hers and, really, not in mine. I've used the never gambit most of my life, and many times since I married you."

"I've never noticed your saying it."

"And there you are, you have a negative focus on Laurie. But that's not all that worries me. I'm afraid you've soured her on other men."

"Soured her on other men? How in the world could I have done that?"

"You are the man in the family. You represent the gender to her. If her relationship with you is bad, it's not going to be easy for her to relate to other men."

"That seems a bit Freudian and quite improbable."

"Well," she sighed, "I don't suppose there's any use arguing with you." She rose. "But I do wish the two of you would get along together better."

Meryl helped her carry the lunch dishes to the counter next to the sink. "Would you like me to take care of the dishes?" he asked.

"Nice of you to ask, but there aren't very many. You go back to your newspaper."

Meryl went back to his chair but not to the Times. Instead he watched his wife at work. It was too bad, he thought, that the argument had lasted so long. She was sufficiently angry at the onset. Margaret took a half turn to place a dish in the dish rack and he gazed appreciatively at her profile. He was very fortunate to have such a beautiful wife. People were always commenting on her lovely facial features, her startling blue eyes, her high cheekbones, and her smooth, creamy skin.

Margaret turned back and his gaze dropped to her body. After twenty-three years of marriage he still had the vivid recollection of the first time he had seen her in the nude. Her figure was just as slim now as it was then. Nor was there any slackness of belly so often seen in women after childbirth.

He was reminded of a line in the Song of Solomon that had puzzled him for years: 'Thy belly is like unto a heap of wheat surrounded by lilies.' Did the ancient Hebrews find big bellies beautiful? The wheat could symbolize fertility and the lilies, due to their shape, vaginas. But a heap of fertility surrounded by vaginas? Perhaps the best explanation would be that the line contained double entendre whose hidden meaning had been lost through the ages.

He stopped his musings and, at a moment when his wife was facing the sink, walked up behind her and wound his arms around her.

"What do you want?" she asked.

"You."

"Oh, I'm busy. You'll have to wait."

"Naturally." He went back to his chair and picked up the Times.

Margaret smiled to herself; she had expected the tone of complaint in his voice. Drying her hands, she hung up her apron and walked over to him. Standing behind him she gently stroked his hair. "You never will learn to know when I'm teasing, will you, Meryl? You never have learned to play the game of love."

"You're right. I never know whether you're teasing or just putting me off."

"Never say never, Meryl. I only put you off when I have the curse."

He turned in his chair, tipped up his head, and carefully scanned her face. "That certainly has a double meaning."

"Of course. Did you think you had a monopoly on double entendres?" She came around and faced him. "But what about Laurie? Suppose she comes home early for some reason?"

"What if she does? Surely she knows that we continue doing what brought her into this world. Chaucer has a couple of relevant lines. I think they're from "The Wife of Bath." They go like this:

'If never a seed is sown,
how can virginity be grown?'

Margaret dropped into a chair next to him. "You assume that Laurie is still a virgin?"

"She often refuses to make full use of her head, so perhaps she's reluctant to make full use of her body."

"There you go again! But let's not argue. I don't know whether she's a virgin or not and I hardly expect her to discuss this with me. I wouldn't with my mother when I was nineteen and I certainly wasn't a virgin at that age."

"Mm. We first got together when you were twenty. I thought you were."

"And where did you get that idea?"

"Well, let's say... your approach to the union was a bit tentative."

"Did you expect me to rush right into it?"

"I've known women who did."

"Psychologically unsound. You'd soon grow tired of them."

"Perhaps."

"Oh, yes, you would. I never rushed into it and after twenty odd years you're still interested."

"That I am," her husband said. He dropped his paper on the table and pulled her up and pressed himself against her.

"My point exactly," she said.

"I thought it was mine but I'll be glad to share it with you." And they walked hand in hand through the little hall into their bedroom.

3

As Laurie walked out onto the Dunhams' dock, she felt the planks sink beneath her. She looked questioningly at Rod.

"It floats on air-filled steel drums. It's mostly muck here. It's a long way to solid bottom."

"It's a pity it's not out in the middle of the lake," Laurie said. "It's so short it would make a fine raft. Couldn't we cut it off at the shore and float it out?"

Rod smiled. "A nice idea but I don't think my mother would go for it."

Laurie sat on the edge of the dock and trailed her feet in the water. "It's a little cold," she said to Rod, who was sitting on the bench behind her.

"It's still early in the season. On a weekday like this there's hardly anybody around."

Laurie surveyed as much of the lake as she could see. There were no boats out and the only sign of life was a lone figure on a distant dock to her right.

Rod had followed the movement of her head. "That's old man Macintosh. He fishes from that dock almost every afternoon. I've never seen him in a boat."

Rod stood and gave Laurie a hand as she got to her feet. "I see you have been raised proper."

"Of course, I know just what to do."

Laurie wondered exactly what he meant by that. "You're carrying oars so I guess we'll swim from your boat."

"No, there's a cove on the other side of the lake with a bit of sandy beach. It's the best place for swimming. We'll row over there."

"Sounds good to me," said Laurie as she helped Rod secure the Dunhams' boat from the buoy to which it was attached.

They were soon out on the lake, Rod rowing and Laurie sitting on the back seat. It was a fine day. A blue, clear sky hung over a darker expanse of blue. In places the placid surface of the lake gleamed as though polished by the sun. All was burnished blue, relieved only by tiny flashes of light as the sun exploded the drops falling from the oars. The two in the boat were affected by the hushed blue calm around them. For a time they sat in silence, Rod rowing as quietly as possible. It was a good time for appraisal.

Rod gazed at the girl seated in front of him. The eyes looking back at him, only partly shaded by long lashes, were of a darker blue and, in this light, even more brilliant than the sun-drenched water upon which the boat floated. He knew that her hair, though now covered by a white bathing cap, was almost but not quite black and showed occasional reddish glints when shone upon. Her face, with its high cheek bones and firm chin, had only the tiniest of flaws. There was the slightest hint of a twist in her upper lip. At first he thought that she was regarding him with a touch of skepticism, or was it amusement? But the tiny twist was always there. It certainly made her face more interesting.

The dark blue bathing suit revealed the shapely contours of her shoulders and legs and accentuated the clarity and smoothness of her skin. The close fitting suit covered rather than hid the luscious curves of her breasts and hips. It was without a doubt, Rod thought, the 'body beautiful.' God! Wouldn't she be gorgeous in the nude?

Rod, in turn, had come under close scrutiny by Laurie. Why was she so attracted to him? Was it because he was so different from her father? Possibly, but in some ways they were alike. Rod had the same ease and confidence as the older man did. Also like her father, he had brown hair and brown eyes, but there the likeness ended. Rod did not have the regularity of features and form of her father. It was these, Laurie supposed, that made people consider her father so handsome.

Rod did have a well-knit, muscular body. But he was more, as she had thought the night before, roughhewn. The legs below the grayish blue trunks were too long in comparison with the short torso above them. He had squarish shoulders and there was something irregular about his face. At first she thought it was the hairline but then decided that one cheekbone was more prominent than the other.

But there was something about him that reached out to her and she found the general effect very pleasing. Rod was also handsome, but in a very different way.

The spell broke and they spoke casually about the friends they had in common and the professors with whom they had studied. "Do you know Millicent Graun?" Laurie asked.

"Of course," Rod said, smiling. Laurie decided to ask no further.

Rod had had a course with her father. "He's a terrific lecturer. Very fluent, I've never known him to be at a loss for a word."

Nor have I, thought Laurie. "Did he ever ask you to write a paper as though you were a journalist?"

"No, why should he have? I don't think anybody in the class planned to be a reporter."

Neither did she. Rod gathered that she was not too fond of her father. Neither was he so he dropped the subject.

Rod turned to check his course. They were nearing the beach. "It looks inviting," Laurie said. "But the shore doesn't curve in where the beach is. It's really not a cove."

"But you can see that the woods surround the beach and come down to the water line. It feels like a cove and everybody calls it one. You can see the whole lake from the beach."

As he turned back to his rowing he asked without a change of tone, "How about a swim in the raw? It's the nicest way to swim. You feel completely free in the water."

Smoothly done, as though it was the natural thing to do on one's first date. She had swum in the nude before with her mother and other girls and she had enjoyed it. "I've never done it before with a boy... with a young man."

"Nothing to worry about. It will be hands off."

Laurie looked back at an empty lake. "I don't suppose anyone can see us?"

"Hardly. There are thick woods back of the beach and no one comes here except by boat. If anyone was coming we could see them before they reached the middle of the lake."

"OK. But remember, hands off."

"I've already promised."

Laurie quickly removed her bathing suit, dropped it on her seat, and slid into the water. Rod continued rowing until he had beached the boat. He left the oars in their locks with their blades inside the boat. Then he removed his trunks, dropped them in the boat, and swam out to join Laurie.

They circled, testing each other's capacity as a swimmer. She's good, thought Rod. "Bet you can't catch me."

He was off with Laurie following quickly in his wake. Then he was gone. When he came up where he expected her to be, ready to splash water into her face, she wasn't there. Then water was splashed into his face by the white cap that came up next to him.

"You're it." Then they were off again, he following her.

"I'm tired," said Laurie after a furious fifteen minutes. "I'm going to float."

"Likewise," Rod said and they both floated companionably on their backs.

Laurie closed her eyes and relaxed, enjoying the coolness of the water and the touch of the hot sun on her breasts. Then there was a bump as something passed under her. At once she turned over and made for the beach.

Rod bobbed up in front of her with hands held high. "Look, Mom, no hands."

"You touched me."

"Not with my hands. It was back to back."

It was more butt to butt, Laurie thought. "I'm going in." And she swam to the boat.

By the time she picked up her suit, Rod had reached the beach. "Don't put on that dry suit while you're still wet. Come and lie in the sun until you dry off."

Logical, Laurie thought and looked back at the lake. Not a boat was in sight. She looked at Rod. He was already stretched out on the sand with his feet toward the lake. She pulled off her bathing cap and patted her moist hair into place. Again she looked back at the lake. It was still very empty. She dropped cap and suit into the boat and walked over and lay down beside Rod, clasping her hands behind her head and closing her eyes. The sun felt good.

For a while they lay in silence, soaking up the sun. Then Rod rolled to face Laurie and propped himself up on an elbow in order to get a better view. She heard the rustling of the sand and then his voice: "The 'body beautiful.' Absolutely gorgeous!"

Laurie reddened but did not open her eyes.

"Let's not waste it all on the sun. There are things I can do that the sun can't."

"Sorry, not interested."

"With you it would be out of this world," Rod urged.

She suddenly knew that she had meant it; she wasn't interested. Not on a public beach in the bright sunlight. Amazed, she heard herself say, "Thank you, but I've had my sex for the day."

"You what? With who?" he blurted out.

And again, "With a ladybug."

"With a ladybug?"

"Yes, you know, order hymenoptera."

Rod's face flushed with anger. She goes this far and then hands me this incredible line. "So I'm second best to a ladybug." He reached over and with two fingers tweaked her nearest nipple. "Can a ladybug do that?"

In a second Laurie was upright. With the side of her outstretched right hand she chopped viciously at Rod's wrist.

"Christ!" he rolled back and nursed his wrist.

Laurie ran to the boat and hurriedly put on her suit. As she was sliding her shoulder straps on, she heard her name called. She looked around. Rod had risen and was posing with his side toward her, head up and feet well planted. He stood with shoulders back, breast out, and belly in. His penis was rigidly erect. "What's wrong with this?"

Laurie did not reply. She jumped out of the boat, pushed it into the water, and turned it around so that the prow faced the lake. Then she got back in, seized the oars, and began to row away. Rod heard the splashing and turned his head but kept his pose. She couldn't row as fast as he could swim. Then something in the corner of his eye caught his attention. He turned full toward the lake. There was a boat out there and it was coming their way. "Hey! You've got my trunks."

Laurie seemed not to hear. She was rowing hard and methodically, making every dip count. The gap between boat and shore was widening rapidly. Rod waded into the water and flung himself into his fastest crawl. When he finally reached up and grasped the back of the boat he was gasping for breath. Laurie was also breathing hard. She stopped rowing and feathered the oars.

Rod hoisted himself up and sat dripping on the back seat. "Quick! Hand me my trunks. There's a boat coming."

Laurie looked at him but said nothing.

"My trunks! They're right behind you." Without taking her eyes off him Laurie fished behind her for the trunks and threw them at him. He caught them, hurriedly put them on, and then looked for the boat. Damn it to hell! It wasn't coming their way. He glowered at Laurie. "That was a dirty trick." He rose menacingly.

Laurie heaved hard on the oars, pulling one and pushing the other. The boat swerved abruptly and Rod nearly lost his balance. He stooped, grasped the swaying sides of the boat, and eased himself back into the seat. They sat glaring at each other like two cats ready to spring.

Rod was the first to soften. He smiled and then his smile turned into a chuckle. Laurie frowned at him.

"Hymenoptera," he explained. "I know it sounds appropriate but the ladybug is a beetle, that's order coleoptera. Hymenoptera are bees. I hope you didn't get stung."

Laurie fixed her eyes on her feet. "Look," Rod said, "I'm sorry I broke my promise. I didn't mean to. But when you go that far and then slam the window down it's a bit frustrating."

Laurie spoke without looking up. "I'm sorry, too. I didn't mean to hit you or to run off with your boat. It just happened."

"Alright, we're even. Let's just forget it happened."

Laurie's face came up lit with its delicately twisted smile. "I'll be glad to forget that it happened."

Rod smiled at her. "At least we had a nice swim."

"A very nice swim," Laurie agreed. Her smile became impish. "The nicest swim I've ever had in the raw."

4

The room that Margaret and Meryl entered was not very large and had only a single rather high window. There was an attached bath, but it only had a shower and Margaret missed her luxurious city tub soaks. "It can hardly be called a master bedroom," she had commented on first viewing the room. "But I suppose you can't expect more from a summer cottage. I'll just have to do the best I can."

There was room for a double bed and she had had it placed near a corner with its back against the left wall. It was flanked by twin maple night tables, each surmounted by lamps with light blue ceramic bases topped by gold colored parchment shades. The bedspread was of a darker blue of a textured fabric shot with threads of gold. Margaret, who had sewn both, had used the same textured material to make the drapes that framed the window that pierced the right side of the outer wall. To the right as one entered, past the adjacent doors of closet and bath, a straight chair of limed oak stood against the wall. To the left of the window was Margaret's dresser and bench and against the adjacent wall Meryl's highboy, all of maple. The seats of the chair and bench were covered with gold colored cloth, the scarf above the highboy with gold cloth bordered with blue. Above on the left wall, Margaret had hung a colored reproduction of a painting by Picasso, one of his blue period, and above the straight chair one of a sunflower by van Gogh. Beneath all this stretched a velvety smooth carpet patterned in several shades of blue. Margaret was proud of the results she had achieved, a cool room but its coolness relieved by bright spots.

Seated on her bench, Margaret began to undress. "Do you know the origin of the term 'missionary position?'"

"I can't say I do," answered her husband from the straight chair where he was also removing his clothes.

"According to an article I've been reading, it came from the South Seas. It seems that the natives there always did it with the women on top. They were amazed to find that the missionaries did it the opposite way, so they called it the 'missionary position.'"

"I understand that some women object to this position. With the man on top and the woman below with her legs spread, they consider it the subjugation of their sex. How do you feel about it?"

"I've never thought about it before," replied Margaret at the closet as she hung up her clothes and extracted her wrapper. "I suppose it can be interpreted that way but I've never objected to doing it in that position."

"Nor have I ever raised any objection to your being on top of me."

"Why should you? Then I do most of the work."

Later, resting from their exertions, they lay uncovered side by side on the bed. Meryl found his desire rising again. He sat up and turned to his wife and with expert fingers caressed her breast with one hand and gently rubbed her belly with the other.

Margaret lay perfectly still with her eyes closed. "Mm, that's very nice," she murmured.

Meryl leaned one ear to her throat. "You're not purring." He withdrew his hand and got off the bed.

"I can't purr in the afternoon, darling. I'm always afraid the doorbell will ring. I'd be embarrassed to go to the door only in my wrapper."

"We all have our hang-ups."

"But I did enjoy it."

"I gather you're not in the mood for seconds?"

"Sorry, darling."

"Then tonight?"

"If I'm in the right mood. You know it always depends upon my mood."

"I know," he said as he went back to the chair where he had left his clothes.

Margaret got off the bed and picked up her wrapper, which had been lying on the bench. "Meryl, you didn't really believe that I was a virgin back then?"

"Of course not, honey. Just a bit of teasing on my part. But by the way, what actually happened between Laurie and the ladybug?"

Now enveloped in her wrapper, she told him. "That's all there is to that affair."

Meryl had begun to dress. One sock was on and he was holding the other one in his hand. After a moment or two he put the sock on and started to leave the room wearing only underwear and socks.

"Where are you going?" his wife asked. "You're not dressed yet."

"I'll be back in ten minutes."

He returned in less time than promised but found no one else in the room. "Margaret," he called.

"I'm in the bathroom, darling. I'll be out in a jiffy."

Meryl placed the piece of paper he was carrying on the bench and returned to his dressing.

The bathroom door opened and Margaret came halfway out, towel in hand. "What is it?"

"You're always in the bathroom when I want you."

Margaret came all the way out of the bathroom and slammed the door behind her with a bang. "And you're always in the bathroom when I want you." She shrugged. "But I'm resigned to it. It's fate, why fight it?" She returned the towel to the bathroom and coming out asked, "Well, what do you want?"

Meryl had only one leg of his trousers on. "Just a minute, honey. I'm almost dressed."

"I thought it was the husband who always waited for the wife to finish dressing."

"Alright, you can read it now if you wish. It's on the bench."

"What is it?" she asked as she picked up the piece of paper.

"Something I just wrote."

She moved closer to the window and began to read what he had typed:

Ladybug, ladybug, come and lie with me.
Both virginal and vaginal your love must surely be.

Deliciously delectable thy titillation,
Erotica exotica but minus copulation.

My God! she thought. Is it going to start all over again? She gazed out of the window, focusing on the familiar and comforting beauty of a lone nearby tree, its branches spreading near the window, its leaves quiescent but ready at the slightest breeze to quiver forth their palate of greens.

"What do you think of it?" her husband asked from behind her.

She turned and regarded him for a moment and then chose her words with care. "I would say that it is a reasonably good example of this genre, especially as far as alliteration is concerned. Obviously, it's a development of Laurie's little joke about the ladybug."

"Precisely. And thank you for the 'reasonably good.' I've never done much in light verse. It's hardly a theme for a sonnet and it certainly wouldn't be effective in free verse."

"Granted," Margaret said, now seated on the bench. "But what impelled you to write it?"

Meryl got up, swung his chair around and seated himself facing its back, his arms resting on it. "I should like Laurie to know that I appreciate her sense of humor and fantasy. I thought I could indicate this by developing her little idea further."

"You intend it as a compliment? And you suppose that it would amuse her?"

"That was my idea. But when I remembered how my little joke had upset you and Laurie at lunch, I thought I had better show it to you first. Do you find anything objectionable in the piece?"

"I'm certainly glad you showed it to me first. At least you know there's a problem, although you don't understand it."

Meryl leaned back in his chair, placing his hands on its back. "You haven't answered my question."

Margaret carefully aligned the side of a box of tissues with the edge of the night table upon which it lay. "Very well. I don't personally find anything objectionable in these lines. In fact, they're fairly amusing. Nor, had we been alone, would I have found the term 'bestiality' particularly offensive. I know about the shepherds lying in the fields with their sheep and I, too, have read The Golden Ass."

"Then why in the world did you react so violently?"

"In defense of Laurie. Call it empathy, if you wish. There was an implied criticism of Laurie and you used a term that most people would find quite objectionable. So I reacted as I thought she would, as she did."

"All she did was to say that she was going swimming with Rod and leave the table."

"Without finishing her lunch. Isn't that enough?"

Meryl stood up and slung the chair from under him. "I'm not fully convinced. Are you sure you're not being overly protective? After all, this is a fairly sophisticated household and Laurie has long passed puberty. Why should my little joke be interpreted as criticism? It wasn't meant that way."

Margaret also rose. "What difference does it make how you meant it? Or how you mean this?" She angrily brandished the piece of paper in the air and then began to pace towards the bed. "She's not going to take it as a compliment. Since you've hardly given her anything but criticism she can't help but react to this the same way. It will be her superior father satirizing her foolish little idea."

"You're never more beautiful than when you're angry," her husband said unexpectedly.

Margaret whirled and faced him. He was smiling. "What's going on?" she asked.

He went to her and held out his hand. "Can I have my verses, please?"

She moved to him and gave him the sheet of paper. He tore it into four pieces, crumpled it into a ball, and deposited it in a wastepaper basket.

"Why did you do that?"

"You wouldn't want Laurie to read it, would you?"

"No, I wouldn't. But what's this all about? Have you been putting me on?"

Meryl laughed. "What a language. You put me off and I put you on." Again he did the unexpected. He came to her and put his arm around her as though to lead her to the bed. "By any chance are you in the mood for seconds?"

Margaret pushed him away. "Meryl, what's this all about?"

"Just what I said, are you in the mood for seconds?" And he took both of her hands in his.

"Wait a moment!" She pulled her hands away. "When it comes to sex, you males are sure persistent. I may be in the mood for seconds and I may not. But you're not going to find out until you tell me what this is all about."

"I'm afraid I haven't handled this very well," Meryl said, going back a step.

"Certainly not the handling," Margaret said and moved back and sat on the bed. "Now, professor, explicate and be brief."

"I suppose you deserve an explanation but I don't think you'll like it. I hope it won't irretrievably damage our marriage."

"Oh?"

"To be brief, I had observed for some time that when you become angry your level of sexuality is raised; you are aroused or are more easily aroused. Your anger seems to act upon you like an aphrodisiac. So I concocted a little plot that I was sure would make you angry, hoping to put you in the mood for seconds."

During this explanation emotions warred for expression on Margaret's face, astonishment, incredulity, and finally, amusement. "And I said you knew nothing about the game of love? Why, you've even developed a new wrinkle."

"I'm glad you're taking it that way. I was afraid you would accuse me of manipulating you."

"And I never manipulate you? Husbands and wives are always manipulating each other. It's one of the joys of marriage. But I don't find the connection you're making too plausible. Certainly every time I lose my temper we don't end up in bed."

"No, sometimes circumstances prevent it. But I'm sure that the cause and effect relationship is there. I've seen one follow the other many times. Take today, for example. You usually won't go to bed with me in the afternoon. But today we had an argument at lunch, you became angry, and we did end up in bed. If I wasn't sure of the connection I wouldn't have bothered to ask you."

"But I'm already dressed. Why couldn't you have put on your little act at bedtime?"

"Because you don't like us to argue when Laurie can hear us."

"You've got me there. But there's one drawback to the whole business. I love to argue. If I really let myself go we'd spend half our life in bed."

"A pleasant prospect," her husband said.

"But you'll never finish your book."

"First things first," he said, advancing towards her.

She halted him with a gesture. "Dear poet and plotter, I have a question." She gave him her most mischievous smile.

"Yes?"

"You write that the love of a ladybug is both virginal and vaginal. This has a nice sound but what does it mean?"

"I haven't the slightest idea," her husband answered. "I've never had an affair with a ladybug." He leaned down and kissed her.

5

Lee Dunham placed a dish she had just washed in the dish rack and wondered if history was repeating itself. What was apparently happening between Rod and Laurie might be a repeat of what had happened between Trevor and Margaret. Of course, this was before she had met Trevor and she had never met Margaret. But she had married Trevor and had been his wife for seven years before divorcing him and he had never made any secrets of his past or present affairs. Like father like son, she thought, but not completely so. Both Rod and Trevor had that peculiar thing, call it male charisma, which attracted women to them. It was this which had drawn her to Trevor although she had never completely understood it. Rod, now twenty-one, had had more than his share of women. Not that she had any particular objection to this; nor during the first few years of their marriage had she objected to Trevor having other women. After all, she had known something about his character before she married him. What brought her to divorce was the growing incontrovertible evidence that Trevor could only use women, he couldn't love them.

The evidence was not all personal. She had become friends with some of Trevor's other women and he had been discussed very candidly. He was so urbane, so sophisticated, so charming that it took a long time to realize that he wasn't the least bit interested in you. His charm persisted even after you had been in bed with him the first time. He must have had some stressful experience during the day that keyed him up sexually but also tired him. What else could explain his behavior, his almost immediate penetration and equally immediate withdrawal? After ejaculation and then after a few crude words of praise, nothing but his back and sleep. At times he made a few gestures at foreplay and whoever was in bed with him the first time was sure that the circumstances were special, that the next time her needs would be taken into consideration, she would be fulfilled and feel loved. It took weeks for some women to learn what he was like and then to avoid him. Some, however, so enjoyed his urbanity and sophistication, his elegance and his exquisitely designed flattery that they were glad to pay for this with a short and arid sojourn in his bed.

Lee wasn't. But almost immediately she had become pregnant. If it hadn't been for Rod she would have spent few of those long seven years with him.

She had always been afraid that Rod would take after his father. From an early age she had trained him to show not only surface courtesy to all but the deeper courtesy of respect for the feelings and needs of others, especially for those of any woman with whom he might have relations. She had thought that he did until Katy called her this morning. Why did she still call her Katy? She had been Sister Domenica these many years. But Rod was Trevor's son and Laurie was Margaret's daughter. Trevor had told her that Margaret had returned to him after the divorce but she had thought that he was merely boasting. By that time Margaret was married to Meryl Crowley and from what she had heard about them, and as a marriage counselor she was likely to hear more than most, the Crowleys seemed to have a very happy and stable marriage. But the parallel between Trevor and Margaret and Rod and Laurie was still there. It worried her. Of course, not all of Rod's genes came from his father nor all of Laurie's from her mother. You couldn't say that the two cases were exactly parallel. They were only half parallel. She was amused at herself, how could anything be half parallel? Her thoughts turned to her father, as they often did when she was low or worried. How she had loved him, Jacob the Talmudist. Wouldn't he have fun with an anomaly like half parallel? "Leah," she could hear him say, "Leah, a half parallel there can't be. What's a half parallel? Nu, I'll tell you: a half cork in a bottle, it don't keep wine. What's a half parallel? Nu, I'll tell you: a half bath, there's no bath. What's a half parallel? You tell me: a single straight line? A single railroad track? Leah, Leah, use your head. A half parallel there can't be."

Fantasizing about her father always made her feel better. Having finished the dishes, she made her way to the living room. It was an old cottage and the floors were of hardwood, now highly polished. The only floor covering was a large oval rug braided in beige, green, and blue. The furniture was sparse, consisting mainly of a sofa, a settee, and a chair. The upholstery of the sofa was forest green, that of the settee a deep brown, and the mahogany Chippendale chair boasted a seat of ultramarine. The only slightly incongruous aspects were the glass tops of the side table next to the sofa and the low and longer table that fronted it.

The most striking object in the room was a majestic full-grown male Siamese cat ensconced on the mantelpiece of the white brick fireplace, his beige fur blending to dark brown at his head, at the lower part of his legs, and at his back near his tail. Although obviously unintended, his beige and brown body together with his sapphire blue eyes almost perfectly matched the general decor of the room. Unfortunately, his majesty was soon dispelled by the oblique stare of his crossed eyes and by his rudimentary crooked tail, a tail that justified his plebeian appellation as Hookie.

As Lee entered the room Hookie jumped from the mantelpiece and sprang upon the chair, rolling over and exposing his belly. Lee ignored him and went to the window from which she could see the cottage's graveled driveway. There was no sign of Rod returning after taking Laurie home. Lee absent-mindedly gave the cat a few belly rubs and without waiting to hear if he was purring, took a seat at the end of the sofa. Hookie turned over, twice circled the seat of the chair, and deciding he was comfortable, curled up to snooze.

Almost immediately Lee heard the sound of tires crunching on gravel and soon Rod was in the room. Lee glanced at him affectionately and thought, as she often did, that his only real resemblance to his father was his tallness. His hair and eyes were a lighter brown and in his angularity of form he resembled neither Trevor, herself, nor even Jacob, but some more remote ancestor.

"Laurie enjoyed talking with you very much," Rod said. "She asked me to thank you again for the privilege of changing clothes here and for inviting her for dinner. She thought your blintzes were terrific."

"That's nice of her. I guess the blintzes are just about what is left of my Jewishness." She sensed the excitement bubbling up in Rod and was not surprised to hear:

"Isn't Laurie wonderful, Mama? She's the most attractive girl I've ever met."

"You say that every time," Lee teased. "You said Clarissa was the most attractive girl you'd ever met, and before that you said the same thing about Beth, and before that about Susan."

Rod flashed his best smile at his mother. "You're almost right, but not quite. I still find Clarissa more attractive than Beth but Laurie so tops both of them that I doubt if anybody could match her. Beth, that's another story. She wasn't necessarily more attractive than Susan but she had her own special quality, a sort of motherliness that I especially liked."

"I'm glad to know that you're interested in other than girls' physical attributes."

"Go on, Mama, you've always known that. Take Laurie, for example. She can talk both sense and nonsense and sometimes she mixes them together in interesting ways. Last night at the Bartons' dance there were more boys than girls. Laurie said she felt sorry for the less popular boys. They wouldn't get much chance to dance. She said they ought to run dances like Noah's Ark, just let them in two by two. And on the way to her house she said that she had seen a litter of newborn Siamese kittens and they were all dirty white except for a smudge on the nose, on the toes, and on the back near the tail. She thought that Hookie must have baked for a long time in a slow oven to achieve his present coloration.

"I've never known another girl who talked like that. She not only has her own brand of humor, but she's beautiful, bright, spunky, can swim like a fish, and rows better than any girl I've ever known. How's that for a varied set of attributes?"

"Very special indeed," his mother agreed. "I also like her very much." Then her voice hardened. "So I want to make sure that you don't hurt her."

Rod was bewildered. His mother had rarely spoken to him in that tone before. "Why should I want to hurt her?"

"Sit down, Rod. I have something serious to discuss with you."

Rod went toward the chair since it was closer to the sofa than the settee. The cat issued a low warning. "Pipe down, Hookie. Since when have I sat on you?" He picked up the cat, placed it on the settee, and took its place.

Lee came to the point without preamble: "Did you know that Clarissa had an abortion?"

Rod's face darkened but he answered without hesitation. "I knew she was going to have one."

"Why didn't you tell me about it?"

"Why should I? I'm twenty-one now and I can manage my own affairs. But the real reason, I suppose, is that I didn't want to worry you."

"I'm your mother. If you're responsible for making a girl pregnant I want to know about it."

Rod's shoulders raised. "How do you know I'm responsible? As far as that's concerned, how did you know she had an abortion?"

Lee straightened up and firmly grasped the arm of the sofa next to her. "Sister Domenica called me this morning. It's known in the Parish that Clarissa had an abortion and it is said that you were the party involved."

A warm flush suffused Rod's face. "It is said! Since when does your Sister Domenica repeat gossip?"

"She usually doesn't. But she is my best and oldest friend. In this case she felt it was something that I ought to know."

"She probably got it from the priest to whom Clarissa confessed."

"I doubt it, that would be a great breach of faith. Things like this have a habit of getting around."

"Also," Rod said with some heat, "things which aren't necessarily true, such as my being the responsible party."

"Aren't you?"

Rod shifted in his chair. "Damn it! I don't really know. I may be and I may not be. It's complicated. Have patience and I'll try to make it as clear as I can."

"Very well, I'm listening," his mother said.

"I don't suppose I ever told you about it in so many words," he said rising, "but I have worked out a particular mode of behavior in my relationships with women." Emphasizing his explanation with gestures, he strode back and forth from chair to doorway, Lee's head following his movements. "In a way, I consider myself monogamous, that is, once I have sex with a girl I never date or sleep with anyone else until one of us calls it quits or we separate by mutual consent. I don't play around, I have one woman at a time, no more. If I have an affair I expect my partner to act exactly in the same manner. I tell her so in advance, she'll be my woman and I'll be her man as long as the affair lasts. And there'll be no one else on either side. Most girls agree, some don't. However much I like them, I don't touch girls after I find out they don't agree."

Interrupting him in mid stride, Lee asked, "What's this all got to do with Clarissa's abortion?"

Rod stopped and addressed his mother directly. "You'll see. I told you to have patience, that it would take a while to explain."

"Well, get to the point. Are you or are you not responsible for Clarissa's pregnancy?"

Still facing his mother Rod continued: "I had that kind of an agreement with Clarissa but she didn't keep it. I found out she was playing around with another guy as well and I quit seeing her. It was just after that that she stopped having her menstrual period."

"And how did you know that?"

"From the horse's mouth." And he continued his pacing. "After I hadn't seen her for about six weeks, Clarissa called me and told me what had happened, that she was going to have to have an abortion. She was pretty upset about it and so was I because I knew she was a Catholic and Catholic women are not supposed to have abortions. We went over things and she was pretty candid about it. She had been in bed with this other fellow two days after I had had sex with her and there was just no way of deciding who was responsible. I told her I had some money in the bank, most of which I'd earned myself, and I would consider myself half responsible and pay half the cost of the abortion."

His mother stopped him again. "No one can be half responsible for a pregnancy." Another anomaly for Jacob, she thought parenthetically. "You must not have handled the contraceptive situation properly or you wouldn't even have considered yourself half responsible."

Rod resumed his chair. "Now, Mama, it really wasn't my fault. You've always said it was the man's responsibility to see that birth control was in place and I agree with you. I always ask the girl first if she's using a diaphragm."

Lee again interrupted. "You mean a pessary?"

"That's the fancy name for it. Most girls don't know it; they call it the diaphragm. As I was saying, if she isn't, I use a condom. I certainly don't want her to become pregnant. Susan is also a Catholic. When I asked her whether she was using a diaphragm, she said she was so I assumed Catholics use them. When I asked Clarissa, she said she had taken care of it so I assumed she was using a diaphragm. When she told me she was pregnant I asked her what type of birth control she had used and she said, `The rhythm method.' `My God!' I told her. `That's hardly reliable.' `So I found out,' she said. Good God! If I ever sleep again with a Catholic girl I'm going to wear a condom no matter what."

Lee had listened to this with some patience. "You probably should. But I happen to know that many Catholic women use a pessary."

"It's a peculiar business," Rod said miserably. "I don't know whether I was at fault or not or if I'm responsible or not. All I can do is to be more careful next time."

"You'd better be. I think Laurie likes you and I suppose the two of you will get together. I have a very special reason for not wanting Laurie to be hurt. I may tell you about it someday, but not now." She rose. "I'm deadly serious about it. If you make Laurie pregnant I'll probably disown you."

Rod also stood up. "That really is serious, but that can't happen right away. She's already having an affair."

"Really, with whom?"

"With a ladybug." And he described what had happened that afternoon.

Lee laughed. "She really gave you a time of it. Quite a girl, Laurie. But what were you going to do about a contraceptive?"

"Oh, that. I had a package of condoms hidden under the back seat of the boat. But if Laurie doesn't leave the ladybug and come over to my side pretty soon I'll just about burst."

"You've got it that bad??" his mother asked.

"Almost." They were both calm now and Rod thought again how wonderful his mother was. You could discuss almost anything with her. And once again he examined her familiar face and form. At forty-two she still had a good figure that was very much erect. At times he thought of her as Rachel coming from the well, carrying a jug of water on her head. More often he thought of her as a queen, probably because of the golden brown braids that circled her head and made him think of a crown. Her eyes were a grayish green and her mouth full lipped. Below them was a determined chin. She was a highly successful professional woman and it showed.

But he thought she was too much alone. Unless he was back home from college she was always by herself, she rarely had a guest. Her main companion was Hookie. The Siamese cat was pretty good company, even Rod would admit, but he was hardly a substitute for a man.

"So why are you looking at me so?" Rod knew she was paraphrasing her father, the only man she apparently had really loved. But he was dead.

As they stood facing each other, Rod asked for the nth time: "Why don't you get married again, mama?"

"We've been over that before," his mother answered. "A second failed marriage and my credibility as a marriage counselor would be nil."

"But why do you have to assume that it would fail?"

"More and more marriages are failing now. I don't want to take the risk."

"OK, then. Just find the right man and have an affair."

"It would get around, and after it broke up it would have the same effect."

Rod was tempted to ask his mother whether she really wanted a man or not, but it wasn't the kind of question you could ask your mother. Maybe for some women having sex with a man was a habit they could kick like that of smoking. At twenty-one he realized there were still some things he didn't know. "At least you have Hookie."

"Yes, he's a very good companion. It's fascinating to watch the wheels go around in his little head and to watch the stratagems he employs to get around me."

"And he does get around you."

"If he didn't at least part of the time, the wheels would stop turning and what would I do then?"

"I guess you'd have to turn him in. Well, I'm going out and sit on the dock for a while. That will be just the atmosphere for some heavy thinking."

"It's still chilly these days out by the water," his mother cautioned. "Take a sweater." She picked up Hookie, who complained about being torn from his nap. "Stop it, stupid. You can sleep on my lap while I'm reading." She settled back in the sofa and took a magazine from the end table.

Rod appeared in the doorway, called to his mother to gain her attention, and then waved his sweater. She waved back in approbation and he left.

6

With her hand Laurie brushed crumbs from their picnic lunch off the blanket on which they were sitting and said, "I don't mind leaving a few crumbs for the insects."

"Food for your ladybug?" Rod asked. Laurie reddened slightly and averted her face. After a moment Rod said, "You're an original."

"What does that mean?" Laurie asked, still looking away.

"You know what it means. We're lying next to each other on a beach in the nude and naturally I suggest we get together and what do you say but, 'Thank you, Sir. I've had my sex for the day.'"

Laurie turned to face him. "I didn't say, 'Sir.'"

"No, I guess you didn't."

"And you asked, 'With who?' That was both impertinent and bad grammar."

"There goes the professor's daughter. And what did you answer?"

"You know what I answered."

"Yes, but would you care to offer a few more details?"

"When I know you better."

"And when will that be?"

Laurie ignored his question and looked down into the wooded valley below. At its bottom trees had been felled and a broad meadow formed. "Rod," she said excitedly, "there's a cow down there."

Rod followed her gaze. "So there is. What's so unusual about a cow in a meadow?"

"It's the first cow I've seen in my meadow."

"Your meadow?"

"Might as well be, the many times I've watched it."

Rod examined the cow critically. It was reclining with its body on the ground as cows do when resting or chewing their cud. It was sitting on its folded legs, the greater part of which could be seen under its sides and it seemed to be resting on its knees. "A rather Japanese-like posture," Rod observed.

Laurie was intrigued. "Why Japanese?"

"Well, geishas kneel like that while making a ceremonial bow."

"Oh, but cows kneel on four legs, going geishas two better."

"Yes, I suppose you could say that the cow was kneeling fore and aft."

"Now you're getting cows and ships mixed up."

Rod got up and moved off the blanket. He stood studying Laurie's face. As far as he could tell she wore no makeup. Perhaps a touch of lipstick to cover that slight twist of her upper lip. Didn't she know that that one little flaw made her more interesting? His eyes then dwelled on the open-sleeved rust colored blouse and finally moved to her slacks, patterned in rust, brown, and white. Laurie remained mute. She felt that his eyes were undressing her. But he didn't have to use his imagination. He had seen her without clothes. Finding a stray crumb on the blanket, she flicked it off with a single finger.

"I think you'd make a good geisha," Rod pronounced.

Laurie looked up at him. "Is that a compliment?"

"You've got it wrong." He came back and sat down next to her. "Geishas aren't prostitutes, they're entertainers, good-looking women who provide witty conversation at a male party."

"A stag party?"

"You might call it that, but there's no striptease. Geishas wear gorgeous kimonos and are there to be looked at and talked to. That's what they're paid for."

"And for nothing else?"

"They dance and play musical instruments."

"You know what I mean."

"Sure, they sleep with men. They're women, aren't they? But not necessarily with a man who was at the party. And it's usually only with one guy. Geishas think it's bad form to sleep around."

"How come you know so much about geishas? Been to Japan?"

"No, read a book about them."

"And you think I'd make a good geisha?"

Rod snaked a dead branch from under a nearby bush and broke it in two. He grinned at Laurie. "Well, let's see. You're certainly good looking, you wear nice clothes, and you dance well. I don't know about music but I can't imagine any geisha carrying on a more interesting conversation."

To cover her embarrassment, Laurie looked down again into the valley below. There was a large splotch of yellow to the left of the meadow and a smaller white splotch to its right.

"Buttercups and daisies?" Rod asked.

"I don't know. I've never been down there."

"Why not?"

"Why should I? If I stay up here I can imagine them to be gold doubloons and white sugar plums strewn over a green velvet carpet. That's much more romantic than buttercups and daisies surrounded with grass and weeds."

"They're probably dandelion blossoms and Queen Anne's lace. They're both weeds. But I haven't the foggiest notion as to what doubloons or sugar plums are."

"Nor have I," Laurie admitted. "But I don't need to know exactly what something is to imagine it."

Rod began to break his branch into small pieces. Then he got up and searched until he found another dead branch and submitted it to the same procedure.

Laurie watched him. His tan arms protruded from the short sleeves of his open-neck blue shirt, which he wore over his blue denim slacks. She didn't have to use her imagination either. He was tall like her father. He had studied with Daddy and Daddy liked him. It wasn't often that she and Daddy agreed about anything. "This is my secret place," she said.

Rod turned toward her. "Where you come up mornings when you can no longer stand your father?"

"Right. No one else seems to come up here. I've always been alone... except today."

Rod searched her face but the message was not clear. "I'm cold. I'm going to build a fire." He hunted in the brush and came back with a third dead branch. He crouched in front of a bare spot, building a little pyre of broken bits of the branches.

Laurie glanced around. Here and there the hot sun rays poured through the chinks in the woods' leaky roof, painting brilliant patches on grass and bushes. "It's not that cold. You really don't need a fire."

"I'm glad to hear you say so," Rod said. He left the pyre and lay down next to her, looking up at the large tree which draped its shade upon them. "Know what kind of tree that is?"

Laurie lay back and gazed upward. "A maple, by the shape of its leaves."

"Good girl." He turned toward her and gathered her to him. She did not resist. He kissed her full on the mouth and then pressed his lips lightly against her neck.

The mingled scent of rotting wood and clover blossoms came faintly to their nostrils. Nearby a bird sang liquidly.

Rod raised his head. "You're delicious." His hand moved to the small of her back and brought them closer together. Now she could feel his erection. She had felt such pressure before but with other men, even with Josiah, it had seemed too urgent, too insistent, too much selfish desire so she had backed off. She didn't know why but this seemed different. It was more an invitation, an invitation to share.

Rod leaned back so he could see her face. "Do you like me?"

"That's a silly question."

"Not so silly, there are many ways of liking a person." His hand softly brushed her cheek. "For example, liking having sex with someone. I'm glad you like having sex if only with a bug."

Rod nibbled at her ear and again pressed her close to him.

She said nothing and for some time they lay in silence. There was a snapping of a twig as some small creature bypassed their clearing. An iodine colored butterfly streaked with lemon fluttered over them in zigzag course like an autumn leaf blown by an indecisive breeze.

Laurie stirred. "You've been mighty quiet," Rod said.

"Just thinking, thinking we ought to be going."

"Why? It's still early."

"I promised Mom I'd help with dinner." That was a lie but it didn't matter.

"Oh." He took her head between his hands and looked directly into her face. She returned his gaze with steady eyes but could not mask a slight blush. Rod kissed the tip of her nose and then stood.

He had done that once before. That night after they had been dancing, when they had reached her cottage in his car, he had placed his arm around her and his hand on her knee. She had said, "No, Rod." And he had immediately removed his arm and hand but took her head between his hands and kissed the tip of her nose. After he had followed her to the cottage door, it was she who kissed him on the mouth before she went in.

He shouldered her knapsack and as they started down she said, "Follow me. This is my private place. I'm not beating a path that might lead someone else here. I never go the same way twice, either up or down."

7

Meryl was already in his pajamas and sitting up in bed reading when Margaret came into their bedroom. He looked up. "Is everything settled?"

"I think so," Margaret replied. "Laurie's staying overnight with Millicent. She's going to a movie with Rod and he'll drive her over there afterwards."

"Good. This place is pretty isolated and I don't like the idea of her staying here alone all night. We're leaving after lunch so she'll have to make her own dinner."

"That's no problem; she's done it before. I've got some rather interesting information from Laurie concerning Rod's mother. Do you want to hear it or would you rather read?"

Meryl put his book on the night table. "Let's have it. I can always read later. But let me guess. She's really a gypsy from Rumania or she's having an interesting affair with the ambassador from Luxembourg."

"Not even close," Margaret said as she began to prepare for bed. "In the first place, she's Jewish."

"With a name like Lee Dunham?"

"Her maiden name was Leah Finkelstein. Everyone but her parents called her Lee for short and after her divorce from Trevor she changed it legally."

"I see she kept her married name."

"Yes, it's probably a better professional name than Finkelstein. She's a relatively successful marriage counselor."

"A very useful trade. So many people having trouble keeping their marriages together."

"Incidentally," Margaret said as she rolled off a stocking, "her father was a scholar in the old country."

"As I remember the custom, his wife probably made a living for him while he studied the Talmud."

"That's what Rod told Laurie. When he came to this country he had to make a living so he opened a pawn shop. But when he had no customers he continued to study the Talmud in his shop."

"Where was this?"

"New York City, Lower East Side."

"And how did this East Side Jewish girl just happen to marry Trevor Dunham, scion of a Boston Brahmin family?"

Margaret answered from the closet. "Apparently she was a very brilliant student and got a full scholarship to Radcliffe. Trevor went to Harvard after he left Juilliard and that's where they met."

"I always wondered about that marriage. I never thought Trevor was the marrying type. You knew him before Lee did; did you ever expect him to marry?"

"No, and he never remarried." She went over to the bed. "Help me with my bra, please."

"You can take it off yourself."

"Of course, but why should I when you're here to help me?" She turned her back and he unhooked it.

As he did he said, "He must have had a lot of other women while he was married to her. Do you understand why she married him?"

"That's not the question. I probably would have married him too, if he had asked me. The question is why he married her."

Meryl slumped down in the bed. "Well, it's a question we can hardly settle. Let's get some sleep."

* * *

As Margaret came into the living room of their city apartment, the telephone rang. The room smelled musty and she would rather have liked to open a window first but the ring of a telephone always drew her. She dropped her tote bag on a chair and picked up the receiver. "Hello."

A somewhat familiar voice said, "Hello, Margaret, this is Trevor."

"Why, Trevor, what a surprise."

"Where the devil have you been, Margaret? I've been in town for a week now and no matter how often I've called I've never found you in."

"Oh, we've just come in for the day. We're spending the summer in the country. What are you doing in Boston? The last I heard you were firmly settled in Florida."

"I am, more or less. I just came up to visit for a couple of weeks. Can we get together, let's say for old times' sake? You know you've always been my favorite and I should get some return for all the money I've wasted on phone calls."

"You haven't changed much, have you, Trevor?"

"Why should I? Ain't I fascinating just as I am?"

"Maybe. It's a matter of opinion, I guess." She sat down on a chair next to the telephone. "I don't know, Trevor. We have plans for the evening."

"So have I and they include you. Just tell your good husband that your old paramour is just pining away for you, my blue eyed princess. Certainly you won't be so cruel as to deny me one night before I return to my monastery in Florida."

"I can just see you in a monastery."

"Oh, the monks find me very decorative. I make a striking figure in Fustian robes and sandals with my long cigarette holder sticking out beneath my cowl."

"How many holes have you burned in your cowl? I don't think I can make it, Trevor. And I don't think I would want to even if I could."

"Miserere, madam. Can't you spare this poor monk a few scraps of love from your bountifully laden table? Have you no pity for one who has hungered for you for so long, at least a week?"

"You must be famished. Incidentally, do you still play the piano?"

"Of course, Gregorian chant in my right hand and a passage from Don Juan in my left."

"Hardly appropriate for four hands."

"For you, my lovely past partner, I'll change my repertory. I've brought your favorites, Brahms' Variations on a Theme by Handel and Milhaud's Boeuf sur le toit."

"Well, Trevor, I'll think about it and call you back."

"Thank you, my dove, princess of my heart, savior of my thighs..."

She cut him off. "Where are you staying?"

"At the Regent. How I hunger for you."

"Perhaps you'd better call room service." She hung up.

Meryl came into the room as she said the last sentence. "Who's the hungry caller?"

"Guess," Margaret said as she went to open a window.

"It's obviously somebody who's staying in a hotel, a relative or a friend passing through, too many to guess."

"It's an old friend."

Meryl examined Margaret's face. She had colored slightly. "Could it be Trevor?"

"Trevor! He's very hungry. He wants four hands as the hors d'oeuvres and bed as the entrée."

"And he's not offering dessert?"

"It depends upon what you mean by dessert."

"A kiss, perhaps."

"Nothing like that. A few crude remarks and he's asleep. It will take some time to chew this over and I want to air out the apartment."

"And I need a drink," Meryl said. "Do you want one?"

"No, but be sure to use a coaster." She left the room and Meryl went to the sideboard. When she returned he was sitting on one end of the couch with a glass in his hand, and there was a coaster on the little table before him. She sat down near the other end of the couch so she could face him.

"How many years has it been?" she asked.

"Since I left the reservation? A dozen years, at least. The last time was when I taught that semester in California and you stayed behind because you didn't want Laurie to change schools. I had Jennifer and you had Trevor, if you want to call it that. I had all of Jennifer until her husband came back from abroad. If I understood you correctly, Trevor has never given his all to any woman." He sampled his scotch and soda.

"It depends upon what you mean by his all. There's a multitude of sweet nothings and he never ejaculates without exclaiming, `You're a terrific lay!' or `You're a wonderful fuck!' or some such compliment."

"That last must be the dessert. I occasionally say things like that myself."

"Of course you do, darling. But then you mean them."

"That's bad?"

Margaret moved to a more comfortable position. "We've been over this before, darling. When we first married you were so damned honest and so convinced of your masculine duty to bring me to an orgasm every time you had one that you nearly broke up our marriage."

"The old vicious circle. You had the same problem as a pianist. You couldn't get yourself to perform in public because there was an expectant audience out there and you weren't sure that you could come up to their expectations. It was pretty much the same thing in bed. You knew I hoped you'd have an orgasm, and would do everything I could to see that you did, so you were afraid you might not have one and thus frustrate my expectation. So you became reluctant to have sex at all." He topped off his glass and placed it on the coaster.

"Thank God you accepted the fact that I enjoyed it whether I had an orgasm or not," Margaret said. "So I occasionally could. You found that anger aroused me but still didn't guarantee that I would have an orgasm."

"I don't believe `accept' is the right term. That's how you feel so I act accordingly. But I enjoy it much more myself when you do have an orgasm. But to get back to Trevor, I thought you were pretty disgusted with him the last time."

Margaret shifted again on the couch. "I was, but I'm very curious. What happens to a rascal in a dozen years? Does he change for the better or does he just become more rascally?"

"He just becomes older," Meryl said.

"Then I'll have a chance to play again. We had developed quite a four hand repertory when we were both at the Juilliard."

"Which you never performed in public."

"Which we never wanted to perform in public."

"And that's the bait?"

"Part of it. And part of it is just pure curiosity. And part of it, I suppose, is every woman's desire to have a lot of sweet nothings poured into her ear whether they are meant or not. Poor darling, it's just not your style."

"No, it isn't. So you are thinking of seeing him?"

"Do you mind very much?"

"That's not the question," Meryl said. He drained his glass and placed it on the coaster. "When we were married we decided not to be possessive. If either of us had extramarital inclinations the other would accept them. We decided that we would remain husband and wife only as long as we both preferred that arrangement to any other. I still stand by that agreement. It's worked for twenty-three years and I don't think your spending one night with Trevor is going to break up our marriage."

"I don't think so either but after twelve years I wondered how you felt about it. Since we survived the Jennifer affair I think our marriage is quite stable."

"What do mean?"

"Well, you've got a very strong sex drive and Jennifer was certainly better in bed than I've ever been. If she hadn't already had a husband I think you might have divorced me and married her."

"Possibly, but it probably would have been a mistake. Anyhow, as you well know, you've been constantly improving as a bed partner. Maybe you can show Trevor a wrinkle or two."

Margaret smiled at her husband. "Thank you, kind sir. But I doubt if I'll ever meet your standard of an orgasm every time. You're the only distinguished professor I know who's still married to his first wife. You're quite out of fashion. I've never understood why you haven't divorced me and married one of your sexy young students."

"Old fashion academic ethics, I suppose. I don't believe professors should make sexual advances to their women students. It's not fair, the professor has grades as a club." As he picked up his glass and the coaster and carried them to the sideboard, he said, "So you see, I'm stuck with you. As for arrangements I just remembered that I have a deadline for a review. It's finished, it just needs proofreading and to be mailed. But it's at the cottage so I have to go back there tonight anyhow."

"But you'll miss the Wycherley play and it isn't staged very often."

"Not really, since the seventeen hundreds. It was published in 1675. Only the New Old Vic would resurrect a play as old as The Country Wife. But our tickets are still at the box office so you call Dick and see if we can't get tickets for tomorrow night. Dick owes me. Did Trevor say anything about dinner?"

"Let's have dinner together. I'll call Trevor and tell him to come for piano music in the evening and let him handle all the rest of it."

"That's good. I hate to have dinner alone. We both have a lot of errands to do so I'll meet you here around five and we'll have dinner early so I can do part of my driving back during daylight."

Margaret stood up and went over to Meryl. "You're such a good husband you deserve a kiss." And she gave him one.

8

"Hi," said Rod at the other end of the line. "What's up?"

"I'm staying overnight at Millicent's. I know it's a good bit out of your way but would you drive me there after the movie?"

"Of course. Your folks are away?"

"They're spending the night in the city." There was a silence at the other end of the line. She broke it. "Come over a half an hour early and we'll have a drink before we go to the movie."

"Sure thing. I've got to shower and change clothes but I should make it."

She hadn't called Millicent yesterday, as she had promised Mom, nor Rod. It had been fast and furious, only ten days since she had first met Rod at the Bartons': swimming, fishing, tennis, dancing, picnic on her hilltop, and now a movie. Some movie that's going to be! Going into her parents' bedroom Laurie swept the bedspread off the bed and placed it on a chair. Then she stripped the bed, folded the sheets and pillowcases, and stored them upon the top shelf of the closet. Then she went to the bathroom and returned with fresh linens, remaking the bed.

Outside the light was fading, dimming the outline of trees and dissolving the silver sheen of the lake's surface. She drew the drapes and closed the bathroom door. The room wasn't completely dark but it would have to do.

She left the room and then returned carrying a large stuffed panda and a double candlestick holding two candles. She laid the black and white panda on the bed with its head on a pillow and placed the candlestick on her mother's dresser at the other end of the room. She lit the candles with a match from a book of matches, dropped the matchbook on the dresser, and looked back at the panda on the bed. She could barely tell where black met white.

Blowing out the candles, she went into the bathroom and turned on its light. Coming out she left the door a little ajar. Then she went back to the dresser and turned to examine the panda again. Now the patches of dark and light were more evident. She snatched up the candlestick and matches, turned out the light in the bathroom, and grabbing the panda, hurriedly left the room.

The doorbell rang. "You sure got here in a hurry," she told Rod as she led him into the kitchen. "Cuba libre is my mother's favorite drink so we always have the makings. Know what it is?"

"Of course. It's mostly Coke with some rum and lemon or lime. But go easy on the rum. I don't hold my liquor too well."

"Could it be that a rakish young fellow like you can't hold his liquor?" said Laurie as she went to the refrigerator.

"What makes me rakish?"

"Trying to make a girl on a public beach in the bright sunlight."

"And what do you call a girl who has an affair with a ladybug?"

Laurie squeezed the juice of a half lemon into a glass. "My father described it as a bit of bestiality."

Rod caught the bitterness in her tone. "That's kind of rough. At times the prof lays it on pretty thick, even in class. It's just his way, I don't think anyone minds much."

"He isn't their father. They don't have to live with him."

Laurie handed Rod his drink and they sat down on adjacent sides of the white topped kitchen table. "My mother has a thing about coasters," Laurie said. "But this tabletop is plastic so we don't have to worry about them."

They both sipped their drinks. For a while Rod watched Laurie who in turn watched her fingers slowly rotate her glass. Then he said, "I'm still curious about that ladybug affair. Your father knows more about it than I do. When are you going to let me in on it?"

"Like I said, when I get to know you better."

"Nothing like being stubborn. I'm never going to find out until you get to know me better. Right? So we'd better skip the movie and take care of that."

"Meaning?"

"We stay here and make love."

Laurie brought her glass to her lips, savored her drink, and carefully replaced the glass on the table. "What about your mother? Suppose she wants to see the movie and asks you to describe it?"

"That's no problem. I've already seen it."

"My! You're sneaky."

Rod waited for her to go on but she said nothing further. He sampled his drink. "Too much rum for a rakish young fellow like me." He went to the sink and poured out half of the contents of his glass, refilling it with a bottle of Coca Cola taken from the refrigerator. Finding a spoon in a drawer, he stirred vigorously. Laurie watched the entire procedure without comment. Rod returned to his seat with his drink. "Better. Too much alcohol and making love becomes difficult." Laurie's face was expressionless. He waited but she did not speak. "Well, if you really want to we'll go to the movie."

Laurie ran her finger along the rim of her glass. Her mouth was like a bud about to open, her lips wanting to break into a smile. "Let's suppose we don't go to the movie and stay here. Would we have to go all the way?"

"Not necessarily. We could continue on the way we were on the hilltop. But in that case you really wouldn't get to know me."

"But I'd know you better."

Rod took a swig of his diluted cuba libre. "Somewhat better, but not as well as I would like you to."

"Well, suppose I let you go all the way just this one time. Will that be enough? Will you be satisfied and not come back and bother me anymore?" There was at least a half smile on her face.

"If you don't like my lovemaking," Rod said stiffly, "I certainly won't bother you anymore."

"Faulty statement. Revision. If I let you go all the way, will you come back and ask for more?"

"Of course, how could I keep away from a girl like you? Day and night I'd come back for more."

"And after that more again?"

"More and more, indefinitely."

Laurie's smile was full blown and mischievous. "It's obvious that I'll never be able to satisfy you so there's no point in getting started. Let's go to the movie." She brought her glass triumphantly to her lips.

"Damn!" Rod exclaimed and threw up his hands. "You're difficult."

Laurie laughed. He liked hearing her laugh. In fact, there wasn't a thing about her that he didn't like, even the teasing he'd been getting. It had been done so nicely.

"Ok," Laurie said. "You make love to me. I know what you did on the hilltop but how will you go about it here?"

"In bed and in the nude," Rod said promptly.

"My! Isn't that a bit unorthodox? Aren't there supposed to be some preliminaries like hugging and kissing on a sofa before one goes to bed?"

"Not at all. It's much more comfortable hugging and kissing in bed and everything feels better when there are no clothes in the way."

Laurie frowned. "I don't know. I may be a bit conservative but I think you're too hasty a lover for me. I vote for the movie."

Rod looked at his watch. "It's a little late for that. I'll do it your way."

Suddenly Laurie's faced brightened. "Sorry, I forgot that you're giving the demonstration. Obviously it should be done on your terms, but you had better come and check the bed first to be sure it's adequate."

9

Laurie lit a lamp and Rod tested the bed by pushing down with his hands in several places. "I find it quite adequate."

"I'm glad you do, otherwise the fresh linen I just put on would be wasted."

"Now who's sneaky?" He tried to pull her to him but she broke away.

"Only in bed, remember?"

Rod returned to the bed and turned back the spread. "I'm warm. I won't need any covers, not even a sheet."

"I guess you're right. I'm warm, too. Must be the rum. Give me a hand but be sure you fold things neatly."

When they were finished Laurie went to the door and locked it.

"Why did you do that?"

"Just in case."

"In case of what? Aren't your folks going to be away for the whole night?"

"In case you try to escape and I have to catch you. I'm a female ogre. When I'm not satisfied with a lover's performance I eat him."

Rod was the first to get on the bed. Since there was a lit lamp on the right night table he stretched out on the left side of the bed, leaving it to Laurie to decide whether or not she wanted to turn out the light.

Then he heard Laurie's voice from the bathroom door: "Rod, please turn out the light."

He leaned over and switched it off. Laurie came out and left the bathroom door partly ajar. The room was now dark except for a thin shaft of yellow light streaming its radiance across the rugged floor. She looked at the bed and Rod. In the obscurity she could only see his outline. She lay down beside him.

Time to ask about contraception, he thought. Damn! How he hated this part of it. He'd wait until just before he'd enter.

"Planning strategies?" Laurie asked.

"No, just a little worried. I just remembered how you chopped my wrist on the beach. It's a bit unnerving to make love to a female ogre who knows karate."

"Oh." Laurie clasped her hands behind her head. "Look, Mom, no hands."

"That's better." He gave her a lingering kiss on the mouth. Her right hand came down and rested lightly on the nape of his neck. It followed him as he kissed her throat. He caught it with his left hand, kissed it, and then held it. With his free hand he began to caress her breasts with soft and gentle strokes.

Laurie closed her eyes, her mind emptying itself of everything but the sensory. Her entire being focused on the touch of Rod's hand.

Even in the dim light Rod could distinguish the darker discs of her aureoles from which her nipples protruded from the lighter skin of her breasts. He teased each firm nipple between thumb and forefinger and then between his lips. Then he cupped each breast in turn. Now, almost imperceptibly, his hand, still softly stroking, moved downwards. There was no sound from Laurie except her even breathing. As his hand passed below her navel she tensed slightly and brought her left hand down and placed it on his. He stopped and waited. Neither spoke. Little by little her hand crept away and his dropped between her open thighs, caressing each one in turn. She murmured something unintelligible and he didn't ask what it was.

Finally his hand came to rest between her thighs. She placed her hand over his and they remained perfectly still.

"Rod," she said softly, "there's something I have to tell you."

"Yes?"

Suddenly Laurie sat up. "What was that?"

"I think it was a car door slamming," Rod said, also sitting up. There was noise at the front door and then the sound of footsteps in the hall.

"It's my father!" cried Laurie in panic.

Meryl came to the bedroom door, grasped the doorknob, turned it and pushed. The door did not open. He tried again without success. Somehow it was locked.

Then he heard his daughter's embarrassed voice, "Sorry, Daddy. The room's occupied."

Meryl cursed under his breath. What an idiot! He had known that the two would be together tonight. He had seen the car outside but this was a dead end and he had thought that there were lovers in it. It had never occurred to him that the lovers would be inside. "Sorry to intrude. It was stupid of me to come home. Forget I'm here. I'll sleep in my study." His footsteps retreated and there was the sound of a door closing.

"There's a good father," Rod said, grasping Laurie's hand.

She pulled her hand away and got off the bed. "Hush!" Her voice was low but vibrant. "You'll have to get dressed and get out of here."

"But why?" Rod said, keeping his voice low. "He said it was alright."

"I can't do it with him here," she said in utter misery. "That's all there is to it. You'll just have to go."

"OK," he said, still keeping his voice low. "If that's how you feel about it, I'll go."

"Then go."

They both hurriedly dressed. As he prepared to leave Laurie said in a stage whisper, "Be quiet as you go out."

"It's hardly a secret," he said at the same pitch level but he did as she asked.

Minutes later Laurie went to her father's study and knocked on the door.

"Come in," Meryl said.

She went in and faced him. "You can have your room now. I replaced the linen and made the bed." She hesitated and then, "I want to thank..." Her throat choked and tears came to her eyes. She turned and quickly went out the door without closing it.

Meryl heard her door close and then low sobbing.

Margaret is right, Meryl thought. He could be incredibly stupid. He then realized that the real basis of his obtuseness was his assumption that Laurie was a virgin and thus wouldn't be having an affair with anyone. And how long, he demanded of himself, does one expect a woman to remain a virgin?

But why had she become so upset? Was he such an ogre? He must try to smooth it over somehow.

He went to Laurie's room and knocked on the door. "May I come in?"

The sobs subsided somewhat and he heard a weak "Come in."

He found Laurie lying face down on her bed. She didn't look up. "Sweetheart," he said and realized that he hadn't called her that for years. "Sweetheart, there is really no reason to become so upset." He patted her shoulder, leaned down, and kissed the top of her head. He was a pretty clumsy father, he thought. "What you were doing was a perfectly natural and normal thing for humans to do. It was something that your mother and I would expect you to be doing someday somewhere. It's something you do in private and you don't want intruders. And fathers who say they are going to spend the whole night in the city shouldn't come barging in at the wrong moment. I'm sorry. I should have had sense enough to stay at a motel."

She turned and looked up at him, her face still wet with tears. "And you won't joke about it?"

He was appalled. Is that why she was upset? Margaret was right, she was ultra sensitive to anything he said. "Of course I won't joke about it. Definitely not," he assured her.

"Promise?"

"I promise." He leaned down and kissed her wet cheek. "Try to get some sleep, sweetheart. We'll talk about it further in the morning if you wish."

He left the room but went to the kitchen, not his study. At times like these he wished he smoked. He imagined that in such circumstances it would be helpful to have a pipe between his teeth. He prepared a scotch and soda, heavy on the scotch, and sat down at the kitchen table to drink it. He knew it was his second one for the day but he needed it.

Things had gone awry. He was good at handling his students, and knew it, but certainly not Laurie. He supposed it was because they were so close and he saw her so often. He'd just have to be less critical and more supportive.

He hadn't yet finished his drink so he took it with him to his study. There he picked up a book and carried it and the glass to his bedroom where he read for some time before trying to go to sleep. When he finally settled in bed he thought he heard the sound of a typewriter coming from Laurie's room. He wondered why she would be typing at this time of night. The question was still on his mind as he fell asleep.

10

Meryl woke somewhat later than usual and quickly shaved and dressed. In the kitchen the table was set only for one and Laurie was standing next to the stove. Her eyes were bright and clear and there was no sign of tears on her cheeks. "I've already eaten, Daddy. Sit down and I'll make breakfast for you."

There was a folder lying to the left of his plate. "What's this?"

"An offering," Laurie said simply.

He picked up the folder and started to open it.

"Wait until you've finished your breakfast, please."

"Very well," he said and placed the folder on the chair next to him. She prepared and served a munificent breakfast, freshly squeezed orange juice, crisp bacon and scrambled eggs, toast and marmalade, and freshly brewed coffee with real cream.

"That was quite a breakfast."

Laurie sat in the chair opposite of him and looked directly at him. "Did you and Mom sleep together before you were married?"

"Yes," he answered without hesitation but hoped she wouldn't ask further.

"That was something I needed to know. Knowing it makes me feel better. Thank you for being willing to tell me."

"As far as I know we weren't unusual in our generation and many of our parents did the same although they kept it pretty quiet. We're slowly getting used to accepting human sexual behavior as it really is rather than what it's supposed to be." He picked up the folder from the chair. "Now, what is this supposed to be?"

Laurie smiled at him across the table. She was even more beautiful than her mother, if that's possible, Meryl thought. As far as that tiny twist in her upper lip was concerned, as Madame Pompadour knew when she applied a black beauty mark low on her cheek, some little flaw was necessary to really validate a woman's beauty.

"You've been trying to get me to communicate in a more organized and orderly manner. You have often suggested that I do this the way a journalist writes a news story. So I've tried my hand at it and I hope you'll find it as well organized as it should be. Of course, it's all imagined. None of it ever happened."

Meryl opened the folder and began to read:

Clipping from the Farmington Clarion Herald, June 2, 1961
By special correspondent

COLOR OF COW CAUSES CONTROVERSY

A dispute is raging in northern Clay County concerning the color of Daisy Belle, a dairy cow owned by Joseph Anderson of Rural Route 2. Anderson has sued his neighbor, David B. Jones, also of Rural Route 2, claiming that he has damaged Daisy Belle by dying her burnt orange. Jones has denied the allegation, claiming that Daisy Belle was still her original color, reddish brown, and entered a counter suit against Anderson for malicious slander. Both suits were heard simultaneously on June 1 by Judge Rubin Perlman of the Clay County Circuit Court, who ruled in favor of Jones. Anderson is appealing the case.

In his suit Anderson claims that the alleged dying of Daisy Belle burnt orange has impaired her ability to give milk of the proper color and her marketability as beef. He asked for damages of five thousand dollars to cover property loss, payment for the time required to find another suitable dairy cow, and mental anguish suffered. In his counter suit Jones also asked for five thousand dollars to cover the damage to his good name and alleged that Anderson, who was being treated for glaucoma, could not distinguish between burnt orange and reddish brown. Anderson was represented at the hearing by Benson Plover, attorney of Farmington, and Jones by Jonathan Blow, attorney of the same city.

Dr. James Weldon, ophthalmologist of Farmington, testified that Anderson was his patient and that he, Anderson, had a very mild case of glaucoma and, as far as Weldon could determine, it has not caused any significant impairment of Anderson's vision. Weldon stated that Anderson definitely did not have anomalous color vision and therefore should be able to distinguish shades of red, or, for that matter, of any other color. Judge Perlman asked the witness to explain the term `anomalous color vision.' Weldon replied that it was the red-yellow color blindness characteristically found in males. Plover asked Dr. Weldon if ophthalmologists had a specific test for determining whether or not a patient could distinguish between burnt orange and reddish brown. The witness replied that he was an ophthalmologist, not a physicist. He assumed that physicists had established the wave length of every shade of color but he did not know whether physicists used the terms `burnt orange' or `reddish brown' in referring to these shades. As to the tests referred to, to his knowledge no such test was available to ophthalmologists.

Dr. Tillson Whitcomb, Professor of Veterinary Medicine at Northeast University, testified for Jones. He attested that dying a cow would produce a variety of deleterious effects. The skin would be denatured and its ability to hold in the animal's heat to activate vitamin D would be impaired, as would be the secretions of the sweat glands through the pores. He further testified that in his opinion no cow could survive dying.

Meryl laughed and looked up. "That's a world champion pun," he told Laurie and read on:

There was laughter in the courtroom and Judge Perlman pounded his gavel for order.

Attorney Blow then asked the witness if the cow had been dyed another color, blue for example, would this be more or less deleterious to its health. The witness replied that the different pigments used in making colors, and the solutions in which they were dissolved, varied somewhat in their effects. It was his considered opinion, however, that no cow could survive dying.

Meryl laughed again, "It's even good the second time."

There was further laughter in the court and Judge Perlman again called for order. He then requested that the witness refrain from making puns. Dr. Whitcomb replied that he was not making puns but statements to the best of his scientific knowledge as requested.

Attorney Plover suggested to the court that an individual who did not know he was punning was not a credible witness. Attorney Blow made the counter suggestion that for the purposes of the court a witness did not need to display a sense of humor, only scientific competence. Dr. Whitcomb then said that if his competence was being impugned he would prefer not to offer further evidence. Judge Perlman ordered the clerk of the court to strike the remarks of both attorneys from the record.

The judge then asked the witness to clarify the term `survive.' Did he imply that the cow would die immediately or after a period of illness? In brief, how long would it take for a cow that had been dyed to die?

Meryl chuckled and then read on.

> There was a slight sound of suppressed laughter in the courtroom, which the judge ignored. The witness replied that it would probably take two to five weeks, depending upon the health of the cow, and the weather. Survival would not be as long during warm weather.
>
> Judge Perlman then removed the court to Anderson's farm where he examined Daisy Belle. Upon moving the court back to the county courthouse he stated that it was his judicial opinion that Daisy Belle's color was reddish brown. He therefore ruled in favor of Jones but awarded him only two thousand dollars and court costs, stating that it was his judicial opinion that Jones' reputation had not been damaged to the amount claimed.
>
> According to Plover, Anderson intends to appeal the case on the basis that it is well known that Judge Perlman is colorblind.

Meryl looked up at Laurie's waiting face. "I'd like to run through it again." As he read through it rapidly he emitted a couple of low chuckles. "Laurie," he said, "this is great. Organization-wise it's perfect even to the punch line at the end. If it were true any newspaper in the country would be glad to print it."

Laurie looked at her father with shining eyes. "Thank you, Daddy. I'm awfully glad you liked it."

"You seem to have a talent for this kind of whimsical humor. You should cultivate it. You must show it to Margaret."

The phone rang and Laurie answered it. "Hello," her voice warmed immediately. "I'm fine, Mom. How are you? ... The movie? I'll let Daddy tell you about it." She held out the telephone to Meryl.

"I'll take it in my study," he said hastily and left the kitchen. Laurie waited until she heard him say, "Hello, Margaret," and then put down the receiver. She wouldn't have listened in even if she had wanted to. This time she definitely didn't want to.

"Laurie, are you still on the line?" Margaret asked at the other end.

"She's hung up," replied Meryl.

"What's this about you and their movie? I don't understand."

"We'll get to that but first, how did it go last night?"

"Oh!" she said rapturously. "We're still a wonderful team in playing the Brahms and the Milhaud. I haven't enjoyed playing the piano so much in years."

"I'm glad."

"But I'd forgotten how long Trevor's legs were. When the bench was placed so that I could reach the pedals his legs were all doubled up and his knees nearly touched the underside of the keyboard."

"And how about the rest of his body?"

"Oh, he's just the old Trevor. His hairline has moved up a bit and he has somewhat of a pot."

"And did you pass on any new wrinkles?"

"Don't be silly. It was just an old rerun, except there was no dessert. I guess it tires him now and he needs sleep immediately afterwards."

"I hope it wasn't too bad."

"Oh, not too bad. As a matter of fact, if you look at it from the right angle, it's rather amusing. How are you? How was your drive home?"

"Things were fine until I got home." Then he told her what had happened the night before.

"What a fiasco!"

"You mean what stupidity on my part?"

"I don't know. I didn't consider the possibility either. If I had I would have warned you. Poor Laurie! Was it Rod?"

"She hasn't said and I haven't asked her. Whoever it was went out quietly and I didn't see him."

"It must've been Rod. I don't think she's been seeing any other boy lately in the lake area. That blows my idea. I called Dick and we have four tickets for tonight. I was thinking of inviting Rod and Laurie to go with us."

"I don't think she'd go for that."

"Nor do I. But I have a better idea now. Let's invite Lee Dunham. She has an apartment in the city or she could stay with us if she wants to. Then we'll get all the parents out of the way and leave Laurie and Rod to their own devices. I'll call her."

"What will we do with the fourth ticket?"

"Well, I could give it back to Dick. But wait a moment! I've got a better idea. I'll invite Trevor."

"Trevor! For God's sake, why?"

"To go to the theatre as theatrically as possible. I'll tell Trevor his two old flames want to see him for the last time and then say farewell forever. Both Lee and I will mean it."

"Do you think he'll go for it?"

"He'll eat it up. I'll call Lee first and see if she's free and wants to come. If she does then I'll broach the question of inviting Trevor. It will be up to her to decide. In any case, I'll call you back before I call Trevor so you can tell Laurie that you're going back to the city."

"Who's the plotter now? Get on with it and let me know."

* * *

"Lee Dunham speaking."

"This is Margaret Crowley," said the voice at the other end of the line. "It was very nice of you to invite Laurie for dinner."

"My pleasure, or I should say, our pleasure. We very much enjoyed having her."

"I've never met Rod but my husband knows him and likes him very much. We three of the older generation ought to get to know each other."

"I'd like that very much."

"Then, if you're free, perhaps you'd like to join Meryl and me in a theatre party. The New Old Vic is playing Wycherley's The Country Wife. It's an old comedy, I think from the Restoration Period, and it isn't played very often. We have tickets. I'm in the city and Meryl is at our cottage. He'll drive you in and we'll all drive back together the next morning."

"That's very kind of you and I accept with pleasure. It seems a very good arrangement."

"I thought you might think so. Well, we have a fourth ticket and, we thought, with your permission only, we should like also to invite Trevor."

There was a shocked silence at the other end of the line and Lee's voice became a little hard. "Margaret, I can call you Margaret can I not?"

"Of course, Lee."

"Well, from courtesy I won't say no immediately. You should know that I haven't seen Trevor outside of a lawyer's office for many years. The last time must have been at least six years ago when we made our final settlement for Rod. Do you know some reason why I should want to see him?"

"I have a reason of a kind although it may not be a good one. You won't be too surprised to know that I was with Trevor last night. He's carrying on just as he did before. It's a bit pathetic and also, I think, a bit admirable. I don't intend to have anything to do with him in the future and apparently you haven't seen him socially for many years. I suppose I am being a bit theatrical but I thought it would be nice if the four of us went to the theatre and then came up to our apartment for a few drinks. In calling Trevor I will tell him that it will be the last time that either of us ever expects to see him. You might call it the last hurrah or a farewell to arms. Now, it's strictly up to you. We'll be glad to have you without Trevor."

Lee's voice became considerably more friendly. "We both know that Trevor, if asked, will come. What's a farewell to arms to him? There will always be other women, at least he thinks so and maybe he's right. How does your husband stand on this?"

"He's with us. He's an English professor, remember? He's got to be for drama."

Lee laughed. "All right, you've talked me into it. If there's trouble the two of you will have to protect me."

"From what I've heard," Margaret said, "you can take care of yourself quite well."

*   *   *

"Well," Meryl said into the telephone, "did she accept?"

"Yes, and she goes along with my idea of inviting Trevor."

"What a woman! Did she understand that we had Rod and Laurie in mind also?"

"I think so, but I can't be really sure. She was the model of tact until I told her I had just been with Trevor and we got on a first name basis. Even then she played it pretty cool. I think we'll enjoy the evening. I told her you'd call and make the arrangements early in the morning. As soon as I can reach Trevor I'll call you back. It's time now to tell Laurie."

"I'll do that. As a plotter you've got me beat to a frazzle."

11

"Don't forget to feed Hookie," Lee said to her son as she got into the Crowleys' car.

"I won't," Rod promised. They all said goodbye and Meryl drove off, leaving Rod and Laurie standing in front of the Crowleys' cottage.

Almost immediately Lee commented, "You have a lovely daughter. She must have many admirers."

"Yes," Meryl said noncommittally. "At school I noticed that Rod was not exactly shunned by the fair sex."

"Oh, he's not unpopular."

Meryl stole a brief sideways glance and saw that she was watching him with an amused smile. He laughed and she joined him.

"Alright, so we gave them the official parental seal of approval. What do you think they'll do now?"

"Argue and then go for a swim."

"To raise their ardor and then dampen it?"

"Oh, there's more to follow. In my profession we call it conflict and resolution."

"That will do for play writing as well. But you don't have the resolution until the end of the play."

"From what I've learned about Laurie from Rod, she'll find a way to delay the denouement until the night."

"Then what act are we in?"

"The second, if you don't count the prologue."

"I gather that you know much more about this affair than I do. I didn't even know there was a prologue."

"I suppose that's because Rod and I are unusually close. For all practical purposes he really has no father."

"I know," Meryl said as he carefully maneuvered the car into the flow of traffic on the Interstate.

* * *

"Well?" Rod asked Laurie.

"I don't want to talk about it out here. Let's go in." This time she led him into the living room rather than the kitchen. She deliberately selected the only easy chair so he had to sit on the couch in order to face her.

He looked at her with foreboding. "I can already tell that I'm not going to like this."

"Like what?"

"Like whatever it is you've got up your sleeve. I doubt very much that it's an invitation to go to bed with you."

"You're nothing if not direct. Isn't it a bit early in the day for that?"

"It's never too early, at least for me."

"I prefer the night," Laurie said. "I think you had some other ideas in mind besides bed when you telephoned."

"Of course, let's go over to my place for a swim—not in the raw this time—and afterwards I'll take you out to dinner, the best place we can find, and back here for cocktails and then let nature take its course."

"Very nice as far as it goes but add the movie we missed last night."

"But I've already seen it."

"Then we'll find one in Farmington that you haven't seen."

"OK," Rod said reluctantly, "I'll add a movie. That's probably what you had up your sleeve."

"And after the movie we'll go to a nightclub and dance and have cocktails, and then home to bed."

Rod exploded. "It's twenty miles to the nearest nightclub and we won't get home until one."

"You're not capable of making love at one o'clock in the morning?"

"Of course I am, if I want to. We've got to the point twice already and I've been frustrated both times. Now you want to put it off further. For all I know we won't get home until two and you'll put me off again. `I'm tired,' you'll say. `I'm going to sleep. See you after breakfast.' And I'll be still more hard up."

"That's an interesting expression," Laurie said.

"But a damn frustrating position to be in. If you don't want to screw why don't you just come out and say so? I might as well leave." He got up and started for the door.

Laurie sprang from her chair, grabbed Rod by the arm, and turned him around to face her. "Don't use that word around me," she said hotly.

"What word?" Rod asked, astonished.

"Screw! Use it with your other women if you want to but not around me."

Rod pulled his arm away. "There aren't other women, I'm just going with you. But why are you getting on your high horse? What's wrong with `screw?' Everybody uses it."

"I don't care, you're not to use it around me. It's what my father calls pejorative. When you say you got screwed you mean that you got done in by somebody. I don't want to be done in by you or any other man. If it can't be done with mutual trust and affection I don't want it."

"OK, I won't use the word. But I doubt if you really want it. But while we're arguing I might as well ask the hard question. It's much harder to ask once you're in bed. Assuming we are going to bed, have you taken care of the contraceptive problem or do I?"

Laurie looked at him strangely. "What do you mean?"

"Damn it! Do I have to spell it out for you? Do you use a diaphragm?..." He hesitated and then, "Or do I use a prophylactic?"

"You mean a condom. Don't call it a prophylactic. I'm not going to infect you."

"I thought you might find the term `condom' offensive."

"Nothing pejorative about it that I can see. But you needn't use one. I'm on the birth control pill."

Rod moved back and gazed at her, his frown lessening. "And how did you manage that? It's only been around for about a year and a half and you need a prescription from a doctor, don't you?"

"All you need is to know the right doctor."

"Are you sure you've taken it long enough? If I make you pregnant my mother will kill me."

"Trust me. I have some interest in the matter, too. Well, you do dance beautifully but we can go dancing some other time. So its swimming, dinner, a movie, and then back here."

The frown on Rod's face was replaced with a smile. "Fine!" he replied.

*   *   *

The three were a little late getting to the theatre and Trevor was already in the lobby waiting. His long dark face, perched above his tall frame, and his long cigarette holder and cigarette jutting jauntily from his mouth made him clearly visible above the heads of most of the crowd. When Meryl returned with the tickets Trevor had taken position between the two women, holding an arm of each. He paraded them to one of the entrances of the theatre and Meryl followed behind, noting the slight swagger with which Trevor moved. Margaret looked back at Meryl in half apology and he winked back at her.

"He's got the tickets," Trevor told the ticket taker, indicating Meryl with the turn of his head. Meryl surrendered the tickets and received his halves and they were ushered to their seats, which turned out to be four ending at the aisle, about a dozen rows from the front.

"Damn good seats," Trevor approved. "Who's got the pull?"

"Meryl," Margaret said as she went in first. Trevor followed and then Lee, and Meryl took the aisle seat.

As Meryl took it, Lee turned to him and smilingly observed, "The usual sandwich of the sexes." Trevor was talking with Margaret so it was natural for Lee and Meryl to converse.

"I had Rod in one of my classes," Meryl said.

"Yes, Rod has talked a good deal about you."

"I hope he had only good things to say."

"Oh, yes. He liked you very much as a teacher."

"And I also liked him as a student. He's unusually courteous for a young man of his generation. By the way, how old is he?"

"Twenty-one. I stressed courtesy in bringing him up. But you're thinking of Laurie, aren't you?"

"Why yes," Meryl admitted.

"He inherited some traits from his father, but he has quite a different character. To be blunt, Rod doesn't use women, he loves them."

Meryl just had time to say, "Thank you for being so candid, Lee," while the lights dimmed and the audience hushed, waiting for the curtain to rise.

*   *   *

Meryl was at the sideboard preparing the drinks. Lee had said that she didn't drink hard liquor after dinner and there were no lemons or limes in the apartment with which to make Margaret's usual cuba libre so she also had opted for wine. Meryl filled two glasses with Chablis and carried them to the women. Then he filled a shot glass with the straight whiskey Trevor had requested and mixed a scotch and soda for himself.

Margaret had been talking with Trevor and as Meryl handed him his whiskey she said, "Why don't you two have a little man talk together and give me a chance to talk to Lee. I've hardly had a chance to say a word to her."

Acting on his wife's hint Meryl gestured towards his study. "Let's go in there and get out of their way. Actually, I haven't had a chance to talk to you either."

The two carried their drinks into the study and Meryl closed the door behind them.

Margaret sat down next to Lee. "Meryl and Trevor won't be in there long so I'm going to pop the question right away. Don't answer it if you think I'm being impertinent, but it's puzzled me for years. Why did you marry Trevor?"

Lee smiled at Margaret and seemed perfectly at ease. "You know the answer to that, Margaret. Would you have married him if he had asked you first?"

"Probably."

"And I'll tell you why you would have. He always had the knack of making the woman he was sleeping with feel she was really tops, she was his favorite and the other women he had were just play things. That was one of the things that kept you coming to him. If you were to marry him that really sealed it, there was no question that you were the top woman in the harem."

"I seem to have asked the wrong question," Margaret said. "Not why you married him, but why he asked you in the first place?"

"I really don't know the answer to that. When I asked him one time he would say it was an `indiscretion' and at another time that it was `a fall from grace.' He wouldn't say more. It was obviously done under an impulse but why a man such as Trevor should have such an impulse I've never been able to figure out. I was married to him for seven years and he never mentioned divorce. I was the one who asked for it."

In the study Meryl was examining Trevor. Margaret was right, he had the long face of the aesthete like those found in a Modigliani painting, with a long slightly hooked nose, not too fleshy nor too thin, and full sensuous lips. Trevor, however, had dark brown eyes, almost black, with hair almost the same shade, which was brushed straight back. His was a powerful figure. "Your son is a very intelligent young man," Meryl said to Trevor. "He also knows how to work. I think he'll go places."

"He'd better," Trevor said. "I'm financing him through college but after that he's going to be on his own."

"There's no question that he'll do well. And from what I've observed in class he does well with the girls, also."

"Like father like son," said Trevor as he sipped his whiskey. "But he doesn't seem to take full advantage of the talent he inherited. I suppose it's because Lee has worked him over with her `sensitivity training' and other folderol so he has as many taboos as the cactus has thorns."

Meryl sampled his drink while he thought of the next question. "Do you see much of him?"

"I did when he was little but Lee has managed to get him away from me. It doesn't really matter. I enjoyed being with him when he was a kid but now that he's grown up and has this holier than thou attitude I can do quite well without him."

Trevor drained the remainder of his drink and grinned at Meryl. "Now that I've spilled it all tell me why you've been pumping me. Has Rod been making passes at your little girl?"

Meryl was embarrassed. Had he really been that transparent? This was Margaret's idea, not his. "That's not exactly how I would put it."

"Oh, so he's already been in bed with her." Trevor placed his empty glass on Meryl's desk. "Nothing to worry about, old man, my son is a most honorable young man, most honorable, most honorable." And without as much as `at your leave' he went back into the living room.

Meryl picked up Trevor's empty glass and swabbed the moisture off his desk with a tissue. Then he carried Trevor's glass and his still half full back to the sideboard. Whatever Trevor was, he was nobody's fool. He had known that any information that they could get from him they could have already secured from Lee or they could have figured it out themselves. If they'd wanted it from the horse's mouth, oh, well, why not? He had nothing to lose and he could get in a couple of digs while he was at it. Meryl wondered what Trevor had meant by `honorable?' In this context he probably meant stupid.

Meryl carried his drink with him as he joined the others. The women were just tasting their wine; they had been so busy talking that they had forgotten about it.

Some time later Lee said it was time for her to leave. She exchanged courtesies with the Crowleys and promised to meet them for lunch the next day. Meryl brought her overnight case but before he could give it to Lee, Trevor peremptorily appropriated it. "I'll see that you get a taxi," he said to Lee, who raised no objection.

Trevor went to Margaret, who extended her hand. "It's goodbye and farewell now, Trevor."

He bent over her hand, kissed it and said, "Fare thee well, my blue-eyed princess of the piano." He then turned to Meryl. "Many thanks, old man. I enjoyed it and don't worry about my honorable son."

Meryl escorted them to the elevator and brought it up for them. When he returned to the apartment he asked Margaret, "How far do you think that'll go?"

"He doesn't expect to get anywhere. He's just acting as Trevor. It's a habit. But what did you find out about Rod?"

"Collating the testimony of the two parents I gather that Rod also attracts women but unlike his father, he doesn't use them, but as Lee put it, he loves them. I gather that means he takes in their needs and considerations as well as his own."

"That's all we can really expect. The rest is up to Laurie."

*   *   *

Trevor followed Lee into the taxi. "It's not wise for a woman to travel alone this time of night," he explained. He gave the address, which he knew well since

Lee was still occupying the apartment in which they had both lived when they were married.

For a time Lee remained silent and looked out of the window. Then she turned to her fellow occupant and asked, "Trevor, I've never known why you married me. All you would ever tell me was that it was 'an indiscretion' or 'a fall from grace.' What does that mean? And why should you, of all people, marry me or for that matter, marry any woman?"

For a few moments Trevor also remained silent. Then he said, "It seems to be my night for explaining but it will be a little difficult because I'm not quite sure, myself, that I understand why I married you."

"Well please try."

"I'll try by using a comparison although I'm not sure it's a good one. I am what people would call a hedonist. But I'm not just a hedonist in behavior or principle. You might call my hedonism my philosophy or even my religion. Now take a devout Christian, a monk living in a monastery who has taken the vow of silence. He's still human and no matter how strong his self control there will be a vestigial desire to speak, to converse with another human. One day, for no apparent reason and with his hardly knowing it, he will speak and thus fall from grace.

"Now in the subconscious mind of this hedonist there seems to have lurked a vestige of the bourgeois urge to marry. I didn't know it was there and therefore I had developed no defense against it. One day, for no good reason, to my amazement, it emerged in full strength and before I could stop myself I asked the woman with whom I was sleeping at the time, who happened to be you, to marry me. That was my fall from grace."

"Not very flattering for me."

"I didn't think it would be."

"Since you considered it an indiscretion on your part, why didn't you leave me?"

"Why should I have? It turned out to be a very pleasant arrangement. You were everything a good wife should be, a good and convenient lay when necessary, a good cook, an excellent housekeeper and, best of all, you didn't object to my having other women. I would have been stupid to leave you."

"And what about Rod?"

"You never asked me to diaper him nor when he got older to pick him up at the kindergarten. As long as he was no trouble why shouldn't I watch the growth of the fruit of my loins? But toward the end of our marriage everything changed. You became a feminist. You now objected to my having other women. And after I had laid you, you wouldn't let me sleep. You insisted that

I wait until I could develop another erection and hold it while you worked yourself into an orgasm. So I quit fucking you. But before I could get around to divorcing you, you obliged me by divorcing me."

"You were very generous. You gave me almost full custody of Rod and support for both of us."

"It was no skin off my back. I inherited more dough than any one man could use. I just told my lawyer to give you anything you wanted within reason and then forgot about it. As far as Rodney is concerned I wasn't likely to want to see him too often and if I did want to I knew that you with your bourgeois morality would arrange for me to do so."

They had now arrived at Lee's apartment house. Trevor told the cab driver to wait and carried Lee's overnight case in for her. As they entered the lobby they could see that the man behind the desk was half asleep, camouflaging his position by holding an open newspaper before his face.

"Good evening, Charlie," Lee said.

And the man with a slightly raised head and half open eyes automatically replied, "Good evening, Mrs. Dunham."

"Good evening, Charlie. Remember me?" Trevor asked. Charlie's head was now fully up and his eyes wide open as he gazed with interest at the two of them. "Of course, I remember you, Mr. Dunham."

Lee extended her hand to Trevor. "Now it's goodbye and farewell, Trevor."

He looked into her gray-green eyes. They were cool and aloof. He bent down and kissed her hand. "And fare thee well, my one and only ex-wife." And looking into her face he smiled and added, "If there be no man God be with you." He turned on his heel and left the lobby.

A final dig, Lee thought, but let him have it. It had been a good evening, she got to know the Crowleys and enjoyed both the play and the scene in the taxi. Margaret was right, there was a certain psychological satisfaction in a theatrically symbolic—and, she hoped, final—farewell.

"Charlie, let's have no misunderstanding. My instructions are still in force. If any time that man comes here-"

Charlie interrupted her. "You mean Mr. Dunham?"

"Yes, Mr. Dunham. If he ever comes here again I'm not at home."

By this time Charlie's head had dropped behind the newspaper. "Yes, Mrs. Dunham," he replied without looking up. Lee picked up her overnight case and went to the elevator and pushed the button.

12

For some time the two had been sitting silently close together on the bench near the end of Dunham's dock, Rod's arm around Laurie. The lake stretched wide and dark before them and the far wooded shore was only a darker ribbon. Above it hung a lemon slice of a moon, its upper half partly obscured by the gauze of a passing cloud. They were alone except for a night bird, an owl, whose hoot seemed to skim toward them across the water.

"I didn't expect you to," Laurie said, "but I'm glad you brought me here. It's very lovely at night." She leaned closer and his arm tightened.

Their silence continued. Tiny wavelets teased from the lake's surface by the slightest of night breezes lapped their low and gentle singsong against the steel drums beneath their feet. As they watched, the cloud receded from the moon and its luminosity increased, making its webbed silvery path across the tips of the wavelets more evident. Finally Rod stirred and asked, "Are you ready?"

"I've been ready almost from the first moment I met you. It's never been a question of whether but of time and place. I think we've waited long enough."

* * *

As they got into bed Laurie turned to Rod and kissed him. "It's the third time we've lain next to each other like this. Let's forget the preliminaries and start over just where we left off last night."

"It's alright with me, if it's alright with you. But you were telling me something just as your father interrupted us."

"Yes," Laurie said, "I'm a virgin."

"What?" Rod sat up. "You can't be!"

"But I am."

"But you can't be. Virgins don't go swimming in the raw on their first date with a guy. They don't lie around with him in the nude."

"This virgin does," Laurie said, her voice rising.

"I don't believe you." Rod swung his legs off the bed. "First you have sex with a ladybug, then you're a female ogre, and now you're a virgin. Damn it! You've got to be pulling my leg."

"There's a bit of exaggeration there," Laurie admitted in a milder tone. "On the hilltop a ladybug crawled up my thigh and I caught it before it became too intimate. So I'm still a virgin and I won't have much trouble proving it."

For a while Rod was silent. Then he said in a more subdued voice, "I've never slept with a virgin before. I'm not quite sure I know what to do."

"What's different about making a virgin?"

"I might hurt you."

"Sometimes I think you are a nice guy." She sat up and kissed the back of his neck. "Quit worrying about it and come on in."

His penetration was slow and careful, and he immediately came out. "Did it hurt?"

"Not much, but I think I bled a little."

"Lie still. I'll take care of it." The lamp on his side of the bed came on and Laurie closed her eyes to avoid its light. Rod plucked tissues from the box on the top of the night table and moments later dropped them into the basket in front of it. The light went out and Laurie felt the bed move as he again lay down next to her. "Everything's under control. Congratulations. You're no longer a virgin."

"I'm not too sure about that; I still feel pretty virginal."

"I don't understand. You bled, so I must have broken your seal."

"I always thought it was called the hymen or the maidenhead."

"You sure come from a literary family. Now most people call it `the seal,' some `the cherry.'"

"I prefer `seal.'" She felt for his hand. "I'm sure the operation was a success but I don't think that's all there is to it. Lots of women have lost their seals without the help of a man, in sports, in accidents—as I lost most of mine when I fell off my bike when I was twelve—and what have you. Aren't they still virgins?"

He felt her fingers fondling his. "I never thought about it before. I suppose they are."

Laurie leaned back on the pillow. "I think you only lose your virginity when a man goes off inside of you."

"Like a firecracker?" Rod asked, amused. "Men don't go off, they come."

"OK, go in and come." When he didn't move immediately she asked, "Aren't you up to it?"

"Of course I am. I'm as ready as they come." He chuckled. "We're getting our terms all mixed up. Well, here goes." But he entered as slowly and carefully as before. When he was fully in he asked, "Are you alright?"

"I'm fine but come closer." She pulled him down upon her breasts and wound her arms tightly about him.

"Mm, you smell good," Rod said.

"I'm wearing a special cologne in honor of the occasion. You smell good, too. Are you wearing anything?"

He managed to kiss the tip of her ear. "Nothing but my birthday suit. What you're smelling is just masculine me."

"I sure like having you next to me like this. I don't suppose there's any way we could get closer?"

"There is if we change position. Loosen your bear hug and I'll show you how." She relaxed her hold and he slipped his left arm under her back. "Now pull up your right leg so there is room for my hip, hold fast and roll toward me." As they rolled he placed a firm hand on her buttocks, imbedding himself to the utmost. She instinctively threw a leg over him, clasping his two legs with her one. They now lay on their sides, each in the other's tight embrace. For a few passionate moments they strained against each other, breast against breast, belly against belly, and pelvis against pelvis.

Then Laurie gasped, "I can't breathe!" In tacit agreement they relaxed their holds but only enough to allow them to breathe in comfort. They lay there entwined and coupled, drunk with sensation, with the mingled awareness of their fresh young bodies. They sensed each other's pulse and heartbeat and the slower rhythm of press and release of abdomen against abdomen as they breathed in and out. And in the warmth within there was the euphoria of envelopment and distension, increased by the foreknowledge of a more compelling rhythm to come.

"God! Are we in touch," breathed Rod, amazed at the quality of what he was experiencing.

"I had no idea it could be like this," Laurie said in an awed tone. "I never felt so whole in my entire life."

Rod could not resist. "Naturally when your hole is filled you'll feel more whole."

"Punster!" She couldn't reach higher so she kissed his chin. "What I meant was, fitted together like this, we make a complete and wonderful whole."

Serious again Rod said, "You put it extremely well. That's exactly how I feel, also."

For a few moments they sensed rather than spoke. Now it was Laurie's turn. "Rod, you're a great lover. I can truthfully say you're the greatest lover I've ever known."

"Thank you. But your great lover can't hold it much longer."

"Oh, what am I doing wrong? Of course." She removed her clasping leg.

Rod said nothing but began to move slowly back and forth within her. Laurie buried her face in the crook of his shoulder and pressed her lips against him. Rod built his crescendo, built it further, and then further. As his thrusts reached peak he felt Laurie's embrace tighten and realized how much he really cared, how deep and visceral his affection for her was, and as he was shaken by his climactic spasms, he cried out, "Laurie, I love you!"

And she responded with kisses softly pressed against his throat and neck.

OPERETTA
LIBRETTO

GADGETS
A Commercial Opera

CHARACTERS IN ORDER OF APPEARANCE

THE OFFICE FORCE (O.F.)————Typists, Clerks, etc.

FERDINAND CASHEW (CASH)————Paymaster and Accountant

MISS PECK (PECK)————Private Secretary to M.T.

MRS. O'RYAN (SCRUB)————The Scrub Woman

HORACE ALGER(HORACE)————The Office Boy

MARTIN THROCKMORTON (M.T.)————The Manager, Eastern Division

SYBIL MANNERS (SYBIL)————Debutante Ward of M.T.

FIRST VICE-PRESIDENT (1st VP)

SECOND VICE-PRESIDENT (2nd VP)

THIRD VICE-PRESIDENT (3rd VP)

PRESIDENT (PRES)
National Gadgets, Incorporated

OLD WORKER————Speaker (O.W.)

ACT ONE

TIME: 1930's—a Friday morning in May—Dawn.

SET: The outer office of the Eastern Division of the National Gadgets Corporation. Cashew's office left front stage partially open to audience. Countertop fenced in by a loosely woven iron grill of dollar signs with window at countertop. Telephone on counter. Open doorway backstage of counter. Immediately past counter, a wall-safe. Back left open doorway to foyer.

Right open doorway to executive offices. Back right Office Boy's desk and chair facing left stage. Vase of flowers on desk. Bench near desk for visitors. Door in rear wall to general offices and shipping room. Also on back wall a time clock. Other props might include photographs of enormous factories with smoking chimneys.

(As the curtain rises, Cashew is discovered busy at the counter of his office. The first contingent of the Office Force enters singing.)

I.1 Scena

O.F: We rise before the break of day
                  And thru the morning murk
                  With eagerness we make our way
                  To be on time to work!

                  Then lighted by the rays of dawn
                  We attack our work with zest;
                  And joyfully we labor on
                  Without a moment's rest.

(The first contingent of office workers go over to their lockers. Cashew comes out of his office.)

Cash: Make certain that you punch the clock.
                  If in this you are remiss
                  Just half your weekly pay I'll dock.
                  Twice amiss, I will dismiss.

(The workers hurriedly line up in front of the time clock and punch in.)

    O.F: Make certain that you punch the clock
                     Or half your weekly pay he'll dock.
                     Twice amiss, he will dismiss.
                     So with emphasis!

                     Mark the date
                     Punch the clock.
                     If once late
                     Your pay he'll dock.

                     With emphasis!

(Cashew retires to his office.)

    O.F: Too soon the day will run its course,
                     Oh! We linger on in sorrow;
                     And leave our desks in great remorse
                     Looking forward to the morrow.

                     And to each legal holiday
                     There but a single flaw is
                     The dreadful drawback that we may
                     Not spend it in the office,
                     Never spend it in the office.

(The second contingent of workers enters. The music and action is repeated from the beginning of the chorus until the second "With emphasis!" The first contingent sings along with the second contingent but does not participate in the action. In the meantime Peck has entered from right carrying a neatly folded newspaper. She goes over to Cashew the moment after the second "With emphasis!")

RECITATIVE

    Peck: How dare you threaten them in this fashion?
                     Such outrageous abuse of authority.
                     I shall report you to the Manager.
                     He'll resent this arrogance, I warn you.

SONG

For you must reck with Miss Peck,
His Private Secretary.
Since at his side it is my pride
To act as guiding fairy.

In me he has implicit trust;
Injustice I will frustrate.

Peck: It's his rule that no one can
Be canned without his mandate.

So don't be in a flutter about your bread and butter.
There is no need for fear.
So don't be in a fluster at this fellow's bluster.
He's merely the Cashier.

He'll pay your wage tho in rage
In his cage he's slinking.
For your Miss Peck, the "Private Sec,"
Will keep your check from shrinking!

(Both contingents had been listening to Peck sing. During the following dialogue they exit one by one through the backstage door and soon thereafter emerge again dressed in their work clothes. The women are wearing vari-colored smocks, the men colored office coats. Both articles of clothing have the initials "NG" embroidered on them in large fancy letters. The men wear enormous eyeshades and have enormous pencils tucked behind their ears. The women, of course, check their makeup. All are chewing gum.)

DIALOGUE

Cash: *(Coming over to Peck)* Miss Peck, you take dictation much better than you give it.

Peck: I certainly won't take it from you, and no one else needs to either.

Cash: They'll take it and like it.

Peck:	M.T. won't stand for it.
Cash:	Your precious manager, all sweetness and light. *(He grabs the newspaper out of Peck's hand and goes into his office with it. As he opens it, he says)* That's what's wrong with this place, no discipline. He never raises his voice.
Peck:	He never has reason to.
Cash:	Reason to? *(He leaves the newspaper on his counter and comes out.)* I suppose it's our regular business routine to send a customer thumb tacks when he orders diaper pins.
Peck:	Well, that was an error.
Cash:	*(Looking around)* Say, where is that dumb shipping clerk? He hasn't been fired?
Peck:	Of course not. But he won't be here.
Cash:	No!
Peck:	No! He was so mortified by the damage he'd done that he resigned. It's been a bad week. So many resignations. *(She counts them on her fingers.)* The shipping clerk, the plumber, the janitor, the night-watchman, the electrician and four traveling salesmen.
Cash:	What a shame. But no one's been hired; who's doing all their work?
Peck:	Horace.
Cash:	That lazy, good for nothing office boy? Why, he must work twenty-four hours a day.
Peck:	Twenty. M.T. insists that he take some rest.
Cash:	Very generous. Of course he insisted Horace accept a raise.
Peck:	Oh, no. Horace volunteered to take over the extra work. The boy believes he has executive ability…
Cash:	*(Finishing her sentence)* …and M.T. is giving him a chance to prove it.
Peck:	Exactly. M.T. always gives youth a chance.

| Cash: | (*Looking at his watch*) I'm afraid the young executive will be docked. |
| | Six o'clock already and he hasn't shown up. |

(*The Scrub Woman has entered through the rear door a few minutes before. She is dressed in her street clothes including her hat.*)

Scrub:	He's napping in the store room. Poor boy, he feel asleep on his feet. Let him rest awhile.
Peck:	No, we'd better wake him.
Cash:	He'll be mortified if he's late.
Peck:	Horace!

(*The whole Office Force takes up the cry. All are quieted by the rear door slowly opening. Horace appears, half asleep.*)

I.2 Scena

Horace:	Thru the fabric of my dreams
	To my drowsy ears it seems
	I hear a chorus
	In tones sonorous
	Calling, "Horace,
	Arise!"

| O.F: | Horace, Arise! |

Horace:	Listen to the admonitions
	Of your various ambitions.
	Don't ignore us,
	Work's before us.
	Hasten, Horace,
	Time flies!

| O.F: | Horace, time flies! |

| Horace: | So from my recumbent state I rose |
| | And gladly with my beck'ning fate I close. |

(*Horace does a bit of shadow boxing.*)

O.F: So from his recumbent state he rose.
To grapple with his beck'ning fate he goes.
And gladly to grapple with his beck'ning fate he goes.

Cash: My! My! What an energetic shipping clerk.
And you were always apathetic to work.
Pray give us some explanation
For this sudden transformation.

O.F: Yes, the explanation
For this sudden transformation.

Horace: If you seek a reason
You'll find it in the season
Of the year.

            Why the former shirker
Horace: Is now a willing worker
You shall hear.

            I'm galvanized by spring;
I'm in love!

O.F: He's in love!

Peck/Scrub: Ah! What a beautiful thing
Is young love.

Horace: Love spurs me on.
Fires brain and brawn.
It urges on ambition
To raise myself above
My low position.

Cash: So this is being in love,
A strange condition.

Horace: She's a debutante,
Known in ev'ry haunt

Horace:	Of wealth and gilded fashion. Ah! She would surely spurn My humble passion.
Peck/Scrub:	Our hearts for you do burn In deep compassion.
Horace:	Love spurs me on. Fires brain and brawn. For I can see quite clearly I need a job that pays a million yearly.
O.F:	Perhaps you'll get a raise, You deserve one dearly.
Horace:	Yes, I know That this romance Needs high finance. Ample dough Will much enhance My wooing stance.
Ensemble:	Yes, we know Etc.

DIALOGUE

Peck:	(*Going over to Horace*) Don't be discouraged. Come, tell us all about it. You'll feel better.
O.F:	Please do.

(*The bench is brought forward and Horace sits on it. All group themselves around him. Cashew returns to his office where he stands behind the counter, apparently reading his newspaper.*)

Horace:	It happened right here in the office, and only yesterday. I was at my desk, busily stamping envelopes, when I heard a voice, (*sighing*) her voice.

Scrub:	What'd she say?
Horace:	She said …"Excuse me."

(All sigh)

Horace:	"Excuse me, may I see Mr. Throckmorton?" I tried to answer…but I couldn't. My lips seemed glued together.
Cash:	*(suddenly from his office)* You shouldn't lick stamps. Use a sponge.

(All turn and glare at Cashew for interrupting)

Peck:	Go on, Horace, we're listening.
Horace:	I moistened my lips and asked, "What is the name please?" "…Just say it's Sybil."
All:	Sybil!
Cash:	So that's who it is. *(He comes out with the paper in his hand. He shows it to Horace.)* There's your girl-friend.

(Horace looks eagerly where Cashew points. He starts to take the paper but Cashew pulls it away and, standing a few feet away, reads for all to hear)

Cash:	SYBIL MANNERS BECOMES ENGAGED Daughter of the late Markham Manners will be married to Charles Chipper To Be June Bride.

(The Scrub Woman holds out her hand and Cashew gives her the newspaper.)

Scrub:	*(Looking at the paper)* But what was she doing here?
Peck:	M.T. is the Trustee of the Manner's Estate.
Cash:	Tough going, Horace, but don't be discouraged. Work hard, save your money, and some day…

(Peck hears a noise in the foyer. She interrupts)

1.3 Scena

RECITATIVE

Peck: Enough of high finance—
    The morning does advance.
    Footsteps echo in the foyer.
    Ah! 'Tis our belov'd employer.

(As Peck sings the last two lines, Cashew exits right. Then M.T. enters from foyer.)

M.T: Good morning, everyone.

O.F: Good morning, M.T..

M.T: Lovely weather we're having.

O.F: Yes, indeed., M.T.

(M.T. crosses to Office Boy's desk, smells flowers and puts one in his lapel. The Scrub Woman takes this opportunity to unobtrusively leave by the foyer.)

SONG

Women: Very seldom do you see
    A boss who so graciously
    Speaks to ev'ry employee.

Men: And you seldom come across
    A more even-tempered boss.
    He is never, never cross.

M.T: You exaggerate, of course.
    You're a model office force.

O.F: Thank you, sir.

M.T: Don't mention it.

O.F: Thank you, sir.

M.T: Don't mention it.
            When the weather is so fine
            I feel exceedingly benign.

Women: When an order's wrongly filled,

Men: We assure you this is rare,

Women: Or the buyer never billed,

Both: You will not hear him swear.

M.T: No, I'd never be so rude.
            Tho I'd like to, I'll confess.
            I continue to exude
            Benevolence unless, unless

            You show the least intention,
            Advocate or merely mention
                ORGANIZING!

            When I think of unionism,
            Bargaining collectivism
            I feel my anger rising.
            And when my wrath bursts into flame,
            The culprit faints in terror!

(One woman faints.)

O.F: It's weeks before she'll be the same
            So badly did he scare her.

M.T: For the folks I hate
            Are those who agitate.
            Don't do it or you'll rue it.

O.F: As the folks you hate
                Are those who agitate
                We'll never, never do it.
                Oh! No, M.T., we'd never, never do it.

DIALOGUE

M.T: Fall in, please. *(M.T. waits a moment while the Office
                Force lines up in two rows or ranks. Now he speaks)*

M.T: Today—

*(He stops, two women are still gossiping. Peck starts for them, but they are
nudged by their neighbors and immediately give M.T. their undivided attention. He continues)*

M.T: Today marks a milestone in industrial progress: the first
                anniversary of our epoch-making Chew for Prosperity
                Plan. *(Peck hands him a folder.)* Your loyal cooperation
                in chewing gum during working hours has produced
                remarkable results. *(He finds his place in the folder.)*
                Production in the chewing gum industry has risen 18.7 %.
                Our sale of gadgets to that industry has increased 36.6%!

(The Office Force applauds.)

                And we have been able to declare an extra dividend!

(The Office Force applauds louder. He hands the folder back to Miss Peck.)

                The entire movement will undoubtedly speed recovery.

*(He walks back and forth before the first rank of the Office Force, giving the
whole the once-over.)*

                Later in the morning you will be reviewed by our Presi-
                dent and his retinue of Vice-Presidents. *(He wags a
                warning finger.)* This means immaculate deportment
                *(He suddenly points at a particularly relaxed clerk and
                commands)* with the toes well turned in.

(The entire Office Force straightens up to a rigid military posture.)

Peck: And no shiny noses.

*(The women hurriedly pull their compacts out of the pockets of their smocks
and repair their noses.)*

M.T: You are all chewing gum?

O.F: *(Demonstrating)* Yes, sir.

M.T: Good. Our President will make a critical analysis of your chewing technique. Of course, you will welcome any corrections he may make.

O.F: Of course.

M.T: Then assemble when I ring and greet our Gadget President with your very best chewing.

(The Office Force marches around the room singing and exits rear.)

I.4 March Song

O.F: We fear no inspection.
Gladly we'll come
To strive for perfection,
Ardently we'll chew our gum.

We have no objection
To a change in style.
Under his direction, surely,
It must be worth-while.

(Peck has secured the newspaper from the Scrub Woman, has carefully refolded it and now presents it to M.T.)

DIALOGUE

Peck: Your morning paper, M.T.

M.T: Thank you, my dear Miss Peck.

(Peck exits to the right. M.T., now alone on the stage, hurriedly looks thru the newspaper and reads the financial section. He sighs and paces to and fro with the paper in his hand.)

Spoken Soliloquy

M.T: The financial section of the Daily Nose
Is the cause of much dejection, of many woes.
And today's quotation on United Soaps
Is the complete frustration of all my hopes.

How can I carry on? All I owned is gone.
And still worse—I've ruined my Ward,
Robbed the purse I was set to guard.

Curse that broker, sleek and smiling,
Who introduced me
To this poker, so beguiling
That it seduced me,
In my market-playing, my gambling lust,
Into thus betraying a sacred trust.

And now in my distress an evil thought
That I held at bay,
That without success hitherto had sought
To have its say,
To consciousness at last has fought
Its noxious way.

The market is bound to rise,
In the safe the payroll lies;
Borrow it for but a day,
By tomorrow you will repay.

No! No! Shall I refute
The world's esteem, my good repute?
Never had I such a thought before,
Of all crimes, embezzling I abhor.

(In a loud whisper)

With that payroll—take one last flyer—
Invest in—say—coal—it must go higher.

M.T: What does the paper say? "Cold snap today."
As it gets cold tons of coal will be sold.
I'll purchase all the anthracite,

M.T: And send the price up out of sight,
         I'll be a millionaire by night.

         Then before the dawn's red gold
         Lights the coming day
         I will this loan repay.
         That is—if it gets cold.

1.5 Scena

M.T: So speculation
         Must lead
         To peculation.

         I fear this morning light,
         The office is too bright.
         For such a deed
         I really need
         The dark and gloomy night.

(He steps into the doorway of Cash's office and looks to see if anyone is observing him.)

         But no one is in sight,
         I must not yield to fright.
         With utmost speed
         I will proceed
         To do what is not right.

(He starts to open the safe. He becomes very nervous.)

         My very life's at stake
         And yet my fingers shake.

(Cashew comes out of right doorway and sees M.T. at the safe.)

Cash: What's this?

(M.T. starts and stops opening safe. Cashew hides behind the upstage jamb of the doorway from which he has just emerged. He pokes his head out when he believes M.T. is not looking his way, and withdraws it when he believes M.T. is. Both sing more or less simultaneously.)

Cash:	What does he seek?	M.T:	Did someone speak?
	In the safe?		Am I safe?
	I'd better take a peek.		Did I hear a window creak?
	O-ho! I fear		It was but fear.
	There's mischief here.		There's no one here.
	If that safe should spring a leak		Have my nerves be come so weak
	We may not be paid this week.		That I start at ev'ry squeak?

(M.T. returns to safe—stops again—becomes very excited.)

Cash:	I have a feeling	M.T:	I have a feeling
	That something's queer.		That someone's near.
	He must be stealing		My head is reeling—
	Or out of gear.		What did I hear?

(M.T. calms himself)

M.T:	I must myself control
	Quiet, troubled soul.

(Opens safe and takes out money. Closes safe and moves out of Cashew's office.)

M.T: So speculation
Has led
To peculation.

—— I'll corner anthracite
And then a boom incite.
I'll be ahead,
Not in the red,
Recovered from this plight.

As night-owls end their flight,
When ears with sleep are tight,
With cat-like tread
I'll leave my bed,
Return to make things right.

But if the market's close
A slump in hard coal shows?

(Addresses himself to newspaper he has been carrying)

O, thou fateful sheet,
As you decide,
Life again is sweet
Or—suicide!

(M.T. buries head in his hands. Cashew quietly disappears. The telephone suddenly rings in Cashew's office. M.T. starts. He looks around. No one else is in the room. The phone rings again. He goes over and answers it.)

DIALOGUE

M.T: Hello, Throckmorton speaking…Oh, hello Sybil…
What are you doing up so early? (He listens for a minute.) Yes… What! Again! But what's the matter with Chipper?…Too rich!…Be reasonable…It's not his fault…now, don't cry…That's a good girl…I'll be expecting you.

(Peck had come from the right just as he answered the phone. She waits, a paper in her hand. As M.T. puts down the phone she speaks.)

Peck: Why all the fuss? It's not the first engagement she's broken.

M.T: But why Chipper?

Peck: Chipper's Cheese,
           Made to Please.

M.T: Can Charles help it if his Dad makes cheese? It's a good business. People have to eat.

Peck: Sybil's wealthy in her own right. She doesn't have to marry into a cheese fortune to eat

M.T: Of course not. But she's not nearly as wealthy as people think. I've covered it well. Not even Sybil knows.

Peck: But if she doesn't love Chipper?

M.T: Now, Miss Peck, let's be practical.

Peck: Practical! I've been practical all my life. What do I have to show for it? A job; a savings account…and…and…

(She begins to cry. M.T. comes over to her. She leans on his shoulder and then snuggles up a bit. He begins to stroke her hair, but quickly removes his hand. Little by little she stops crying.)

Peck: There's nothing like a good cry. (*She takes M.T. by the arm.*) M.T. don't be practical.

I.6 Duet

Peck: Sybil is so young and pretty,
           To be his would be a pity.

           Let her wed whom e'er she pleases,
           Why be fed on Chipper's Cheeses?

           For I know that true romance
           needs no finance.

           High or low one loving glance
           All dough supplants.

M.T: I am sure she would not relish
          Being poor for it is hellish.

          Therefore I'll let no one court her
          Whom in style cannot support her.

          For I know that good finance
          All pleasure grants.

          Minus dough there's not much chance
          For sweet romance.

          It is rash for one to marry
          Minus cash the deal to carry.

Peck: Why not woo and wed on credit?
          Why do you so greatly dread it?

Both: For I know
          Etc.

DIALOGUE

Peck: I had quite forgotten *(She hands him the paper she has
          been carrying)* a second complaint about a shipping
          delay.

M.T: A second complaint? Unheard of! Let me see it.

I.7 Scena

M.T: (*Reading letter out loud*)

IN RE ORDER OF ABOVE DATE
TO BE SHIPPED EXPRESS FREIGHT

IN CONFUSION WE HAD TO WAIT
A WEEK FOR THIS CRATE
OF DOG COLLARS.

IN CONCLUSION WE WISH TO STATE
WE SEEK A REBATE
OF TEN DOLLARS.

YOURS TRULY, C. DOOLEY,
TOGS FOR DOGS.

When this occurred before
I spoke no word nor swore.
But these mistakes must halt.
I'll have Horace here before us
And find out who's at fault.

Peck: If Horace made this sad mistake

M.T: Of this there is as yet some doubt.

Peck: His job is surely not at stake,
You'll only bawl him out.

M.T: Well, I never, never fire
When it is the first offence
For it's always my desire
To be impartial, hence

No one is badly treated
'Less the error is repeated.

M.T: But then my wrath bursts into flame,
     The culprit hides in terror!

Peck: I hope that he is not to blame
     For this repeated error.

M.T: Horace!
     Horace! Come here!

(Horace partially opens the rear door and then sings from behind it.)

Horace: As I gaily was at work
     At my duties as Shipping Clerk
     I heard a bawling,
     A sound appalling,
     M.T. calling,
     "Horace! Come here!"

(Horace comes slowly out.)

M.T: I have here a note from C. Dooley.
     He's complaining of lack of speed.

     Do not fear but answer me truly,
     No conniving,
     Who caused this crate to be so late
     In arriving?

Horace: I cannot tell a lie.
     It was I!
     It was I!

M.T: Horace, why do you ignore
     A statement I have often made before?
     I do not mind a lone transgression
     But you will find that in succession
     I will not tolerate
     Another collar crate
     Shipped late!

Horace: In contrition
          I my folly see
          Repetition
          Is not our policy.

          Forgive me!

M.T: No!

Peck: Forgive him!

Horace: Forgive me.
          Indeed the fault was mine
          But I have saved on twine.

TWINE SONG

1.

Horace: With economy in view
          I made one winding do for two.

Peck: With economy in view
          He made one winding do for two.

M.T: I follow you,
          Use one for two.

Horace: But as the crate was being weighed
          The single strands quite quickly frayed.
          It was returned.

Peck: It was returned.
          It was returned to him for packing.

2.

Horace: Being a thrifty employee
          I made two twinings do for three.

Peck: Being a thrifty employee
            He made two twinings do for three.

M.T: Of course I see.
            Use two for three.

Horace: But yet it seems it hardly paid
            For once again it quickly frayed.
            And was returned.

Peck: And was returned.
            And was returned to him for packing.

                        3.

Horace: But I knew a collar crate
            Could not be needing strands quite eight.

Peck: But he knew a collar crate
            Could not be needing strands quite eight.

M.T: You knew no crate
            Needed strands quite eight?

Horace: So on I toiled still undismayed
            To find a fraction that's unafraid
            Of being returned.

Peck: Of being returned.
            Of being returned to him for packing.

                        4.

Horace: Now that I report to you
            That seven strands for eight will do.

            That twelve percent of bills you've paid
            For twine is now by skill defrayed.

            Please change your mind,
            About this sacking.

Peck:	Please change your mind. Please change your mind about this sacking.
M.T:	If what you say is really true, If seven strands for eight will do, I cannot refuse you, I indeed excuse you.
Horace:	Thank you, sir.
M.T:	Don't mention it.
Horace:	Thank you, sir.
M.T:	Don't mention it. When the firm has saved on twine I feel exceedingly benign.
Horace:	Ah, you seldom come across A more even-tempered boss. He is never, never cross.
Peck:	Ah, you seldom come across A better boss.
M.T:	Ah, you fill my heart with joy You're a model office boy. But take my advice Don't make this error thrice. Forget it and you'll regret it.
Horace/Peck:	As to your advice In re my (his) doing it thrice I (He) never shall (will) forget it.

THE ABOVE MATERIAL IS DEVELOPED INTO A FINALE.

(M.T. and Peck exit right. Horace exit by rear door. The stage is empty for a moment and Sybil then enters from stage left. Seeing no one around she takes off her furs and sits on the bench. Etc.)

I.8 Song

Sybil: From party to party, from place to place
                 I've played and I've travel'd at a furious pace—
                 But I'm sick at heart
                 From playing the part
                 Of a foolish, frivolous play-girl.

                 I'm tir'd of being
                 A gay butterfly.
                 I wish fate would clip my wings.
                 I'd much rather sing
                 A sweet lullaby
                 Or wash out a baby's things.

                 I've flirted in Paris, I've gambled in Nice
                 But not for an hour has my soul been at peace.
                 There's no greater curse
                 Than the overstuffed purse
                  Of a foolish, frivolous play-girl.

                 Were I but poor
                 I'd soon be wed,
                 A workingman's humble spouse.
                 I'd find life's allure
                 In making his bed,
                 In keeping my lov'd one's house.

DIALOGUE

(Peck enters from right carrying a number of papers. She sees Sybil sitting on the bench.)

Peck: Good morning, Miss Manners.

Sybil: Good morning, Miss Peck. May I see M.T.?

Peck: Of course, he's expecting you.

Sybil: Thank you.

(She exits to the right. Peck watches her go, then absent-mindedly fixes a hair pin. She goes over to Horace's desk and pushes a buzzer, which sounds loudly. Horace comes quickly in. He wears heavy work gloves and carries a pair of pliers. There is a smudge of grease on one cheek.)

Peck: *(Putting down the large number of papers she had been carrying as a pile on Horace's desk)* Rush orders, Horace.

(Horace rapidly takes off his gloves, puts on an eye shade, tucks a pencil behind his ear and begins to shuffle through the orders, stamping them with the various rubber stamps that litter his desk. Peck stays and silently watches him as he works with a great show of energy. A moment or two passes.)

Peck: What efficiency. I'm sure you have great executive ability.

Horace: *(Stopping and lifting his head)* Thank you, Miss Peck. I only wish I were one now—then I could propose to Sybil. *(He drops his head.)* But she would surely laugh at me—a mere office boy. *(He furiously continues at his work.)*

Peck: Nonsense. You're a very important person. For all practical purposes you're a great executive already.

Horace: At my salary?

Peck: But think of your glorious future. You have the makings of a great man...like Lincoln...like Jackson... like...HENRY FORD. The similarity is obvious. They all started in some menial capacity.

Horace: Like Office Boy?

Peck: Or janitor...night-watchman. Why, you hold so many menial positions you're bound to be a great man.

Horace: Oh! Miss Peck, do you really think so?

Peck: I'm sure of it.

Horace Then I'll propose to Sybil at once. *(Horace leans back in his chair and from the beautiful smile that creeps over his face you can tell that Sybil is accepting his proposal. Peck starts out)*

Peck: She's in M.T.'s office now. *(Horace starts)* I'll tell her you have a message for her. *(Peck quickly exits right.)*

(Horace looks wildly about as though to escape, but then seizes a piece of paper and begins to write. Sybil enters quietly from right and stands in front of Horace's desk.)

Sybil: Yes?

(Horace raises head and seeing Sybil rises. His legs will not support him so he supports himself with his hands on his desk.)

Sybil: Are you ill?

Horace: A little feverish, I think. My cheeks grow hotter and hotter—my temperature rises—but I have a sinking feeling in my stomach.

Sybil: Indigestion?

Horace: *(Ignoring her question)* My heart burns, my veins vibrate, my brain is on fire—but I have cold feet.

Sybil: *(Feeling his brow)* Poor boy. What ails you?

Horace: I'm in love.

(He steals a look at what he has written and then continues)

Love has given me strength and vision. Ambition seethes within me. Love is my spark plug, fuel for my engine, ergs, volts, watts, power. Sybil, I am only an office boy but lifted up by your love I shall scale the heights of Wall Street.
Sybil! Will you marry me?

(At this moment the buzzer sounds; Horace hesitates. The buzzer sounds again.)

Horace: Excuse me. (Horace exits rear.)

Sybil: What a queer feeling. Can his illness be contagious? My heart has been deaf to the pleadings of an authentic Chipper Cheese…and now it quivers at the voice of a mere office boy.

A mere office boy…how could I have said this? Is he not the Prince Charming of my dreams? Does he not offer me all those glorious experiences my wealth has denied me?

A little cottage, all my own, with no obsequious servants to annoy me. A jolly washing on the line, with

Horace: undies long, short and medium, decorated with rakish patches by my own two hands.

Protecting his familiar feet from the winter's cold by plain and fancy darning, and guaranteeing the privacy of his pants by strong and well-placed buttons.

All these honest, simple pleasures Horace offers me. Together we shall plunge into the ennobling struggle for existence. Shoulder to shoulder we shall stand, gallantly meeting sickness, unemployment…and other acts of God.

But wait—if I marry Horace he will no longer be poor. With my fortune at his disposal there will be no need for struggle—he will no longer be the Horace I love.

I.9 Scena

Sybil: Must I ever be oppressed
By vested interest?

If I take him for my mate
My stocks and bonds and real estate
Again will separate us two.
The moment that I say "I do"
The workingman I just had wed
A cap'talist becomes instead.

Must I ever be oppressed
By vested interest?

(Horace enters from rear)

Horace: Excuse me if I am abrupt
This bell again may interrupt
This prolonged proposal.
I know I list as bankrupt stock
But fortune soon will loudly knock
And deposit funds at my disposal.

Horace: I have a rendezvous with destiny.
            Sybil, will you invest in me?

Sybil: Horace, I love you.

Horace: She loves me!

Sybil: Yes, I love you.
            But I cannot marry you.

Horace: What irony is this?
            What imperfect bliss?
            She loves me
            But she cannot marry me?

Sybil: *(Kissing Horace on the forehead)*

            Please take this testimonial
            That my love is true.
            But intentions matrimonial
            Will not at present do.
            Indeed we should be mating
            But my financial rating
            Permits us no debating.
            Intentions matrimonial
            Will not at present do.

(They sing more or less together.)

Horace: *(Showing his empty pockets)*

            My portion patrimonial
            Would scarcely nourish you.
            So intentions matrimonial
            Will not at present do.

            Indeed we should be mating
            But my financial rating
            Permits us no debating.

Horace: Intentions matrimonial
Will not at present do.

Sybil: Were I but poor   Horace: Ah, she has refused me.

I'd soon be wed,   I knew that she would
spurn

A workingman's   My humble passion.
humble spouse.

I'd find life's allure   Love spurs me on.

In making his bed,   Fires brain and brawn.

In keeping my lov'd   It urges on ambition
one's house.   To raise myself above
My low position.

Both: Indeed we should be mating
But my financial rating
Permits us no debating.
Intentions matrimonial
Will not at present do.

Sybil: Love, I know   Horace: Yes, I know

Will look askance   That this romance

At high finance.   Needs high finance.

Deadly dough   Ample dough

Will ruin all chance   Will much enhance

For true romance.   My wooing stance.

There's not much   This romance

For true romance   Needs high finance

With deadly dough.   How will I know?

(There is an instrumental postlude in which Horace returns to his desk and sits staring at the blotter. As Sybil leaves, she glances back at him, glances back at him a second time and then exits left. Horace sighs. He again begins to stamp papers with rubber stamps. Peck enters quietly from the right. Horace sees her and answers her unspoken question.)

DIALOGUE

Horace:	She loves me.
Peck:	Congratulations.
Horace:	But she can't marry me at present. Financial reasons.
Peck:	Oh! Then you only have to wait 'till you're a great executive.
Horace:	I'm afraid I'll never be one. I keep making mistakes. And the harder I work, the worse it gets.
Peck:	*(She looks at the right door to see if M.T. might have heard Horace.)* You must concentrate, Horace.
Horace:	I've tried everything. I've worn blinders. I've held my breath. But nothing helps. I've done the only thing left for me to do.
Peck:	You're not resigning?
Horace:	Oh! No, I've invented a machine to do my work.

(He takes a large roll of paper out of a desk drawer and unrolls it. Peck looks over his shoulder as Horace reads aloud.)

PLAN FOR A MECHANICAL OFFICE WORKER

One-eighth horse-power, air-cooled and radio-controlled. Completely equipped with conditioned reflexes, super-salesmanship, self-starter and automatic self-correcting device.

Peck:	It looks good to me.
Horace:	See, I sit here…push this row of buttons…and no mistakes.
Peck:	Why don't you show it to the President? I'm sure he'll be interested. *(A bell rings in the Executive Offices right. M.T. enters from right.)*

I.10 Scena

RECITATIVE

M.T: The President has come.

(Horace puts away plan. Peck exits right.)

M.T: Horace, to the rear.
            Gird each worker with his gum
            And bring him chewing here.

(M.T. exits right. Horace exits rear. Then the Three Vice-Presidents enter from foyer left.)

TRIO

All: Three Vice-Presidents are we.

1st VP: I'm One.

2nd VP: I'm Two.

3rd VP: And I am Three.

All: Or as frequently is heard:

1st VP: I'm First.

2nd VP: I'm Second.

3rd VP: And I am Third.

1st VP: As Shakespeare said, "what's in a name?"

2nd VP: Our work, our duties are the same.

3rd VP: To warm a chair for a handsome fee.

All: Three Vice-Presidents are we.

(Buzzer rings. M.T., Peck and Cashew enter from right. Horace and Office Force enter from rear. Horace sits at his desk. Office Force forms two rows or ranks.)

M.T./Peck/
Cash: How do you do?

VPs: Pleased to meet you. The President will soon be here.

(M.T., Peck and Cashew give the Office Force the once-over)

M.T: Straighten your rows.

Peck: Powder your nose.

Cash: Turn in your toes.

All three: Everyone pose.

Executive
Sextet: Let ev'ry office resident
            Now greet his Gadget President.

(Fanfare. President enters from foyer left. Applause.)

O.F: We greet our Gadget President.

Pres: I'm here for a friendly call.

O.F: Flexing strong and willing jaws.

Sextet: They'll masticate as you dictate.

All: And eradicate all flaws.

O.F: We're here for inspection,
            Gladly we've come,
            To hear your correction,
            Ardently we chew our gum.

O.F: We have no objection
              To a change in style.
              Under your direction
              Surely, it must be worth while.

1st VP: Jaws are biting, teeth uniting.

2nd VP: Lips are writhing, nostrils tense.

3rd VP: Hearts are pumping, pulses thumping.

All three: They are eager to commence.

Sextet: Hearts are pumping, pulses thumping.
              They are eager to commence.

(The ensemble divides into two parts, each singing one of the sets of the verses below and they join on the last two lines.)

ENSEMBLE

We're here for inspection.
He'll quickly teach us how to chew
Gladly we've come
To chew with ease and grace.
To strive for perfection,
We'll learn exactly what to do
Ardently we chew our gum.
To shift our gears, to change our
Pace.

We have no objection
He'll bring to mastication
To a change in style
An innovation—the latest style.

Under your superb direction
It will be worth while.

DIALOGUE

Pres: *(To Office Force)* Thank you, thank you, thank you very much…but please restrain yourselves. The artistic gum-chewer cultivates a perfect emotional equilibrium. His features match the solemn serenity, the philosophic impassivity of that master cud-chewer, the cow. Please arrange yourselves in appropriate positions and ruminate until we are ready.

(Horace and the Office Force carry out his instructions. The President makes a cursory inspection of the Office Force. He is followed by M.T. and the three Vice-Presidents as a sort of color guard. The President stops before an Old Worker.)

This man is not chewing gum.

M.T: Attention! *(The Old Worker stands to attention.)*

Pres: My good man, why are you not chewing gum?

O.W: It's my false teeth, sir. The gum gets under my plate.

Pres: I see. You realize, of course, that you are depriving the Corporation of business and that your position and salary are intimately bound up with the amount of business we do?

O.W: I know that, sir. It worries me. If I try to chew, I spend all my time taking my teeth out, removing the gum and putting my teeth back in again. I don't get my work done.

Pres: That won't do.

O.W: No, sir. It's a dilemma, sir. It's bad for business either way, whether I chew or I don't chew.

M.T: Have you thought of getting a new plate? One that the gum can't get under?

O.W: Yes, sir. I've priced one. I'm saving up the money, but it will take another nine months.

Pres: And we must lose your business for nine months?

O.W: You'll excuse me, sir. But I suggest that the Corporation loan me the money so that I can buy the plate now. I'll pay it back in installments at whatever interest you wish.

Pres:	Would that be a large loan?
O.W:	About sixty dollars, sir.
Pres:	The Corporation is always happy to cooperate with its employees in all matters which will help business but I am afraid I could not authorize such a large loan myself. I would have to secure the assent of the Board of Directors. I do not believe that they would loan such a large amount to a mere clerk. Should you be an executive, that would be a different matter. In that case, the Board would be glad to loan a larger amount at a very low interest. Is there any chance that you might be promoted?
O.W:	I doubt that very much, sir. I have worked here for 28 years and there is no sign whatsoever that I might be promoted.
Pres:	Then I am very sorry, but I am afraid that I will have to ask Mr. Throckmorton to give you a week's notice. We must replace you with someone who is capable of chewing gum.

(The President joins M.T. in the center of the room.)

Pres:	That is something new. In my inspection of the other divisions of the Corporation, I found no one who is not capable of chewing gum. Anything else unusual around here, M.T.?
M.T:	Well, there have been quite a number of resignations here lately.
Pres:	Merely seasonal unemployment. Spring fever. You can't blame people for leaving a stuffy office in such lovely weather. I should have been a scientist, a biologist, one never encounters interesting phenomena in an office.
Cash:	*(Loudly whispering to M.T.)* How about Horace?
Pres:	*(Overhearing)* Horace? Who's Horace?

(M.T. points to Horace who reclines at his desk in a particularly ruminative pose.)

Pres:	*(Examining him from the distance)* Can't see anything phenomenal from here. What's wrong with him? Some rare occupational disease?

M.T:	*(Going over and placing his hand on Horace's shoulder. Horace continues to ruminate as though M.T. was not present.)* I have shown great faith in Horace. I have put him in charge of sales, of supplies and of shipping.
Pres:	Really? How many men does he have under him?
M.T:	None. He's in sole charge. He's been most efficient until this morning when something happened to his morale: he duplicated an error.
Pres:	*(Coming over and examining Horace more closely)* Undoubtedly a case of split personality. Perhaps a few fatherly words of advice would improve his morale.
M.T:	Horace! *(Horace immediately gets up from his desk and steps forward.)*
Pres:	My son, what profit it a man that he be loaded with honors, yet lose his job?
Horace:	To err is but human, sir.
Pres:	But un-businesslike, Horace. Un-businesslike.
Horace:	The flesh is weak, sir, and this mortal machine is prone to slip a cog now and then.

(Horace produces his Plan)

I.11 Song

Horace:	The human machine is too weak, too erratic.
	It leaks and it creaks and it suffers from static.
	No matter how often it may be inspected
	And pepped up and stepped up, adjusted, corrected—
	It constantly rattles thru life's daily battles
	For never, ah! Never can it be perfected.
	For man is but human tho ever so clever.
	He'll make some mistake in the highest endeavor.
	By striving and struggle this can't be prevented,
	Defeated, deleted, annulled, circumvented.

Horace:	He'll stay inefficient, by nature deficient, Until a mechanical man is invented.

Behold then in characters diagrammatic
A plan for a worker who's all automatic;
Who cannot make errors in adding up digits;
Who ne'er gets an itch, has a day-dream nor fidgets;

Who will not haunt restrooms, whose fingers are tireless;
Who, ten at a time, can be guided by wireless.
Just give him a brush-up, a shine and an oiling,
And he will forever and aye, go on toiling.

DIALOGUE

Pres:	*(Takes plan from Horace and looks at it. VPs look over shoulder.)* H'm, rather complicated.
1st VP:	Very complicated.
2nd VP:	Would be expensive to install.
1st/3rd VP:	Very expensive.
Pres:	*(To Horace)* Have you ever built one?
Horace:	No, Sir.
Pres:	It probably won't work, they rarely do. *(To VPs)* When is our next Director's Meeting?

(1st VP whispers to 2nd VP, who whispers to 3rd VP, who looks through a little book to no avail.)

1st VP:	It's rather far off.
2nd VP:	But not too far off.
3rd VP:	But not soon.
Pres:	*(To Horace)* Be glad to consider it at that time. Now, young man, follow me closely. I will demonstrate how to achieve the maximum efficiency with the material at hand, *(indicating the Office Force)* imperfect as they may be.
	Pass out fresh gum.

(VPs exit left into foyer. Peck passes container for old gum, M.T. passes out fresh gum and Cashew passes waste basket for wrappers.)

Pres: Wait, don't chew it yet. Let it steep a while—improves the consistency.

(He begins to lecture) The rhythmic chewing of gum during the act of labor has many beneficial results. All the activities of the body and mind—the motions of the limbs, the telegraphic operation of the nerves—the very heart's throbs—become coordinated and move inexorably to the regularly recurring beat. Nervous strain is eliminated, relaxation induced, and work is found much less taxing.

(The VPs wheel in a giant Metronome and take off cover.)

Pres: My experiments have shown that the average, unskilled masticator can sustain a rhythm of about 80 Metronome Mälzel or about 40 complete operations a minute. (The President sets Metronome at 80 and lets it tick for a moment.) For demonstration purposes we will try a slower tempo—say—Larghetto.

(He sets the Metronome accordingly. The three VPs come forward, line up and commence to chew in time to the Metronome's ticking.)

Let us analyze their technique. Only two motions are used: one, the jaw compresses the cud of gum, two, the tongue turns the cud over—and a fresh surface is presented to the molars. This alternation gives us that age-old formula: *(In time with the Metronome)* Chew, turn it; chew, turn it; chew, turn it; chew, turn it.

It is the tongue motion that we are interested in. *(He watches the VPs chew for a moment.)* This is nature's mechanism to see that our food is properly chewed. But gum is not nutritious. Can this incessant revolution of the gum be wasted motion? Let us experiment.

(To VPs) Eliminate the tongue motion.

(They do as told and immediately run into difficulties.)

Pres: What happens? The gum wears thin; it is sliced in half; the teeth click. There is no resilience, no bounce. So, we have concrete proof: the tongue motion is not wasted motion. But perhaps we can eliminate some of it.

(The 1st VP flashes his pocket watch at the President. The President smoothly picks up the cue.)

But time is flying. Sufficient to say, I carried on intensive laboratory research on this subject for twelve months—I completely demolished two tons of gum.

At long last my experiments were rewarded; I established the average mean ratio for the emasculation of gum: .333 and a 1/3 revolutions per mastication.

(Applause. Cries of Marvelous! Bravo! Etc.)

Pres: Or, in colloquial language, one can chew three times before the gum wears so thin as to require turning. So we have our new formula: Chew, chew, chew, turn it. Chew, chew, chew, turn it. (The VPs demonstrate) A device of two-fold efficiency, alternately rests the tongue and jaw muscles, and yet speeds up the entire process by .375%.

(Applause. Cries of Astounding! Ingenious! Etc.)

Pres: One word of warning before we commence. No emotional display. It is unwise to smile while chewing. (VPs demonstrate. One bites his tongue.) Or to frown. (VPs demonstrate. Others bite their tongues.) Or injuries will occur.

(The VPs wind up the Metronome. The President takes out a baton and raps on the Metronome for order. The Office Force straightens up. The President's baton comes down and the ballet commences.)

I.12 Chewing Gum Ballet

Exec. Sextet: Chew, chew, chew, turn it.
See how quickly you can learn it.
Do not smile, do not frown.
Move your jaws straight up and down.

(Someone bites their tongue.)

(Action and music is developed.)

Pres: Now pretend you're working
             At packing, typing, clerking.

(Office Force pretends to work.)

O.F: How relaxing, how relaxing.
             Work is much less taxing,
             Much less taxing.

Pres: Now, if you please,
             Shall we go a little faster?

O.F: A little faster? Of course.

Pres: They're a model Office Force.

Exec Sextet: They're a model Office Force.

Horace: When you're really keyed up,
             No one minds a little speed up.

O.F: When you're really keyed up,
             No one minds a little speed up.

(President conducts an accelerando to a climax ending with a gum glissando. The President and Executive Sextet applaud.)

RECITATIVE

Pres: A very good performance. At this new tempo we can
             handle a much greater volume of business—if we can
             get the business. Ah! All my work—my experiments—
             gone to waste unless we get new orders.

O.F: Get new orders. Get new orders.

Pres: How?

1st VP: Advertise.

Pres: Too expensive.

O.F: Too expensive.

2nd VP: Lower prices.

Pres: With our overhead?

O.F: With our overhead?

3rd VP: Reduce overhead expenses.

Pres: That's it. Reduce overhead. Lower prices. Gain volume.

O.F: Reduce overhead. Lower prices. Gain volume.

Pres: But how?

M.T: Cut wages.

3 VPs: Cut wages.

Pres: *(To Office Force)* Cut wages?

(There is a grand pause in the music. The members of the Office Force look at the President and each other. They hesitate, but finally they sing)

O.F: Oh, that's all right.
               Anything for the dear old firm.
               We'd never fight
               Or emulate the treacherous worm.

               For we're a model Office Force.

Pres /
Exec. Sextet: That statement we'll endorse.
               They are a model Office Force.

O.F: We're glad to make the sacrifice,
              To keep your stock on par.
              So lower ev'ry gadget price
              And sell them by the car.

Cash: These hypocrites deserve no praise,
              Their devotion is pretended.
              I'm sure they'd rather have a raise
              Than pile up profits to be dividended.

O.F: You malign us. You malign us.
              Never have our brains recorded
              A single thought so mean and sordid.

              Tho at five we must be waking,
              Tho from gum our jaws are aching,
              Tho you cut the wage we're making,

              With willing hands and joyous heart
              We shall always do our part.
              WE SHALL ALWAYS DO OUR PART.

(The above is developed as a finale.)

CURTAIN

END OF ACT ONE.

ACT TWO

TIME: The same day, late afternoon.

SET: The shipping room. Piles of crates, boxes, etc. There is a waste high pile of crates at the back of the room. Doorways left front and right front. Door in rear wall a few feet right of left wall. The sun floods through a window at the back of the room. There is a large thermometer on the wall indicating 90 degrees Fahrenheit.

(M.T. is on the stage as the curtain rises. He carries his jacket and a newspaper, mops his brow and is looking at the thermometer.)

II.1 Scena

M.T: At ninety Fahrenheit
      Who'll buy my anthracite?

      Sun shining bitter bright,
      Cloudless sky,
      Have pity on my plight.
      Must I die?

      Howl wind, come snow.
      Freeze, blizzard blow.
      Chill the smiling face of spring,
      Bring the frost's intemp'rate sting.
      Dim the sun and strain his rays,
      Make men long for a warming blaze.
      Freeze mankind and sell my coal,
      Or the flames of hell will sear my soul.
      Sun shining bitter bright,
      Cloudless sky,
      Have pity on my plight.
      Must I die?

(M.T. puts pistol to his head. Cashew enters right and sees him.)

DIALOGUE

Cash: Stop.
Where's your pride?
A business man of your reputation
Shooting himself
For a mere $ 12, 847.39?

M.T: (Taking down pistol) Howd'ja know how much it was?

Cash: I saw you at the safe
But I won't tell.
Surely the Manager can touch the firm for a loan.

M.T: *(Raising pistol again)* But I can't even pay the interest.

(As Cashew pleads with M.T. he comes closer to him as though to take the gun away from him. M.T points the gun at Cashew who retires and M.T. puts it to his own head again.)

Cash: Wait!
Think of the firm,
Of your responsibilities.
You can't recoup your losses when you're dead.

Wait!
Think of the investors in N.G. stock.
Think of the widows and the orphans.

(M.T. wipes his forehead, closes his eyes and prepares for the final dispatch.)

Wait!
Wait!
Have pity on the worms.

M.T: *(Opening his eyes)* The worms?

Cash: Yes, the worms.

(During the following song M.T. holds the gun ready at his head, relaxing and taking it down little by little as Cashew explains.)

SONG

Cash: The worms limp out for they have the gout
And cannot travel quickly.
The worms crawl out and squirm about
For they feel extremely sickly.

For those who die in bankruptcy
With the worms will not agree.
For the worms digestion, you will see,
Depends on Dun and Bradstreet.

So pity, pity the race of worms,
There are so many bankrupt firms.
So pity, pity their poor insides,
There are so many suicides.

Each little beast who hoped to feast
On honest vermicelli
Will meet his doom and find his tomb
Within your wormy belly.

Let any worm but gnaw your skin
And ptomaine poisoning will set in.
For you'll have died in grievous sin,
Unblessed by Dun and Bradstreet.

So pity, pity the race of worms,
There are so many bankrupt firms.

Cash / M.T: So pity, pity their poor insides,
There are so many suicides.

(M.T. looks at his gun, shudders just a bit, shakes his head and puts it away.)

DIALOGUE

Cash:	*(Coming over and putting his arm around M.T.)* A most humane decision.
M.T:	But I'll go to jail!
Cash:	Don't worry. I'll cover it up.
M.T:	Nothing dishonest?
Cash:	Of course not. We'll issue nine payroll checks, one each for Horace's extra jobs, endorse them, deposit them to the firm's credit, and—presto!—no deficit.
M.T:	But…uh…
Cash:	*(Walking him to and fro)* Look. If we had no Horace, we'd have to issue the nine checks anyway. And if it weren't for you (jabbing M.T. with his finger) he'd never been put in sole charge.
	So why hesitate? It's the businesslike thing to do and…
Cash / M.T:	What could be more honest?

(M.T. sits down on a packing crate with a sigh of relief. He takes out two cigars and hands one to Cashew. They both light up.)

Cash:	Of course I shall expect the usual commission.
M.T:	Of course.
Cash:	Fifty percent.
M.T:	Outrageous, sir. Ten.
Cash:	Fifty. And I'll throw in a valuable piece of information.
M.T:	And what's that?
Cash:	Sybil's in love again. With Horace.
M.T:	What? So that's why this sudden ambition. Wants to marry Sybil, does he? I'll fix him. I'll fire him.
Cash:	You can't.
M.T:	I'll fire him, I tell you.
Cash:	You can't. You'd better let me handle this matter too.
M.T:	You'll stop Sybil from marrying Horace?

Cash: I guarantee it.

(They start out of the room)

M.T: Cashew, how can I repay you?

Cash: (As they exit right) Don't worry, you'll pay me.

(Immediately after their exit Sybil slowly enters left.)

II.2 SONG

Sybil: What have I done to merit
High heaven's hilarity?
Why was I doomed to inherit
This load of prosperity?

Why did not Father bequeath it
To some worthy charity,
Rather than crushing beneath it
His blameless posterity?

1.

If M.T. would allow it
I'd find some good cause and endow it.
I'd set up the Sybil Foundation
For watch-dogs who need a vacation,
For bridesmaids who can't afford bonnets,
For poets who have to write sonnets,
For kiddies who've lost all their marbles,
For robins who've worn out their warbles.
Each check thus bestowed
Would lighten my load
Of unwanted prosperity.

2.

I'd subsidize needy romancers
To think up the very best answers
To the questions that floor ev'ry mother
When Junior keeps asking another.

Sybil: Like "Why can't a dog go to heaven?"
      Or "Mama, how lucky is seven?"
      Or "Why do you always say maybe?"
      Or "Tell me how God makes a baby."
      Each check thus bestowed
      Would lighten my load
      Of unwanted prosperity.

3.

      I'd make a substantial donation
      Towards the moral and health education
      Of savage and ignorant races
      Who never wear garters or braces.
      I'd trade them white trousers for g strings,
      Insure them from snake bites and bee stings,
      Provide them with nicely wrapped doses
      Of gargles to cure halitosis.
      Each check thus bestowed
      Would lighten my load
      Of unwanted prosperity.

(Sybil sits on a crate and props her chin on her hand. Cashew enters right. He looks to see if anyone else is in the room and then goes over to her.)

DIALOGUE

Cash: Poor girl, it is tough to be broke, especially the first time.

(Sybil raises her head and looks at him.)

      I told M.T. not to invest your funds in United Soaps—
      slippery stocks at their best—and now they have gone
      down, down, down.

(Sybil starts to speak; he goes on before she gets her first word out.)

      But you should worry. *(With a wave of his hand)* You're
      going to marry Chipper—and a good thing too, you've
      no idea what it's like to be poor.

Sybil: But I have.

Cash: But have you? Listen:

II.3 SONG

Cash: If you are lucky,
              Patient and plucky,
              You'll land a position,
              A counter career.

              'Steen bucks and commission
              Retailing tin thimbles
              At Woolworth's or Gimbel's
              Year after year.

              You'll suffer in silence,
              Tho itching for violence,
              It's no ma'am, and yes sir,
              Three aisles to the front.

              A father confessor
              To finicky matrons
              And crusty old patrons
              Who mumble and grunt.

              Oh! The life of a shop girl is no bed of roses.
              She's dead on her feet by the time the store closes.
              She works like a horse and gets, for her pains,
              A few measly dollars and varicose veins.

              If you get married
              Expect to be harried
              By armies of vermin
              And curious mice,

              By babies who squirm in
              Their diapers and wet them,
              By neighbors who pet them
              And offer advice.

              From cooking and cleaning,
              From child-birth and weaning,

Cash: You'll grow gray and toughen'd,
A bony old nag.

Your hands red and roughen'd,
Your knees raw from scrubbing,
Your back bent from tubbing,
A worn out old hag.

Oh! The life of a house wife is no bed of roses.
Her work never ends for her shop never closes.
She slaves day and night and gets, for her pains,
As many free boarders as heaven ordains.

(Cashew waits for her reaction to his song, and she remains silent for a few moments. Then she asks:)

DIALOGUE

Sybil: There isn't any chance of my stocks going up again?

Cash: Not a chance.

Sybil: It was nice of you to tell me.

Cash: You're not very appreciative. I love wedding cake.

Sybil: I'm afraid it won't be that kind of a wedding.

Cash: Say, who're you marrying, anyhow?

Sybil: *(Skipping off stage right)* Horace!

Cash: Wait! You can't do that! *(He runs after her.)*

(Horace enters from left stage pushing a two-wheel hand-cart. He stops at a pile of cartons and packages, and as he sings he carefully piles them high on the cart. He uses one hand to balance the cart and the other to pile cartons and packages on it and to check them off on bills of lading strapped to his leg. When not using the oversized pencil he keeps it behind his ear.)

II.4 Scena

Horace: I've been conscientious;
           I've swept under benches;
           I've picked up pins.

           I've delicately dusted,
           And nothing's bent or busted,
           Except my shins.

           I've dittoed and dotted;
           Meticulously blotted;
           I've crossed my T's.

           I've smiled very brightly,
           And always most politely,
           Said, 'Excuse it, please.'

           No doubt I am deserving
           In a dozen different ways
           But it 's just a bit unnerving
           To ask him for a raise.

M.T: *(From offstage right)* Horace!

(Horace starts to leave to answer the call but the hand truck won't stay up by itself.)

Horace: Coming!

(Horace tries again to balance the truck without success. He begins to unload it, singing as he does so.)

Horace: I've been conscientious,
           I've swept under benches,
           I've picked up pins.

M.T: *(Again from offstage right)* Horace!

Horace:	Coming!
	I've delicately dusted, And nothing's bent or busted, Except my shins.
M.T:	*(Coming closer)* Horace, where are you?
Horace:	No doubt I am deserving In a dozen different ways, Yet it 's just a bit unnerving,
M.T:	*(Appearing at the door)* Horace.
Horace:	To ask him for a raise.

DIALOGUE

M.T:	Why didn't you answer me? Are you deaf?
Horace:	No, sir. I was…busy, sir.
M.T:	Busy? Day-dreaming, more likely. The water-cooler isn't working. Fix it. *(He starts off)*
Horace:	Yes, sir. *(M.T. is nearly offstage)* Excuse me, sir.
M.T:	*(Turning around)* Yes?
Horace:	Is it a job for a plumber or an electrician, sir?
M.T:	What difference does it make? You're both. Fix it.

(He starts off again)

Horace:	Yes, sir. Excuse me, sir.
M.T:	What now? *(M.T. comes over to Horace.)* Well? What is it?

(Horace finally gets up his courage)

II.5 Scena

Horace: I work from break of day, sir,
'Till half the night is gone
And only stop to pray, sir,
For strength to carry on.

And if I doze I dream, sir,
Of things I have to do
Then when I wake I beam, sir,
To find my dreams come true.

M.T: Can the chatter.
What's the matter?

Horace: And if by chance I err, sir,
It's not from lack of skill.
It's due to wear and tear, sir,
I err against my will.

So listen to my plea, sir,
With all these facts in mind
And try your best to be, sir,
Benevolent and kind.

M.T: Can the chatter.
What's the matter?
Have you made another error?

Horace: Another error?

Oh, no! Sir!
I'm asking for a raise.

M.T: *(Unable to believe his ears)* A what?

Horace: If you please, sir.
I'd like a raise, sir.

M.T: A raise!

     A raise!

     Of all the brazen impudence.

     Twice you ship a collar crate late.
     You make us pay a ten dollar rebate.

     You waste our time on crackpot inventions.
     You annoy my ward with your unwanted attentions.

     You'd like a raise, would you?

(M.T. advances and Horace backs until he is against the left wall.)

     YOU'RE FIRED!

(M.T. stalks out right.)
(Horace is stricken. In the meantime, attracted by M.T.'s shouts, Scrub Woman and Office Force have opened the rear door and have been watching. They now come on stage. Two clerks help Horace to a packing case on which he sits.)

Horace: How could he be so cruel to me?
     I'm hurt beyond repair.
     In stunned surprise my poor heart cries
     Unfair! Unfair! Unfair!

O.F: Agree we must it's quite unjust
     But hardly our affair.
     So let there be neutrality
     When trouble's in the air.

Horace: In dismal mood I sit and brood.
     It's more than I can bear.
     My tortured brain cries out in pain
     Unfair! Unfair! Unfair!

O.F: Our sympathy we offer free
          But firmly we declare:
          "We take our stand in no man's land
          When the trouble's in the air."

(Sybil hurriedly enters. She is dressed for travel and is followed by Cashew who is loaded down with her suitcases. She falls on Horace's neck)

DIALOGUE

Sybil: Horace, I love you!

Horace: I know that.

Sybil: But I've come to marry you.

Horace: Sybil! *(They embrace but Horace immediately tears him self away.)* No.
          (He bows his head.) I haven't a job.

Cash: What did you do with them all? You had nine.

Scrub: M.T. fired him.

Cash: *(Dropping the suitcases with a thud)* The double-crosser.

(He sits on the suitcases and begins to mop his brow.)

Sybil: Please marry me, Horace.

Cash: *(Wringing out his handkerchief)* All this perspiration wasted. Well, I'll fix him. *(He goes over to Horace)* I'm surprised at you. Where's your loyalty to the firm? Don't we make Grade-A diaper pins, extra-fancy rubber nipples? We need your orders. It's your duty to marry her.

Horace: Duty? I gave my all to the firm. I slaved! I sacrificed! And now…fired.
          But he'll not get away with this. *(He strides up and down.)* I'll go to the President. I'll write letters to the newspapers. It burns me up.
                    I SEE RED!

(Everyone draws back, shocked.)

Scrub: That's no way to act, laddie.

II.6 Scena

Scrub: When you're caught in a lay-off,
            Can't pay the rent.
            When you've seen your last pay-off,
            Ain't got a cent.
            Don't rave, rant or riot,
            Try a brand new diet
            And live on love.

O.F: And live on love.

Scrub: Oh! Love and kisses
            Will feed the missus.
            It's delicious, nutritious,
            Full of vitamin A.

            And words like "sweetie"
            Are rich and meaty.
            A "darling" a day
            Keeps the doctor away.

            So when life leaves you stranded,
            High up and dry,
            Leaves you cold and empty-handed
            Under the sky,
            Don't rave, rant or riot,
            Try a brand new diet
            And live on love.

O.F: And live on love.

Horace:
(*To Sybil*)   If you only have one hat?
               If there are runs in all your hose?
               If you have to wear the same old clothes?
               Won't we have a spat?

Scrub: (*Coming between them*)
                Your sweet caresses
                Will buy her dresses.
                The latest fashion
                Is Passion with a capital P.

Horace: (*As before*) If we stay home ev'ry night?
                If we never see a show?
                If you have to sit at home and sew?
                Won't we have a fight?

Cash: (*Coming between them*) Oh! All your troubles
                Are merely bubbles
                If you've learnt the art of loving
                From "A" to "Z."

(*Horace and Sybil embrace.*)

O.F: If you've learnt the art of loving
                From "A" to "Z."

All: When you're caught in a lay-off

                Etc.

(*President enters from left front followed by his three Vice Presidents. He goes over to Horace and thumps him on the shoulder. Horace turns and the President shakes his hand vigorously.*)

DIALOGUE

Pres: Allow me to be the first to congratulate you. You're a
                great man.

1st VP: A pioneer.

2nd VP: A trail-blazer.

All three VPs: A genius.

Pres: *(Holding Horace's plan aloft for all to see)* Your inven-
             tion works.

*(Two clerks place Horace on their shoulders and carry him in a triumphal
procession around the room. Another clerk appears on top of the pile of
crates at the back of the room.)*

Clerk: Awright, everybody. A great big Gadget for Horace.

(He leads them in a cheer using the traditional college gestures.)

1st group: He's a Gadget.

2nd group: A Gadget.

All: He's famed and extra fine.

1st group: He's a Gadget.

2nd group: A Gadget.

All: A leader in his line. Horace! Horace! Horace!

(Now beginning softly and increasing in volume)

1st group: Gadget.

2nd group: Gadget.

1st group: Gadget.

2nd group: Gadget.

All: Gadget! Gadget! Yea!

*(Immediate applause. The cheerleader jumps down and Horace is placed on
the pile of crates.)*

O.F: Speech! Speech!

Horace: Thanks. (He looks at Sybil.) This means a lot to me. It
             means a lot to all of us. My machine can do any job,
             even the managers'. Why, we can connect the whole of-
             fice up on a single circuit and take turns pushing but-
             tons. Why, it's…

*(By this time the President has given the three VPs the high sign. They
climb up behind Horace, shut him up and pull him down. The President
appears in Horace's place. In the meantime Peck and M.T. have entered
from right.)*

Pres: ·   Let us give praise where praise is due: to the man whose
             unfaltering faith in Horace's genius made this happy
             day possible. A…what'ja call it? *(He turns to the VPs)*

2nd VP: *(Whispering)* A Gadget.

Pres: Oh, yes. A Gadget for your beloved manager, Martin
             Throckmorton.

(The president leads them in the same cheer where he substitutes M.T. for Horace. Once the cheer is over, M.T. takes the place of the President on the pile of crates.)

M.T: Words cannot convey
             My appreciation
             For this ovation.

             I can only say,
             I don't deserve it.
             I don't deserve it.

(Loud applause by Cashew. All turn to stare at him and he stops applauding.)

M.T: If I showed Horace any special consideration, it was
             due to the peculiar qualities he displayed. If any of you
             would care to give a similar demonstration of your
             executive ability, and can make the grade, I am sure you
             will earn the approbation of the stockholders, the Presi-
             dent, and myself.

(The Office Force look at one another.)

M.T: Don't be hesitant. Consider it a general invitation.

II.7 Scena

O.F: Thank you, sir.

M.T: Don't mention it.

O.F: Thank you, sir.

M.T: Don't mention it.

        When I earn your gratitude,
        It puts me in a mellow mood.

O.F: Very seldom do you see
        A boss who unselfishly
        Tries to help each employee.

        Ah! You seldom come across
        A better boss.

(In the meantime Cashew has been pacing back and forth.)

Cash: Ah! You seldom come across
        A more competent boss
        At handing out the applesauce.

        He's just a sordid speculator,
        A puffed up peculator,
        A misappropriator
        Of the firm's funds.

Pres: Sir. This is a serious accusation. If I understand you,
        you're calling the man a thief.

(As this has been going on M.T. has climbed down from the pile of crates.)

Cash: I meant exactly what I said.

Cash: He's made away
           With the whole week's pay.
           The firm's $12,847.39 in the red.

Pres: There's no denying
           Your talent for detail,
           But if I find you're lying,
           You'll surely land in jail.
           You deny it, of course?

Cash: If he says it isn't so,
           He lies.
           I saw him take the dough.

(M.T. has a short struggle with himself and then sings:)

M.T: I cannot tell a lie.
           It was I, It was I.

O.F: Can it really be?
           Was it he? Was it he?

Pres: M.T., why do you ignore
           A statement I have often made before?
           A slight irregularity
           I regard with charity
           But a payroll at a time
           Is definitely a crime.

M.T: Before you pronounce my sentence
           Be sure of my deep repentance.

Pres: *(Turning away)* It's easy to repent
           When the money's spent.

Peck: Spare him, sir, o spare him.
           Count the love we bear him
           As evidence in his defense.

Peck: Tho we strive forever
            The sum of our endeavor
            Can never measure his benevolence.

(She chants in liturgical style)

DIALOGUE

Peck: If he had installed the water-cooler and had not fur-
            nished us with wooden coat-hangers

O.F: It would have been enough.

Peck: If he had furnished us with wooden coat-hangers and
            had not sent us Christmas cards

O.F: It would have been enough.

Peck: If he had sent us Christmas cards and had not given us
            a ten percent discount on the firm's merchandise

O.F: It would have been enough.

Peck: If he had given us a ten percent discount on the firm's
            merchandise and had not taken up a collection for us
            when we were sick

O.F: It would have been enough.

Peck: How much then are we indebted to him for the mani-
            fold favors he has bestowed upon us

Peck / O.F: *(In unison)*   He installed the water cooler;
            He furnished us with wooden coat hangers;
            He sent us Christmas cards;
            He gave us a ten percent discount on the firm's
            Merchandise;
            And always took up a collection for us when we were sick.

(The VPs begin to pass their hats. Peck catches their eye and stops them.)

Peck: How then can we fail him
            In his hour of need?
            Can we let them jail him

Peck: Through our petty greed
                When one week's pay
                Will do the deed?

(The three VPs sit down on crates and pull crates before them. They take paper and pen from their pocket and hurriedly make out subscription lists.)

Peck: I'll lead the way.
                Who'll follow?

(She signs)

Three VPs: Right this way:
                One week's pay.

Three VPs: Sign
                On the dotted line.

(The Office Force hesitates. They look at Peck and the Vice Presidents.)

                Sign
                On the dotted line.

(The Office Force hesitates a bit longer then, having made up their minds, go over and form three lines in front of the VPs and then begin to sign the subscription lists.)

O.F: We're glad to make the sacrifice
                To keep you out of jail.
                We'd hate to see you pay the price
                When we can furnish bail.

DIALOGUE

Pres: Very touching. Very touching.

Cash: But you said it was a crime. He'll be punished?

Pres: *(Going over to M.T.)* M.T., you are no longer manager. *(M.T. bows his head.)* You're Fourth Vice-President.

II.8 Scena

M.T / VPs: Three Vice-Presidents no more,
Three Vice-Presidents are four.

1st VP: I'm one.

2nd VP: I'm two.

3rd VP: I'm three.

M.T: And I am four.

All four: And now that he's been kicked upstairs
Four figure-heads will warm four chairs
And charge cigars to the company.
Four Vice-Presidents are we.

RECITATIVE

Peck: *(Going over to Cashew)* So you thought you'd get away
with it?

SONG

————   But you must reck with Miss Peck
His Private Secretary.
For at his side it is my pride
To act as guiding fairy.

(As the Office Force repeats what she has sung, she goes over to M.T. and takes his arm. He smiles down at her.)

O.F: At his side it is her pride
To act as guiding fairy.

DIALOGUE

Pres: (*Going over to Cash*) And you, sir. I'll have no industrial spy within the National Gadget Corporation. Your employment is terminated. Pay yourself a week's salary and leave.

Cash: With what? (*He stalks off stage left.*)

M.T: (*Going over to Horace*)
Circumstances alter cases.
Take her, my boy,
And make her happy.

(*He returns to Peck and asks*)

M.T: How would you like to join me in saying I do? (*They embrace.*)

(*Horace attempts to embrace Sybil. She pushes him away and then kisses him on the forehead.*)

II.9 SONG

Sybil: Please take this testimonial
That my love is true
But intentions matrimonial
Will not at present do.

Indeed, we should be mating
But your financial rating
Permits us no debating.
Intentions matrimonial
Will not at present do.

DIALOGUE

Pres: I don't quite follow the discussion.

Sybil: I don't want to marry a rich man. I want to marry a poor man.

Pres: Oh! I can easily take care of that. *(To M.T)* This invention, I understand, was perfected on company time?

M.T: That's so.

Pres: *(To Horace)* And you haven't acquired a patent?

Horace: No, Sir.

Pres: *(To Sybil)* Then, my dear, I assure you it's quite alright to marry him.

Sybil: *(Falling on Horace's neck)* Horace!

(Horace does not embrace her.)

Sybil: Don't you love me?

Horace: Yes, I love you. But I have no job. I can't support you.

Sybil: Horace, I love you. I shan't mind starving a little.

(They embrace.)

II.10 Finale

Ensemble: When you're caught in a lay-off,
Can't pay the rent.
When you've seen your last pay-off,
Ain't got a cent.

Don't rave, rant or riot.
Try a brand new diet
And live on love.
Etc.

(The above is developed into a finale, but as the music seems to be reaching its conclusion and the audience expects the curtain to momentarily fall, the music ends on an unresolved chord. There is a short pause.)

II.11 Scena

RECITATIVE

Pres: *(To Office Force)* There's one thing I forgot to mention:
With this new invention
The services of an office force will no longer be required.

Three VPs: In short, you're all fired!

1st VP: Whether you're a typist

2nd VP: Or whether you're a clerk

3rd VP: You are now out of work.

Three VPs: You're all fired!

(For a moment the Office Force remains in stunned silence.)

O.F: We have been hurt we do assert
We're hurt beyond repair.
There is no doubt our hearts cry out
Unfair! Unfair! Unfair!

Pres: Agree I must
It's a bit unjust
But hardly my affair.

At times we hire;
At times we fire;
In biz all is fair.

O.F: In a dismal mood we stand and brood
It's more than we can bear.
Each tortured breast cries out protest
Unfair! Unfair! Unfair!

Pres: My sympathy I offer free
Pres: But firmly I declare:
             Making profit is my only biz
             I have no other care.

(The Old Worker now appears on top of the pile of crates at the back of the room.)

O.W: Enough is enough!

(He chants in liturgical style.)

             If we had worked a twelve hour day but had not taken a
             ten percent cut in our salary?

O.F: It would have been enough.

O.W: If we had taken a ten percent cut in our salary but had
             not purchased gum?

O.F: It would have been enough.

O.W: If we had purchased gum but had not chewed till our
             jaws ached?

O.F: It would have been enough.

O.W / O.F: We worked a twelve-hour day;
             We took a ten percent cut in our salary;
             We purchased gum;
             We chewed till our jaws ached.
             That was enough!

DIALOGUE

O.W: So what are you going to do about it?

(As the scene continues, the Old Worker climbs down from the crates and disappears.)

O.F: *(In unison)* We'll organize! We'll strike!

Pres: You can't strike. You've been fired.

O.F: *(In unison)* Then we'll picket. We'll boycott the firm's
             merchandise, we're burned up.

             WE SEE RED!

Pres: Shocking! You must be Reds, totally un-American!

(The Office Force draws back in shocked surprise.)

O.F: *(In unison)* Oh! Sir, don't say that!

II.12 Scena

O.F: I'm not a Red, I've never said
             Anything un-American.
             I've never bought or even thought
             Anything un-American.

             Although I eat neither bread nor meat
             I'm on my country's side.
             Although I thirst my country's first.
             I take my leave in pride.

II.13 FINALE

(Now all come forward and sing a truncated version of the finale.)

Ensemble: If you're caught in a lay-off,
             Can't pay your rent.
             When you've seen your last pay-off,
             Ain't got a cent.
             Don't rave, rant or riot.
             Try a brand new diet
             And live on love.

             AND LIVE ON LOVE!

CURTAIN

(As soon as the curtain in down Cashew comes from behind it at stage left and a man wearing a fedora with the sign "Author" stuck in the ribbon of his hat comes from behind the curtain at stage right. As they advance to meet in center stage there is a crash of brass and a simultaneous clash of cymbals to alert the audience to their presence. Once they have the audiences' attention they speak.)

DIALOGUE

Cash: So you're the author of this thing?

Author: I wrote the words, not the music, so I suppose I can be called its author.

Cash: You didn't treat me very well. Towards the end I was fired.

Author: You're the villain of the piece. You can't expect to be treated very well.

Cash: And at the very end you fired the entire office force.

Author: That seemed to be what the plot required.

Cash: I thought this was supposed to be a comic operetta.

Author: Comic and satiric. I think it high satire when the whole office force after sacrificing in everyway for the welfare of the corporation is rewarded for this by being fired.

Cash: You carry satire too far. Every comic operetta I have seen or heard has a happy ending.

Author: As does Gadgets. The usual one, the lovers finally get together.

Cash: And have nothing to live on. You can't tell me that when in addition everyone is fired that's a happy ending.

Author: Possibly not.

Cash: Possibly not! That's not a happy ending and not what the audience is accustomed to expect in a comic operetta and if the audiences' expectation is not satisfied that will get around. Then the audience will dwindle from performance to performance, the show will have

Cash:	to close and it won't have had much of a run. I wouldn't like that much nor would the rest of the cast.
Author:	Neither would I.
Cash:	Then do something about it.
Author:	Like what?
Cash:	Rewrite the ending so it's a happy one.
Author:	That's rather a tall order.
Cash:	You can do it, the rest of your book works well.
Author:	Nice of you to say so. Well, I'll see what I can do but the result is likely to be totally absurd.
Cash:	So what! So is the whole of your so-called opera. Get on with it.
Author:	Alright.

(They retrace their steps and disappear behind the curtain. After a moment the curtain rises. On stage are the president, Horace and Sybil.)

DIALOGUE

Pres:	Horace, you have been reinstated as has everyone else who was dismissed.
Horace:	I am glad to know that, Sir. I was quite upset when so many people were fired because of my invention.
Pres:	No need to worry about that now. It is concerning your invention that I wish to talk to you. You created it on the corporation's time and it therefore legally belongs to the corporation. I can't do anything about that. However, in doing this you made such a large contribution to the corporation that we are prepared to offer you a royalty of twenty percent on all profits made through its manufacture, sale or use. This should make you quite a rich man.
Sybil:	I shouldn't like that. If he's to become rich I shan't marry him.
Horace:	Then with thanks I must refuse your most generous offer. I would rather have Sybil than all the wealth in the world.

Sybil:	Horace!
Horace:	Sybil!

(They are about to embrace.)

Pres: Hold it for a moment, please. The profits from Horace's invention will be so large that we feel obliged to share it with our employees by giving all of them a 20% increase in salary. Sybil, will you not at least allow Horace to receive this?

Sybil: Will we then be able to afford a servant?

Pres: By no means, even with this raise an office boy's salary will be much too meager for that. I'm afraid you will have to do all your housework yourself.

Sybil: Good.

(The two now embrace. The office force begins to enter from stage right. Horace and Sybil disentangle themselves and hand in hand exit stage left. The office force forms in informal groups at stage right, standing at ease.)

Pres: I'm glad you have come. You have been a most loyal office force.

(Cashew enters from left and stands quietly listening.)

Pres: *(continuing)* You have worked long hours, always chewed gum while you worked and accepted a pay cut. We now wish to reward you for these loyal acts. You are no longer required to chew gum while you work unless, of course, you so desire. The pay cut is rescinded and instead you will all receive a 20% increase in your salary. *(He holds up a hand)* Further, since the automatic worker that Horace invented can do your work much more efficiently than you can you will need to come to the office only four hours a week and still receive your full pay. While there your only duty will be to push the appropriate buttons to make this machine operate.

SONG II.13.

OF: Thank you, sir.

Pres: You are quite welcome.

OF: Thank you very much, sir.

Pres: You are, indeed, quite welcome.
             When the firm's future is so bright
             To share the profits is only right,
             To share the profits is only right.

RECITATIVE

Pres: *(Facing audience)*
             And now that every wrong's been righted
             And not a person slighted…

(Cashew interrupts)

DIALOGUE

Cash: Beg pardon, sir. Are you really certain that no one has
             been slighted? What about Miss Peck, the Scrubwoman
             and, in particular, Horace?

Pres: All taken care of, Cashew. Peck is marrying M.T. and
             no longer will be with us. The Scrubwoman was close
             to retirement and we really no longer needed her
             services. We offered her early retirement and she ac-
             cepted. We found her pension to be highly inadequate
             so we doubled it.

Cash: And Horace?

Pres: He was offered a 20% royalty on all our profits on his
             invention. Since Sybil then rejected him, he refused this
             so he could marry her.

Cash: Love conquers wealth. I wish them Godspeed.

Pres: As do I. She did allow him to receive the 20% increase
           in pay we are offering our workforce and which, unfor-
           tunately, you will not receive.

Cash: May I ask why not, sir?

Pres: You are considered a member of the executive team.
           The Board of Directors has decided that no executive
           can receive an increase in salary or any other financial
           advantage until the board is satisfied that the promised
           raise to the non-executive employees is fully funded.
           However, since you have been so solicitous of the wel-
           fare of others without mentioning your own I shall
           recommend to the board that they make an exception
           in your case and allow you to receive a commensurate
           increase in your salary.

Cash: I would much rather, sir, that you do not do this. I feel
           the board is quite justified in coming to this decision
           and I shall be glad to abide by it.

Pres: You should be commended, Cashew.

FINAL FINALE II.14

Pres / Cash: *(Facing audience)* Now that everything's been mended
              It's time this operetta was ended.

(While the orchestra continues to play, all members of the cast not on stage join those on the stage. The principals, the president and three vice-presidents, Horace and Sybil, M.T. and Peck, Cashew and the scrubwoman form a line facing the audience just back of where the curtain would fall. The office force forms two ranks center-stage immediately behind the principals.)

Principals: *(in unison)*
            Thus our story happily ends, happily ends, happily ends.
            Of many things we've made a joke, made a joke, made a joke
            And at others taken a poke, taken a poke, taken a poke.

            And now that we have made amends, made amends,
                made amends

Principals: We hope you still remain our friends, remain our
friends, remain our friends,
We hope you still remain our friends.

*(While the orchestra continues to play the principals divide into two groups
of five and face in opposite directions. Nearing their respective sides of the
stage each group files part way upstage and then makes an about face. In the
meantime, the two ranks of the office force move forward until the first rank
occupies the place where the principals had been.)*

O.F.: *(in harmony)*

Thus our story happily ends.
Of many things we made a joke
And at others taken a poke.
And now that we have made amends
We hope you still remain our friends,
We hope you still remain our friends.

O.F.:   *(in unison)*

This is all we have to tell, have to tell, have to tell
And no matter where you dwell, where you dwell,
where you dwell
And whether you buy or whether you sell, buy or sell,
buy or sell
We, indeed, do wish you well, wish you well, wish you
well.
We, indeed, do wish you well.

*(The two ranks of the office force about face and return to where they stood
before and then about face towards the audience. In the meantime, the two
groups of principals retrace their steps and again form a line at the front of
the stage facing the audience.)*

Principals: *(in harmony)*

This is all there is to tell
And no matter where you dwell
And whether you buy or whether you sell
We, indeed, do wish you well.
We, indeed, do wish you well.

All: *(at times in unison and at times in harmony)*
       Now it's time to say farewell, to say farewell, to say fare-
       well,
       We to you and you to us, you to us and we to you.
       Its time to say farewell, farewell to Gadgets,
       To say farewell to Gadgets, The Commercial Opera.
       To say farewell, to say farewell!

CURTAIN

THE END

VIGNETTES
&
SHORT STORIES

The OB

I t's hot as hell, Jerry thought, as he turned onto his back. But that wasn't what was keeping him from sleeping. The heat hadn't fazed him the summer before but then he had just come to New York and things were going good. He had told the agency that he was twenty-one and had gotten away with it. They had come up with a first class job, working as a teletype operator at the Battery office of the Penn Railroad. It had been a responsible job. When he typed an order, carloads of fruit were shunted onto barges in Jersey and towed through the harbor to wherever he sent them, sometimes all the way around into the East River. He particularly liked working the evening shift, for at times there was nothing to do and he could read. But the best part was the pay, a hundred and twenty-nine a month. He had saved a good deal of it. With that, the morning's stint at the cafeteria for his meals, and the fifty bucks a month from home, he had gotten through the school year quite nicely.

But that was last year, 1928, before the Depression hit. Now things were really tough. Even his Dad was having trouble; he had to cut his check to forty. The rent for his furnished room was thirty a month and he had to send out his laundry so there wasn't much left. Tuition at the Juilliard was two hundred a year. He figured he could pay half of it by giving blood at St. Luke's hospital. They paid fifty dollars a pint. He had given blood once this last year and he figured he could do it twice in the coming year. But he still had to find another hundred dollars.

At the beginning of the summer Jerry had gone back to the Penn office. During the day shift the summer before, every desk had been filled but now that big office was half empty. Even some of the old timers were gone, even Jake who had covered for him when he had sent a couple of cars of apples to the wrong pier. Jerry wondered how Jake was making out.

Well, he had found work—and he was lucky to have it—a full time job at the cafeteria. Full time, hell, with a half-day Sunday he worked a seven day week. Jerry turned on his side and tried to sleep. No dice. Through the open second story window he even heard the hum of an occasional auto rounding Grant's Tomb on the Drive, a sound that had never bothered his sleep before. His dad had often told him that he had to shift his brain into neutral in order to sleep. His kept slipping into reverse.

He glanced at the illuminated dial of the clock. Ten to five. Apply at seven, the want ad had said. He gave up the struggle and let his mind race back to the first time he had seen Eddie in back of the call window of the parking garage reading a magazine. If he could only get that job.

Then the campaign: the casual borrowing of a match, the innocent interest in the job, and the slow accumulation of information. Hours, evenings seven to one. Perfect. The pay, fifteen weekly. Duties, checking cars in and out, calls on the switchboard. And here he was working a lousy split shift, six to ten and four to eight-thirty for fifteen a week and his meals, doing all of Vance's dirty work, dish washing, mopping, and—ugh!—cleaning pots. If he could only get Eddie's job he would take a stint from five to seven at the cafeteria, just for his meals, and then go around the corner to the garage. He'd be free during the day, have time for classes, for practicing and doing his music theory. Also, and this was a bonus,for reading on the job. Altogether he'd have a hundred a month and meals, which would easily take him through the school year. There might even be some left over.

And Eddie with his soft spot at the garage wasn't even going to school, wasn't doing a damn thing, just putting in time until something better showed up. When they were fast friends Jerry popped the question. "Sure," Eddie had said, "I'll talk to Pilcher for you when I quit. I ought to pick up something better any day now."

That had been two months ago and in the meantime Jerry had taken no chances. He sat up in bed and looked across the room. Eddie's sleeping figure was only dimly visible. Hardly the ideal roommate. In his mind's eye Jerry filled in the details: the fly-catcher mouth, the protruding bare feet, the dirty socks slung under the bed. What a guy, nothing keeps him from sleeping. Fired without notice, reads the want ads and finds his own job advertised and doesn't even snore.

Jerry slid off his pajama top and put on his bathrobe. Wrapping his towel around his neck and putting his shaving things in a mug, he made his way down the long narrow hall to the bathroom. These days he was always the first roomer up and he tried to be as quiet as possible.

Washed and shaved, he headed for the garage. As he crossed Claremont Park the stars were dimming into their pinholes in the retreating dark of the sky. Intent on his problem he hardly felt the cooling breeze coming off the

Hudson. Should he tell Pilcher that he knew Eddie? It was dangerous; Pilcher had fired Eddie. But he had a talking point; he knew the job. Pilcher wouldn't have to break him in.

A few steps past Broadway he stopped and looked across the street at the parking garage. Wedged between two brick walls of apartment houses, in the half light its gray stone front loomed like a misplaced fortress. The only light was in the coal window through which Jerry could see the night man dozing in Eddie's chair. No one else was around.

Jerry was hungry. It was only six, the time he had breakfast at the cafeteria. Vance would be mad as a wet hen when he didn't show up. To hell with that, Jerry thought, as he turned into Amsterdam Avenue where he knew that there was an all-night diner. As he spooned his cereal he watched the counter man spread cracked ice in the salad bar. He ought to be behind the counter with Vance, cracking ice for the butter crock. Damn! How long would he have to work for that sanctimonious bastard? That sign he pinned behind the swinging door: 'Cleanliness is next to Godliness. If you can't be Godly, be clean.' So he had been a Baptist minister; that didn't keep him from serving half-spoiled butter.

When Jerry returned he was dismayed to find a crowd of men waiting in front of the garage. He had forgotten that others could read the ad, that there was a Depression for others, too. What should he do? Should he talk to Pilcher down here before these men? They wouldn't know who Pilcher was so he would probably go upstairs to interview in his office. Jerry shouldered his way through the crowd and went into the garage, hoping he looked like someone who owned a car. No one followed him. He climbed the metal stairs to the landing outside of Pilcher's office. As he watched through the window the crowd grew. He counted thirty-one. No, another one just came. Thirty-two guys after his job. Well, maybe they needed it, too, but he had worked for it, planned for it, smelled stinky socks for it. It was his job.

Finally he saw Pilcher coming across the street toward the garage. Would he speak to them downstairs? Would he ask them to come up with him? No, he was coming up the stairs alone.

Then Jerry realized he was scared; he had been working up to this for a full two months and he was scared. What would he say? What about Eddie? Pilcher was at the head of the stairs. Jerry forced himself forward. "I'd like to apply for the job."

Pilcher looked him over coldly. "Haven't I seen you around here before?"

Jerry wavered. "Yes, I know the job. You won't have to tell me what to do."

"Yeah, I place you now, the kid who was always hanging around Eddie." He motioned with his thumb. "Well, scram. No friend of Eddie's gets this job."

ARRIAGE

It was spring on the campus of Midwestern University. Loraine was late for her lesson and took a shortcut across the lawn next to the Music Building. She did not notice two long legs jutting out from the shade of a tree, legs that belonged to a young man who was reading a book concerning philosophy. She stumbled over the aforesaid legs and found herself in a somewhat inverted position. The young man, his reading interrupted, was immediately attracted by the seductive whiteness of her glistening thighs. Dropping his book, he brought her to her feet and embraced her.

"Not now," Lorraine said, "I've got to get to my voice lesson."

"Quite right," said the young philosopher, "first things first." He picked up his book, tucked her arm under his, and went with her into the building.

He was waiting when she came out from her teacher's studio. "I am desperately in love with you," he told her. "Will you marry me or at least live with me?"

"Love me and love my animals," Lorraine said and took him home and introduced him to her four pets: her cat, her catamount, her dog, and her dogie. The young man did not much care for animals but he was a philosopher. He let the cat claw him, let the catamount take a small bite out of the flesh of his upper left arm, let the dog treat his leg as a fire hydrant, and fed the dogie a few blades of grass that had adhered to his trousers.

"You pass," said the possessor of the white thighs. "I'm Lorraine. Who are you?"

"I'm Aldo," said the young philosopher. "I'll move in tomorrow and pay half the rent."

"That's very generous of you considering that there are six of us."

"Oh, I think I'll enjoy the ménage." But not the menagerie, he said to himself. "But I doubt if you'll want a one armed lover. What about the catamount?"

"He'll have to be satisfied with an initial sample and go back to his diet of raw hamburger."

"But why doesn't he eat the dogie?" Aldo asked.

"Silly. The dog is a shepherd and the dogie is a white Brahmin calf. The dog thinks it's a sheep. He wouldn't let the catamount touch her."

For two years they lived happily in this two room, ground floor apartment. Of course, everyone had to make some compromises. The selfish humans took the living room for themselves so they had access to the kitchenette, bathroom, and the front door. The four animals were restricted to what had been the bedroom. Aldo did almost all his studying at a carrel at the library and Lorraine most of her vocalizing, to the relief of her pets, in a practice room at the Music School.

Lorraine was a strict Catholic and Aldo became accustomed to being awakened at dawn once a month when she prepared to go to Mass. He went with her to Midnight Mass on Christmas since he enjoyed the music. She went to confession twice a year.

"Do you tell the father about our fornication?"

"What else do I have to confess?"

"Nothing I know of but doesn't he require some severe penance?"

"Only the reciting of a few Hail Marys and Our Fathers."

"Is that all for fornication?"

"Well, I'm careful to pick a confessor who I know is engaged in the same activity."

Aldo was a Jew who had become a Buddhist. When he was home there was a good deal of reciting, "Om, om, om." Lorraine rather enjoyed this and wanted to join in as a form of vocal exercise but he forbade it. It made it difficult for him to concentrate on thinking about nothing, which is the purpose of the recitation.

They took turns in taking the animals for their twice daily walk. The practical Lorraine had arranged with a gardener for her pets to have free use of his compost heap in return for the resultant manure. The compost heap began to take on the odor of what the poetic Chinese farmers described as "night soil" but the neighbors had no recourse since the garden was outside of the city limits. The only problem was that the dogie was passionately fond of eating flowers and if not restrained walked away with the stems of a couple of carnations hanging from her lips.

They also took turns in cleaning the animals' room and grooming them. Aldo managed this latter task by distracting the catamount with a large ball of catnip and grooming the dog only after it had visited a neighboring telephone pole or fire hydrant.

Lorraine was very attached to her pets and being very particular about their health, frequently took them to be examined by a veterinarian named Patrick Donahue. Patrick was an excellent veterinarian but he had a paradoxical philosophy concerning the treatment of animals. Patrick was a vegetarian, and as such he refused to treat animals which humans ate but was quite willing to treat animals which ate other animals. He had no objections to treating the cat, the catamount or the dog but he drew a line at treating the dogie since humans ate them, usually in the form of veal cutlet. However, Lorraine managed to persuade him that the dogie was merely a pet and since she would live her entire life with Lorraine, no one would ever have the opportunity of eating her. So Patrick relented and was kind enough to treat the dogie, especially when she ate some of the deep piled rug in Lorraine's bedroom, taking it for grass.

Lorraine's voice teacher, Mary Veronica Jones, had an international reputation. She had recently sung with a symphony orchestra in a German speaking area of the Alps. One of the violinists in the orchestra called himself Dieter. Both of his parents were Italian and his real name was Domenico but he changed it to Dieter because he preferred the thinner air of the Austrian Alps and therefore spoke mostly German, leaving it to his brother, who preferred the thicker air of the Italian Alps, to speak his parents' language. Dieter played the violin extremely well. He had a particularly supple wrist, which made his bow arm the envy of the remaining violinists in the orchestra in which he played. As Dieter grew older his wrist grew suppler and suppler, to everyone's amazement.

Mary Veronica Jones had only sung a few notes when Dieter fell in love with her. It was not because she sang well but because she was sixty-three. All his life it had been his ambition to marry a woman who was sixty-three. Dieter also found her name, Mary Veronica Jones, to be most unusual and exotic. He managed to talk the conductor of the orchestra into introducing him to the singer, whom he invited to join him in a stein of beer and some Viennese pastry. She gladly accepted for she found singing in the Alps made her very thirsty and she was absolutely mad about Viennese pastry. As courtesy demanded he waited until she had emptied half of her stein and then proposed marriage. He did this in proper fashion, getting down on his knees. Unfortunately, he placed one of his old knees on a sharp stone, which threw him off balance so that he fell upon his right hand and broke its wrist.

Dieter was immediately rushed to the hospital, where the surgeon carefully set the broken bone, and placed his wrist in a splint. Impressed with Dieter's courtliness, and sorry that the old man had hurt his wrist, Mary Veronica Jones delayed her return to the United States and paid him a daily visit in the hospital. When it became evident that Dieter's wrist would never again be supple enough for playing in the symphony orchestra, and when she had been assured by many of his friends that he baked the most delicious Viennese pastry imaginable, Veronica Jones married him and took him back with her to a place he found rather queer, Prairieton, where Midwestern University is located.

Dieter loved Mary Veronica but he was most unhappy in Prairieton. The land was pancake flat and if there was a mountain anywhere nearby he was unable to discover it. Hardly anyone spoke German and the air was much too thick. Every few months he insisted on going back to the Alps whether Mary Veronica went with him or not. Being seventy-three, he found that he could get along without her for almost two months at a time. This is probably because he had never married before and had not gotten into the habit.

Mary Veronica could not leave her job at the university whenever she wanted to but she humored Dieter and spent as much time with him in the Alps as she could. She did find one advantage to living there: she didn't need to use a tape recorder to check up on her singing. Whenever she practiced, particularly vocalizes, she had only to listen to her echo.

In the meantime, Lorraine and Aldo were faced with a problem. The little dogie had grown into a great dogie, a large Brahmin cow. She not only severely restricted the space available for the other three pets but the humans began to have difficulty getting her through the bedroom door.

"I know that your mother divorced your father long ago," Lorraine said, "and is now teaching Marxism in Bulgaria so she can't help. But isn't your father still a big shot in computers? Couldn't you put a small bite on him so we could move into larger quarters?"

"I was thinking of something larger than a bite," said the philosopher. "If you'll marry me I am quite sure I can rip him off for a few thousand. We could buy a two story house, live upstairs and arrange the ground floor for the animals. We might even be able to hire someone to take care of them, a zoological groom so to speak."

"Marriage certainly seems indicated," Lorraine said. "But who can we get to marry a Catholic and a Buddhist?"

"A veterinarian."

"You're kidding!"

"Not at all. Patrick Donahue can marry us. He's a minister. He has a card he bought for five dollars by mail from some invented religious cult that makes him one and entitles him to celebrate marriages. Since the constitution doesn't define religion, it's perfectly legal. All we need is a license."

"But will he do it?"

"How can he refuse? You're one of his best clients."

Patrick agreed and it was arranged to have the marriage at the little ecumenical chapel provided by the university for such occasions. This building was six-sided like the Star of David since Judaism is also the basis of the Christian and Moslem religions. Rising skyward from equally spaced points of the star were three miniature structures: a Catholic cathedral tower, a Protestant church steeple, and a Moslem mosque minaret. The remainder of the building was covered with a Buddhist pagoda-shaped roof.

They invited only a few friends. Mary Veronica was delighted and invited all to a reception at her apartment after the wedding.

One day before the wedding occurred Lorraine was having her singing lesson. At Mary Veronica's request Dieter had come to the lesson to coach Lorraine on her pronunciation of German. After Lorraine had sung Brahms' "Sapphische Ode," Mary Veronica turned to Dieter and asked, "Have you noticed how much her breath control has improved in the last few months?"

"*Ja wohl*," Dieter responded. Mary Veronica turned to Lorraine and said, "You've been sleeping regularly with Aldo, have you not?"

"Why, yes," Lorraine said, surprised. "But what's that got to do with my breath control?"

"Oh, the connection is well established and it will be still better after you've been married for some time," Mary Veronica said. "Frazzini definitely established the correlation in his twenty year study at La Scala in the 1940s."

"I haven't noticed any improvement in your breath control since we married," said an aggrieved Dieter.

"Now, Dieter," Mary Veronica said, coming over and kissing him on the cheek, "you must remember that you're my third husband. Anyhow, Frazzini established that it was in the thirteenth or fourteenth year, depending upon the sex, that the diaphragm remains reasonably stable." She smiled at Lorraine. "You have a few years yet to go, my dear."

In bed that night Lorraine duly reported this conversation to Aldo. He was not pleased. "Stud service for Brahms?"

She pulled him to her. "Just an unanticipated by-product of the main event."

Lorraine's pets were of course invited to the wedding but had to observe it outside through a window, chaperoned by the newly employed zoological groom. Each pet had been carefully washed and brushed and the necks of the smaller animals adorned with white, pink or blue ribbons surmounted by braided bows, each bow of color appropriate to their sex. Two similar bows adorned the horns of the cow as well as her tail, making her a symphony of pink and white. She watched with her head thrust through the window while the cat sat on her neck and watched through her horns. The catamount and the dog watched with their front paws resting on the sill.

Since the ceremony was only to last fifteen minutes the decorations within were somewhat sketchy. The altar was flanked on either side by wrought iron candelabras filled with electric bulbs simulating candles. On the altar was a vase containing only three white lilies. It was feared that a larger number of more colorful flowers might tempt the great dogie to break her way through the window.

The ceremony was scheduled to begin at four. Unfortunately, Patrick was scheduled to do some emergency surgery and it was only at three fifty-eight that he was able to change into his ministerial garb and leave for the chapel. He did his best to make it in time and in the process secured a traffic ticket that cost him more than his ministerial license. Arriving at four fifteen he launched into an abbreviated but sonorous recital of the formulae and remarks appropriate to the occasion, had the bridal couple exchange rings, and then declared them man and wife. All present were then regaled with a musical sandwich, the slices of bread being provided by one of Mary Veronica's other students, a sizzling *puertorriqueña* called Concepción Rodríguez, who sang two settings of "Ich liebe dich," one by Grieg and the other by Beethoven. Dieter listened with pleasure to the German although even with his coaching it still had a slight Spanish flavor. Patrick provided the middle of the musical sandwich, singing "Tell Me That You Love Me" as a sing-along with the guests.

After receiving everyone's congratulations, Lorraine and Aldo along with the groom took their pets home and settled them for the evening. Little by little the guests found their way to Mary Veronica's place. Here a terrific spread had been provided including various Viennese pastries freshly baked by Dieter and a quantity of Mozart kugel which Mary Veronica had carefully preserved since her last trip to Salzburg. There was also to be a case of champagne but it had not as yet arrived. The guests were discouraged from eating until they had champagne to drink with the food. When the champagne did arrive, and was iced, they were discouraged from drinking it until the newlyweds were first toasted with it. Time passed and the guests began to grumble. Some shame-facedly sneaked cans of beer out of the fridge.

Back at the just possessed home of the newlyweds the adornments had been removed from the animals and instructions given to the groom. Then on the floor above there was the reenactment of the drama that had occurred two years previously. In the living room Aldo lay on the grass rug dressed only in a blue figured pajama top and reading a book on philosophy which he had not dipped into for some two years. Then Lorraine rushed into the room dressed only in a sheer pink nightgown and stumbled over Aldo's legs, assuming the proper inverted position.

"What beautiful thighs," Aldo said. He drew Lorraine to her feet and embraced her.

"So far so good," Lorraine said. "Now carry me to our new bridal bed." It was a king size bed, with the most expensive of mattresses, and they felt so comfortable that for a while they forgot about Mary Veronica's reception.

When they finally did arrive, she was quite cross with them for holding up the party so long but the champagne was immediately opened and soon everyone felt in much better spirits.

"What in the hell took you so long?" Patrick asked. "It's an hour and a half since I married you."

"We were consummating our marriage, what else?" Aldo answered.

"It feels quite different when you're married," Lorraine testified.

Patrick raised an eyebrow and turned to his wife. "Did you feel anything different after we married, hon?"

His wife smiled at him over her third glass of champagne. "Only that I missed that little tang of wickedness that I used to feel before."

The champagne, the Viennese pastries, and even the Mozart kugel disappeared with miraculous rapidity and most of the guests soon felt the necessity of going home while they were capable of doing this.

Mary Veronica had had very much too much and was out on the sofa where she snored lightly with that elegant tone quality that only the trained vocalist can produce under such circumstances. A wife who is dead drunk is of no use to a husband, even to one who is seventy-three. Dieter decided to make a play for Concepción. Manfully supporting her on his lap, he confidentially informed her of his wide acquaintance with the impresarios in Austria. "But how do you expect to have a stage career with a name like Concepción Rodríguez?"

"My full name is Concepción María Rodríguez Monte. I shall be known as María del Monte."

"But here del Monte is already a famous brand of canned food."

"Then when I come back to the United States I shall already be famous."

Just as Dieter was about to slip his hand under Concepción's skirt she noticed Mary Veronica's comatose condition and jumped off his lap. Going to the bedroom door she knocked violently. "Break it up, kids. Mary Veronica has passed out and we'd better get her to bed." The three women undressed Mary Veronica and put her to bed while the men made a show of putting things away and tidying up the living room.

"She'll probably be out all night," Concepción said. "Dieter may need some help with her. I'll stay."

"OK, call us if you can't handle him," Lorraine said and she and Aldo and the Donahues made for the door. At that moment Patrick's beeper buzzed. He dialed a number on his cellphone and listened. "Dr. Donahue speaking." He listened. "Pretty much what I expected. Tie them up and I'll patch them up in the morning."

As they went out of the door Lorraine asked, "What was that all about?"

"It was your groom. With all of the excitement I expected your pets to go on a rampage. The great dogie is stuck in a window trying to get to your flower patch outside, the catamount has his teeth in her flank, and the dog's jaws are securely fastened around the catamount's leg. I had given the groom some anesthetic ampoules to stick in them just in case. I'll do what I can to put them back together in the morning."

"But the cat?" asked Lorraine in alarm.

"It's disappeared. But she'll be back and there'll be more business for me, a litter of kittens."

$\mathcal{S}$QUIRRELS *in* $\mathcal{S}$HORT $\mathcal{S}$UPPLY

In 1930 the Juilliard School of Music conferred the Diploma in Clarinet on Gerald P. Reinecke. This piece of vellum certified that the recipient was an able clarinetist. In 1930 it had no further value. It couldn't help Jerry find work because there was none. There just weren't any jobs for players of orchestral instruments. The larger cinemas no longer needed orchestras—the Vitaphone, the earliest form of sound movie, had taken care of that some years earlier—and, with the onset of the Depression, symphonies in cities large and small were folding.

When there is nothing better to do, go back to school. But in 1932, when Jerry completed his Bachelor's Degree in Music Education, the Great Depression had dug itself even deeper. There were no openings for music teachers in public schools. There were no openings for music teachers in private schools. There just weren't any openings.

Jerry had to eat and he had to find some way of making music. While working on his degree he had earned part of his keep conducting recreational music—rhythm bands for the younger kids and a glee club for teenage girls—in a settlement house in the Kip's Bay district of the New York City East Side. He liked working with kids and the people of the settlement house liked what he did with them. So he talked them into backing him in organizing a music school for the children of the neighborhood. It didn't pay much, and at times he wasn't too sure he was making music, but he did eat.

The settlement house helped him secure a grant from a music foundation which he used to buy instruments to lend to the children and to make up the difference between what the school charged for lessons and what he paid his friends among the Juilliard students to come down and give them. Most of the parents were receiving Home Relief—that is what Welfare was called in those days—and could pay very little. Only when the father was regularly employed, as was the father of Angelina Maglioni, did the school ask for the full fee, one dollar.

Angelina had come to him saying that her father had heard of the Music School and wanted her to learn to play the cello. That was in late February of 1933 and she had just passed her twelfth birthday. Jerry had tested her ear and sense of rhythm and had been much impressed so he had bought a cello and begun to give her lessons. He started all players of orchestral instruments himself. With his slender budget he couldn't afford to pay any part of the cost of lessons by others until he was reasonably sure it was worthwhile. In Angelina's case, it very soon became apparent that it would be, and he made an appointment to visit her parents. He preferred this to having them come see him. By visiting them at home he could better judge how much they could afford to pay toward the lessons. He didn't much care for this part of his job—he tried not to act like a case worker for Home Relief—but it had to be done.

As Jerry turned west from First Avenue into the street on which the Maglionis lived, he heard the snort of a tug boat in the nearby East River. This was a familiar sound and it always seemed to him that it came from under water, as from the throat of some sea monster.

A sea monster in the East River?

Jerry enjoyed arguing with himself. Why not? he replied. It's not really a river, it's an arm of the sea.

But in all that tar, oil, and garbage?

Maybe it lives on the stuff.

What kind of a monster would that be?

Oh, a giant tapeworm, flat, thin, slimy and a couple of blocks long.

Ugh! But since when do tapeworms snort?

The shriek of an elevated train braking into the station on Second Avenue boomeranged around the corner and assaulted his ears.

With a start Jerry returned to the reality of the shadowed street. Only the opposite row of tenements was illumined by the afternoon sun, which also shone on the number he sought. As he stepped from the curb there was the grinding of wheels on rails, and the clangor of the passing train flowed into the street and washed over him. Shaking his head to clear his ears, he walked into the welcome quiet of the hall.

He climbed the two flights and paused to look around. It seemed to be the usual layout. The two doors at the ends of the hall would lead to the front and back apartments. High in the wall between them were two windows barred with wooden dowels. These, he knew, would lead to inside rooms. When the tenement was built the law required that each room have a window but did not specify what the window must face. The two apartments would be mirror images of each other, each having a large room with two outside windows, a smaller room with one outside window, and an inside room with a window to the hall.

A third door led to a closet at the head of the stairs that contained a toilet. Tenements had no bathrooms. Jerry quietly opened the door and looked in. It was just what he had expected. His gaze rested upon the worn wooden seat and traveled up the long pipe bracketed to the wall to the high tank, down the long metal chain to the wooden handle that one pulled to plunge the water down the pipe to flush the bowl. It was strictly utilitarian and not too roomy. He would hate to have to replace the rubber bulb in that high tank. As he closed the door he reminded himself that this high water closet within a closet had not been designed purely for the profit of builders of tenements. There must have been a time when it was standard. He had once sat enclosed and closeted in an identical model in an old court house in his native eastern Kansas.

He hadn't thought to ask whether the Maglionis lived in the front or the back. Since he was already at the back door he knocked at it.

It was opened by Angelina. "Hi, Mr. Reinecke. My folks are waiting for you in the living room. That's the front door."

"Thanks, Angelina." So the Maglionis occupied the entire floor. This meant six rooms for mother, father, and four children. Not too bad. He knew families of five who could only afford three rooms. Well, the Maglionis should be able to pay the full fee for lessons.

In the living room he was welcomed with a glass of chianti. Through the windows open to the warm spring air, window boxes flaunted the bright red of geraniums. Thin shafts of sunlight slanted down between chintz curtains and scrawled their yellow on the green fiber carpet that spread across the uneven plank floor. In a corner, its shiny pipe angling up to a high chimney hole, stood a cold stove, cold and black.

Jerry slowly became aware of a delicious aroma floating in from the kitchen. Apprehended in a sniff, he immediately had a steaming bowl of pasta thrust into his hand.

He twirled strands of spaghetti onto his fork. "Your Angelina," he told the Maglionis, "is a very musical girl."

"Of course," Mr. Maglioni said, "she comes from a very musical family. My grandfather, he played the cello in the opera orchestra in Milan. We listen much to opera."

Jerry followed his gesture and first saw the old but carefully polished mahogany wind-up phonograph flanked on its table by two neatly stacked piles of records, still in their original tan envelopes now worn, a bit torn, with the black of the records peeping out of their sides. From the centers of the uppermost envelopes, between blocks of print advertising new issues, wide, round, red eyes stared stolidly at the ceiling. Victor Red seals? Jerry's father had a whole collection of them. Caruso singing Rigoletto? Pagliacci? "La donna é mobile?" "Vesti la giubba?"

"My family, it is also musical," Mrs. Maglioni said. "My uncle played the accordion. It was beautiful."

Mr. Maglioni's hand sliced an expressive half circle in the air. "The accordion is good, Mama, for a dance orchestra but not for an opera orchestra, not for the kind of orchestra Mr. Reinecke is going to have. For that, a cello is better."

"I'm afraid we don't teach the accordion," Jerry said.

"A dollar a lesson is OK," Mr. Maglioni said. "But fifteen dollars deposit?" He spread his hands. "That's pretty steep. That's half a month's rent."

"That's less than we paid for the cello," Jerry said.

Maglioni turned to his wife. "We'll have to eat less scaloppini, Mama, more pasta, more minestrone."

"Mario!" she said reproachfully.

He turned back to Jerry. "OK, she say no bargaining. We pay the fifteen dollars. You know, my father, he also played the cello. Learned it in the old country. I used to listen to him play when I was a kid. He sang with the cello. But he died when I was fourteen and I had to go to work so I never learned it. Angelina will have to be the cello player in the Maglioni family."

"This time a woman plays the cello, not a man," Mrs. Maglioni said.

Maglioni lifted one shoulder. "What can you do when a woman gives you only girls? But on the cello Angelina can sing like a man, from bass to high tenor. She can be both Rufo and Caruso. Mama, give Mr. Reinecke another glass of chianti."

"This is very good chianti," Jerry said. "What bootlegger do you use?"

"Bootlegger? I can afford a bootlegger? I get it from my cousin in Jersey. He made wine in the old country. This Roosevelt. Now beer is legal but not wine. Is he a German?"

"Dutch, I think," Jerry said. "But you'll get your wine soon. You'll see; Prohibition is on its way out."

Things had gone well but as Jerry descended the stairs he was surprised to find that he was not elated. It must have been the second glass of chianti. Sometimes alcohol gave him a high, sometimes a low. He never knew which it would be or why.

Outside the sun was brightening only the upper half of the row of tenements from which Jerry emerged. After the cheerfulness of the Maglioni living room everything below seemed drab and tinged with gray, the pavement a grayish black, the sidewalk a grayish white, the garbage cans a rusty, iron gray. Further down the street Jerry could see a few strips of mottled green, narrow rectangles between walk and wall where weeds warred with grass.

He remembered the extravagant greens of his childhood: the leafy greens of a line of shade trees, the grassy green of broad lawns, the sculptured green of bordering hedges. And everywhere the floral colors of spring: on the front porch the blatant red of sunlit tulips; edging the brick walk that halved the front lawn, the golden butter yellow of daffodils; the tiny white blossoms sprinkled like dew drops along the privet hedge; the lavender blue drapery of morning glories hung over the lean-to built against the back yard board fence in which he and his sister had kept their bicycles.

From this back yard he had once seen a squirrel cautiously picking its way from tree to tree along the telephone cable strung across the back alley, a furry little tight rope walker balancing itself with a plume of a tail rather than a pole. He wondered if Angelina had ever seen a squirrel. The Maglionis, like most families he knew, had no telephone. In the Kip's Bay district both squirrels and telephones were in short supply.

Depressed by the shadowed gray of the street, Jerry lifted his head for a glimpse of the Maglionis' geraniums. His eye caught other hints of color and scanning the walls of the tenements, he discovered that the Maglionis were not the only family celebrating spring. Among the green of scattered window boxes the sun picked out patches of red, gold, and white, and here and there a few flecks of blue. As Jerry walked away he began to whistle.

UNCONSCIOUS

Betty smiled at me over her empty daiquiri glass and said, "We certainly were a bunch of unconscious kids, weren't we, Jerry?" I had just asked if she had remembered that night in my apartment but I didn't like her answer so I didn't say anything. What I asked about happened twenty years ago—in the Fall of 1931, to be exact—but I was quite sure that I had been completely conscious of her presence in my bed and of that of Rachel also. If Betty had been unconscious, where was I and what was I doing? I felt like asking her, "Who was unconscious?" but I didn't.

Betty had called her husband to tell him she would be home an hour late. My watch told me that the hour had passed. "I think it's time to break it up."

She looked at her watch and it told her the same story. "An hour sure passes fast when you're talking about old times," she said.

I paid for the drinks and picked up my clarinet case. She hoisted her violin case from the corner where it had been leaning and we left the bar. Outside she said, "It was nice to have a chance to talk with you, Jerry." She shifted her violin case to her left hand and offered me her right.

I didn't take it. "What's happened to your famous good night kiss?"

She smiled at me again. "I'm married now, Jerry." She patted my arm and that's how we parted. It was more of a taunt than a question. I hadn't expected her to kiss me.

I watched her walk away. She was short and bottom heavy and I was surprised that she hadn't put on weight after having those two kids. I had liked Betty. She had been such a warm and companionable sort of girl—she still had that good-humored smile—and she had been so easy going. But now?

As I walked back to my hotel I passed Radio City Music Hall. There were few lights in that massive building now. There had been plenty of bright lights earlier in the evening when Betty and I were playing in the orchestra. I had never played the Music Hall before. I was in town for a few days to see relatives and some shows. A friend in the orchestra had called me and had asked me to sit in for him one night. Betty was in the first violin section. We hadn't seen each other for years. After we had played the last bar for the Rockettes we went out together for a couple of drinks and to talk about the old Juilliard days.

It had been very enjoyable but she never mentioned that night in my apartment. I had waited until the end of the hour to ask her about it. Although I didn't like it, her answer didn't surprise me. I had heard the same line before from another former girlfriend and I hadn't swallowed it that time either. Hell, sex is fun. Every aspect of it is fun, something you share, when possible, with others.

Back in my hotel room I began to prepare for bed. But that bit about being unconscious still irked me, so naturally I began to review the past.

—— Betty and I had been in some classes together at the Juilliard and we played together in the symphony orchestra for about three years. We did a good deal of kidding around after classes and rehearsals and sometimes we took walks in Riverside Park. But I only dated her once.

She lived with her parents in the east Bronx, a few blocks from the end of the Pelham Parkway subway line, and I had a furnished room on Riverside Drive near the Juilliard. To pick her up I had to take the West Side subway from 125th Street down to Times Square, then the shuttle across 42nd Street to Grand Central, and then all the way up on the East Side subway to 241st Street. Then we rode back to Times Square where I took her to the Paramount to see a movie and a stage show. After a snack it was all the way up again to 241st Street. By the time I had walked her home and had gotten back to the subway, the expresses had stopped running and there were only locals every half hour.

I hadn't looked forward to that long ride home. I thought of getting off the subway when I reached Manhattan and taking a street car all across town on 125th Street. But I didn't know how often they came along at night, if at all. So I sat and sat, and as I sat the still, heavy air of the subway rested harder and harder on my eyelids until I could hardly keep my eyes open. I didn't dare make myself comfortable in a corner with my feet up on the seats and my back against the partition or even to sit leaning against the side of the car for fear of falling asleep and missing my stop. So I sat bolt upright and did what I could to keep awake.

I'm astigmatic so I can't read a book or a magazine on a train. It didn't bother me to read the multicolored ads stripped in above the windows, but this didn't use up much time and it took even less time for me to decide that no matter what the green and yellow ads said I didn't have halitosis and I had no need for Listerine. Nor could I make much time pass by counting the number of yellowish tan fiber seat cushions filling the elongated bench of a quarter section of the car or the number of white enamel hand straps hanging down above them or the multiplying of each of these numbers by four to get the totals for the car and again by three to get the totals for the three car train.

What did take time was waiting for the shuttle to move and for the uptown local to come at Times Square. When I got back to my room I figured I had spent nearly four hours on the subway. Betty had a first class good night kiss but I didn't think that alone was worth so much time riding the trains so I never dated her again.

Soon thereafter I was able to afford my first apartment. It was a one room and bath in Greenwich Village on the top floor of a four story walkup. The small room was rectangular with a window at one of the room's narrow ends and the doors to the hall, closet, and bathroom bunched together at the opposite end. The fireplace filled most of one of the long walls and my bed was lengthwise against the other. I had a small desk with a chair and a bureau, and my kitchenette consisted of a bookcase with a two-burner hot plate upon it. All the furniture was second hand but I was determined to make the place as attractive as possible with what little money I had. I painted the furniture a dull black and placed an emerald green pottery luncheon set in the kitchenette-bookcase. My bedspread was made of *mate* sacks sewn together and my curtains of natural theatrical gauze. I had threaded a design through the curtains with red and yellow yarn and talked a girlfriend into sewing me matching pillow covers in red and yellow percale with a design identical to that of the curtains. Finally, I splurged and bought a good-sized color reproduction of a Degas ballet girl, trimmed in passe-partout, and placed it above the fireplace.

It was very cozy and I would have felt completely at home if the guy in front hadn't played Ravel's *Bolero* on his phonograph every minute that he was home. It's a good piece but is very repetitive and certainly can't take that many consecutive hearings. It was years before I could stand listening to it again.

I was very proud of my new place and advertised that visitors were welcome, but hardly anyone came. Most of the students of the Juilliard lived in the neighborhood or with their parents in other boroughs than Manhattan. The Village was out of their way. Then one night, when I was thinking about going to bed, the doorbell rang and I pushed the buzzer that opened the downstairs door. A whole crowd seemed to be climbing the three flights but it resolved into Betty, her girlfriend, Rachel, and their two dates. I had an extra chair, a folding chair that I kept in the closet, but the boys had to sit on the bed. While the girls admired my decor I hosted with wine in paper cups.

They hadn't visited very long before one of the boys said, "I think we'd better take the girls home."

"You've only been here a few minutes," I objected but I knew what he was thinking. Rachel lived near Betty and they all had a long ride ahead of them, especially the boys.

"Look," I said, "this thing opens to be a double bed. It will manage three. Betty and Rachel are welcome to sleep over if they want to." I looked at the boys. "It's two against one and they really won't be in any great danger."

Betty giggled. "I know Jerry; I'm not so sure. What do you think, Rachel?"

"I'm for it," Rachel said. "It's too late for an express and I'm sick of long subway rides on locals. Anyhow, I'm big and strong." She frowned at me and flexed her right arm. Actually, she was only an inch taller than Betty.

"I'll keep far away from you!" I said in mock fear.

Rachel looked at the bed. "Quit your kidding; how could you do that?"

The boys raised no objections. I didn't think they would and although they hadn't fully earned them each got their goodbye kiss before they left.

"I'm afraid three's a crowd," Betty said. She was merely repeating an old saying which had become popular again at that time. There had been a very successful musical running on Broadway: *Three's a Crowd*, one in which Libby Holman had given the first performance of the song "Body and Soul." There was a sophisticated popular tune if I ever heard one. It went through almost the entire circle of keys during the B section.

"Not at all," I said, replying to Betty's remark like the gentleman I was. "I'll sleep in the middle, on the crack."

"We get first dibs on the bathroom," Rachel said.

"OK," I said, "I'll make up the bed while you're in there." My bed was a wide version of what was then called a studio couch. There were two mattresses, a separate one on top and a lower one attached to the box spring. I rolled out the lower spring and flopped the top mattress over upon it. The bed now occupied most of the room. I put on clean sheets and pillow cases, the only extras I had, and spread my only blanket over them. I had only two pillows so I pushed them close together.

The girls came out in their slips. They made an interesting contrast: Betty fair, with fine, light brown hair and Rachel olive-skinned with hair as black and coarse as that of an Indian. They were different in figure, too, Betty with more bottom and Rachel with more bust.

While I brushed my teeth I wondered what the devil I was doing. Why had I invited two girls to stay overnight? My instinct, I realized, was beguiled by Rachel. I had only met her once before, briefly in the Juilliard cafeteria. I had been attracted by her bold and brash manner and filed a note of interest in the back of my mind and had promptly forgotten it as one does with things one files. But my instinct apparently had access to my files. But what in the hell could I do with two girls in one bed?

When I came out of the bathroom in my pajamas both of the girls were already in bed. Betty was lying on the inner half, near the wall, and Rachel on the other half, near the edge.

"It was very thoughtful of you to leave space for me," I said. "But how do I get in?"

"Oh," Rachel said and got out of bed. I slipped in, Rachel turned out the light, got back in, and pulled the covers up over us. All three of us were now lying there on our backs and by some miracle we weren't touching.

Under the circumstances it seemed the best thing I could do would be to go to sleep. I wasn't accustomed to sleeping on my back and I had forgotten one characteristic of this bed. The two mattresses do not match. The half of the bed near the wall is lower than the other half. This meant that I had to continue to do a balancing act or I would slide toward Betty. I achieved balance without touching Betty by digging in my elbow right next to my body. I lay there for quite a while, listening to the breathing of the girls and wondering if they would fall asleep. They didn't. I wondered why. Their parts of the bed should be comfortable and I found one blanket warm enough. Maybe they weren't accustomed to sleeping on their backs either. I remembered that a lot of women slept on their stomachs. Men didn't, for obvious reasons.

After a while I came to the realization that they must be expecting something. Perhaps, as host, they were expecting me to offer them some small courtesies. Although I was expecting nothing in return, I saw no reason not to oblige. I placed a hand on Betty's slip over her left breast. There was neither a sign nor a sound from Betty. I moved to her other breast. Reaction ditto. I checked her straps but there was only one. No bra. For comfort or accessibility? I slipped my hand under her slip and felt her left breast. It was like half of an oversized delicious apple swathed in velvet but the nipple was flabby.

I ignored it and made a little love to both. Still no sign from Betty. Thinking I had given sufficient attention to one girl, I turned to the other. The girls were good friends and I would make it even Steven. I didn't want to break up their friendship. If you live at the end of the subway line in the east Bronx you really need a friend.

I applied the same procedure to Rachel. Her breast was larger than Betty's but not as firm. But the nipple stood up like a tower.

I lay back and considered the situation. There had been a lot of laughing and giggling in the bathroom while I was making the bed but I had given it no heed. Obviously, a conspiracy was in effect. They must have decided that I couldn't keep my hands off of them but I also couldn't go too far with three in a bed. Thus, no bras. But how far would they allow me to explore? A tantalizing question.

I returned to Betty. After proper attention to her breast I moved my hand toward her navel. I didn't reach it. She turned over and presented her back to me. OK, now Rachel. She turned on her side just as I reached her navel.

I was now more comfortable. I could lie on my side in back of either girl. Of course, if I went back from Betty to Rachel I had to climb a bit, but it was worth it. I returned to the attack. I picked up the hem of Betty's slip. Immediately her hand came down and pushed mine away. Rachel's hem came up without resistance and she let me feel her leg and thigh until I reached her pubic hair. Then she gently withdrew my hand and pulled down her slip. Good old instinct!

To get any sleep I had to lie on my side and nestle up to one girl or the other. I dozed off but I don't remember behind which girl it occurred. I don't think they got much sleep either.

When the first daylight crept from behind the blind and percolated through the gauze curtains, I came fully awake. I had a ten o'clock class. I patted each girl gently on her behind and said, "Rise and shine." The girls were apparently annoyed at being awakened so early so there was a pillow fight. I think Rachel started it by hitting me over the head with one.

I put the bed together and set up my card table, serving what breakfast I had. I think it was canned orange juice, toast with marmalade, and tea. I don't drink coffee. It was all very pleasant. Then the girls got dressed and before they left each gave me a goodbye kiss. I noted that Rachel was no slouch at this, either. If you live at the end of the subway line and want dates I suppose as a minimum you have to develop a first class goodbye kiss. But Rachel's was different from Betty's; her lips were parted. As they left Betty said, "See you soon." And Rachel said, "Me too."

Several nights later there were two in my bed and one of them was Rachel.

Back in my hotel room I had reviewed the past and I was now quite sure that I knew the answer to the question that I had not asked Betty in the bar, "Who was unconscious?" Obviously, it was neither Rachel nor I. And when the three of us were in bed Betty was hardly under anesthesia. So the answer was simple, no one.

The  DARK SPOT

L eave her alone," Kevin shouted angrily at the yapping Chihuahua on the other side of the fence. When he turned Whitey had already retreated around the corner of the house into the back yard. He found her lying in her favorite spot in the shade of the old apple tree, her right ear drooping and her muzzle on her forepaws.

He sat down and stroked her head. "Don't pay attention to him. We love you."

"Kevin," his mother called from the house.

"Coming." He gave the dog a final pat. "Take it easy, girl. I'll see you after school."

In the kitchen his mother handed him his lunch box. "I've made you a deviled egg sandwich. I know you like them."

"Mm, thanks." Then his face clouded. "That Chihuahua has been teasing Whitey again about the dark spot in her ear."

"Kevin, dogs don't talk."

"Sure they do, Mom. Remember how Whitey used to talk to her pups?"

"Well, maybe."

"What else could it be?" Kevin asked.

"Perhaps she's afraid of that Chihuahua."

"A dog that small? It's because she's a Westie. She knows Westies are supposed to be white all over, no dark spot, not even in the ear. She's ashamed of it and when that Chihuahua starts yapping about it she runs away. Couldn't you get Uncle Bob to look at her? Maybe he can rid her of the spot and she won't have this trouble."

Uncle Bob was his mother's brother and a veterinarian. "Honey, that spot's probably been in there all the time and we just didn't notice it. I've checked her ear; it doesn't hurt her. But I'll be glad to take her to Uncle Bob on Saturday."

"But today's Tuesday."

"I'm sorry, but I can't take off from work when she's really not sick. Now hurry, school buses don't wait and if you're not going to be here when I get home don't forget to leave a note so I'll know where you are."

"I won't." She said that every morning but he had forgotten a couple of times and didn't want to worry her. As he left the house he was careful to fasten the latch on the gate in the high picket fence surrounding the yard. Then he ran for his bus.

"Each of you draw an animal," instructed Mrs. Adams after recess. "Draw one you've seen pretty often so you'll really know what it looks like and then color it. When you're finished we'll pass it around to see if the rest of the class knows what animal it is."

"I'll bet you'll draw Whitey," said Dotty who sat next to him.

"Of course. She's the animal I see the most." He saw her in his mind's eye and then sketched her outline. He was pretty good at drawing, and at least they would know it was a dog. He took out his paint set and began to fill out the outline with white.

"She said to color it," Brad said. "White's not a color."

"Sure it is," Kevin said. "But she'll have a black nose and brown eyes." He suddenly realized that Whitey wasn't white all over even with the dark spot in her ear. But no one expected even a white dog to have a white nose and white eyes. If he could have drawn her so that the inside of her ear showed he would have painted out the spot.

Everyone in the class knew Kevin had painted a white dog. He wasn't sure if it was because he drew well or because he talked so much about Whitey that everyone knew who it was.

As usual he walked home from the bus with Brad. "Doesn't our picket fence look neat?" Kevin asked. "We just finished painting it."

"Not bad," Brad said as he continued down the street. "Of course, you would paint it to match your dog."

"So what!" Kevin retorted. He liked Brad but he wished he would stop kidding him about Whitey. She was a wonderful dog. He opened the gate. Whitey came bounding around the corner of the house to greet him as she always did when she heard the gate latch click. She put her paws up against him so he could tickle her ears, which were standing straight up. Then the Chihuahua appeared in the neighbors' yard and began to yap. Whitey's ears drooped and she dropped on all fours and ran around the house to the back yard.

When Kevin came out after putting his things away he found her lying in her usual place under the apple tree. He sat down next to her and put his arm around her. "We've got to get rid of that spot. I'll just paint it out." There was some paint left from the job on the picket fence. He could use that but he'd have to be careful not to spill any or Mom would be upset.

Soon he had everything he needed sitting on a double length of kitchen paper towel stretched out next to Whitey. There was a little brush from his water paint set, the big can of paint, the stick with which to mix it, and the old screwdriver which already had paint on it with which to open the can. He tore off a piece of paper towel, bunched it into a ball, and gently pushed it down into Whitey's right ear. "That's to keep paint from getting down in there," he explained. Whitey trusted him and didn't complain.

He pried off the cover of the can and carefully mixed the inch or so of paint still in its bottom with the stick. He dipped the little brush down into the paint and then held it over the can until it stopped dripping. Turning to Whitey, he held up the tip of her ear with his left hand and began to paint out the spot with his right. The spot wasn't very large so it didn't take long.

"That ought to do it. It's quick dry paint so it'll dry fast." He held up the tip of the ear with one hand and stroked her all the time with the other. He tested it with a finger. It seemed to be dry. "OK, no more spot."

Working carefully, he removed the ball of towel from her ear. It was a good thing he had thought of it; there was one spot of paint on it. Dropping it on the toweling next to the little brush, he placed the cover on the paint can and pounded it into place with the butt of the screwdriver. Then he went into the garage and placed everything back exactly where he had found it, the wet mixing stick on top of the can. Back in the yard he folded the paper towel around the little ball and the paint brush and placed them in the garbage can next to the kitchen door. He'd have to buy himself another brush but it couldn't cost much; he had some money.

He found Whitey's ball in her doghouse and threw it down the yard. She dashed after it and triumphantly returned with it, her ears standing straight up. He felt warm inside. She was the old Whitey again. Then he tried the front yard to see what the Chihuahua would say but the other dog didn't appear.

He meant to tell Mom all about it at dinnertime but didn't. Somehow he didn't feel as good about it as he had before. He told himself that it was because he hadn't checked it out with the Chihuahua yet but as he got ready for bed he realized what really bothered him. The paint took care of the spot alright but was there any chance that it might hurt Whitey's ear?

He checked Whitey the next morning before he left for school and she seemed fine. But when he came home she didn't come running at the sound of the gate latch. Hurrying around the house he found she was in her doghouse, a bad sign.

"Hi, Whitey. Something wrong?" There was no sound from the doghouse. He sat at the little doorway and looked in. Her right ear was drooping again. He reached in and touched it and she whined and drew away. He picked up the ear by the tip so he could look at the place he had painted. She made a low noise in her throat. The ear was still white inside but it seemed swollen. He touched the spot and she whined and pulled away. Her ear hurt. There was no question about that. He didn't feel warm inside now but cold and empty. He loved Whitey. In trying to help her he had hurt her. She needed to go to Uncle Bob. Mom didn't get home 'til six and by that time the animal clinic would be closed, so he'd have to get her there himself.

Up in his room he got the dollar bill he kept in a flat box in his desk drawer and emptied his coin bank. There were only five quarters and a dime. The clinic was all the way across town and they couldn't walk it. They'd have to take a bus. He wondered how much that would cost.

He put the money in his pocket and went down to the kitchen and took Whitey's leash from its hook. Outside he called, "Come on, girl." She came out obediently but slowly and he put on the leash. As they were about to go out the gate he remembered. He went back into the house and wrote on the pad next to the telephone: Whitey's ear hurts her. Took her to Uncle Bob. Kevin.

They waited at the bus stop for quite a while. When the bus finally came Kevin picked up Whitey and held her in his arms. The door opened and a man stepped out but before Kevin could get in the driver said, "Sorry, kid. No dogs allowed." The door closed in his face and the bus drove off.

A car pulled up next to him. It was a small car, fire engine red, and the only person in it was a little old man with gray hair and a cheerful face. "Your dog sick, son?"

"Yes, sir. There's something wrong with her ear. Got to get her to my Uncle Bob's animal clinic but it's all the way cross town on Highland Avenue."

"I can take you most of the way. Hop in."

"Thanks," Kevin said. Then he remembered and drew back. "Thanks just the same, mister, but my mom said I shouldn't get in cars with strangers."

The old man frowned. "That's hardly a compliment." Then his face became cheerful again. "Come to think of it, your mother's right. Tell her I said so." And he drove off.

Kevin decided to wait for another bus. When it came and the door opened he got in before it could close. The driver was a stout man with red hair and laugh wrinkles around his blue eyes.

"Please, sir, my dog's sick and I've got to get her all the way cross town to Highland Avenue, to the vet's. Please let her ride with me. I'll pay for both of us."

There was only one passenger in the bus, a large Black woman sitting two seats back with a bulging shopping bag at her side. The driver turned to her. "What do you say, ma'am?"

"A sick dog don't feel no better than a sick human. Let it ride."

"OK, kid," the driver said, "but sit all the way in the back and keep the dog quiet."

"Whitey won't cause any trouble. How much?"

"Fifty cents. No charge for dogs."

"Thanks a lot, mister, and to you, ma'am," Kevin said as they went up the aisle.

"Something wrong with Whitey?" asked Rebecca, the receptionist, as they walked into the clinic.

"Her ear hurts. Can Uncle Bob see her right away?"

"He has a patient with him now but I'll get him to squeeze you in before the next appointment."

"Thanks." Soon a man with a beagle came out of Uncle Bob's office and Rebecca told Kevin to go in.

"What's wrong with my favorite West Highland White Terrier?" Uncle Bob asked.

"Her ear. It had a dark spot inside of it and the Chihuahua next door kept teasing her about it so I painted it white."

"Oh," Uncle Bob said, "not too good an idea."

"I guess not," Kevin said.

Uncle Bob took a wad of cotton out of a jar and moistened it with liquid from a big bottle. Then he began to rub the inside of the dog's ear. She whined. "Steady, old girl," Uncle Bob said. Kevin came over and held Whitey.

"There," Uncle Bob said, "all the paint's off." Kevin looked inside the ear.

"The dark spot's all gone," he said excitedly.

Uncle Bob looked at the wad of cotton that he held in his hand. There were some dark specks on it. "The spot you painted over must have been made by ink or by a dark colored paint. Any chance she got into some fresh paint recently?"

"Oh. A little while ago our neighbors painted their fence and I took her out for a walk right afterward. It's an ugly dark brown."

"Then that's what it was."

"Well, I'm sure glad it's gone," Kevin said. "Thanks an awful lot, Uncle Bob."

"You're welcome. Wait around and I'll give you two a ride home. Does your mother know you're here?"

"I left a note," Kevin replied and was very glad to be able to say he had.

"What time will she get home?"

"About six."

"Well, I can't leave until after six so I'll have Rebecca call her at work and let her know we'll be late."

As Uncle Bob stopped his car in front of the gate of the picket fence, he said, "Painting animals in drawing class is all right but leave the real ones alone. Don't forget that."

"I sure won't," Kevin promised. As he ran into the house with Whitey at his heels he called, "Mom, Whitey's spot's gone."

The MATING of INGWA and TSLU

N ulu! nulu!" shouted the five other three crests surrounding Tslu as they pecked at him while thrusting out their talons in a gesture of disgust. "Nulu! nulu!" They chorused.

Pushing his way through them Tslu ran sobbing up the winding, rocky path which led to the cave of Mua, their class mother. Hearing the taunts of his classmates Mua came out and sat on a stone in front of the cave awaiting his arrival. Upset as he was Tslu did not forget the ceremonial bow due his class mother although his beak barely touched the ground.

"What is it?" asked Mua as she folded him in her arms and pressed him against her ample sternum.

"Why do they call me nulu, nothing? I am not nothing, I am Tslu."

"Yes, you are Tslu," said Mua soothingly. "But you are also nulu and it is not your fault. Only the silly three crests will taunt you about it. When they are older they will know better."

"But nulu means nothing," persisted Tslu. "Why am I called nulu?"

"You do not know?"

"No," he sobbed angrily. "Not even a three crest Rashkiki would ask questions about something he already knows."

"Then I must tell you," said Mua. "You are called nulu because the egg from which you were hatched had only one yolk and you, only you, were hatched from it."

"But what happened to the other yolk?"

"No one knows. Such an egg occurs only in many moons and the Rashkiki who hatched out of it brought with him no Rashkika to live on this island, a Rashkika who would hatch at least one egg. You brought no Rashkika with you and therefore you will not be allowed to participate in the hatching of an egg. Thus you are nulu."

"But I'm just like the other three crest Rashkiki. When I have eleven crests I also could hatch an egg with a Rashkika."

"Of course, but this you will not be allowed to do. Your egg did not contribute a Rashkika. The group will only have five eggs to hatch, not six."

"But I had nothing to do with it!" wailed Tslu.

"That is true," said Mua. "It is hard but that is the way it must be. That is the way it is. You are nulu and there is nothing that can be done about it. That is the Rashki way. You were hatched alone from your egg and lost the right to hatch an egg in turn with a Rashkika. It is a great misfortune."

Tslu stopped sobbing and pulled himself away from Mua. "Perhaps a Rashkiki will die," he said hesitantly.

"That does not happen very often," said Mua. "You intend to kill one of your classmates?"

Tslu stood as tall and as straight as he could, the three little red crests standing high on his back. "No, I wish to hatch a Rashki, not kill one."

"It would not do you much good if you did kill one. You would just be drowned."

"And that I know." Fiercely he said, "I shall become the best of fishers. I shall play kali better than any other Rashkiki. I shall be the best weaver of fishing nets. They shall see how good I am and they will let me take the place of another Rashkiki."

"Perhaps." She did not wish to discourage him. "You will at least be greatly honored if not allowed to hatch an egg."

Sitting alone in his nest during the red dusk Tslu remembered with bitterness what Mua had said that day. It was not true and it would never be true! Since then seven red moons had emerged from the sea far to the west and slowly moved overhead, each adding its tint to both the light and the dark before plunging into the sea far to the east. He now had ten crests but he had never been honored. He had practiced and practiced until he could beat any other Rashkiki in a game of kali. The only result was that now no one would play the game with him. He had woven better fish nets by using the tough tendrils of the barbar bush which were more flexible than vines—an idea no one else seems to have had—and spent much time on the sea rocks at high tide, catching many fish. But he was still nulu. The Rashki took the fish and did not even thank him, that is, all but Ingwa. She never thanked him in so many words but before she turned away she looked directly into his eyes and opened her beak as though to speak.

There was a rustle nearby and he wondered who was there. Most Rashkis slept during the dimly lit dusk period when only the red sun was in the sky.

Of the two suns the white sun was much larger and more brilliant than the red. For a short period every eleven days the white sun blotted out the red and the rays of the white sun then clearly defined the entire landscape. The Rashki called this period the white morn. The two suns rose almost simultaneously but in different regions of the sky. The white sun was the first to set and the red sun remained alone in the sky for quite a time before it also set. During this period, which the Rashki referred to as the red dusk, for some reason the sun's rays were even dimmer.

"Who's there?" he called.

"'Tis I, Ingwa."

"And what are you doing out at this hour?" he asked harshly, knowing that his tone of voice did not reflect his true feelings. Ingwa was the only one of his classmates who had always been kind to him and he thought her beautiful. He could not see her well because of the red dusk. Forms were now indistinct and merely loomed, producing almost no shadows. Nevertheless, he could imagine the lovely curve of her sternum and the fine articulation of her tiny red nails which were almost luminous when she moved.

"Tslu, why do you sleep here alone? Come and join the rest of us. There is an empty nest next to mine under the long ledge."

Knowing she would not recognize it he waved his talons at her in a gesture of caring. "No," he said and his tone was now a little less harsh. "I'm a curious fellow. It is low tide and while the other Rashkiki sleep I go to meet the sea and then follow it back to shore."

"But that is very dangerous. You may be drowned or caught and eaten by one of the sea creatures who remain as the tide goes out."

"What difference will that make?" asked Tslu, his tone becoming harsh again. "I am nulu. Nothing will be lost. The number of newly hatched Rashki will remain the same whether I live or die."

"I cannot deny that. But why do you live alone? It must make you unhappy. And why do you no longer fish?"

"You ask silly questions. It is because I am nulu that I live alone. Now I fish only for myself. If I fish for others they take my fish and offer no thanks. Nor do you."

"I have always been grateful for the fish you gave me but I could say nothing. It is against custom to thank a nulu."

"That is, one cannot thank nothing for something."

"You hurt yourself with your pride and bitterness. But you had better get some sleep. I understand that you and Psko have been selected to gather the yelt tomorrow. This is difficult and you will need all your strength."

"Yes, one of us may not return. If it is a nulu nothing has been lost. Thank you for warning me, Ingwa, but you had better go back to your nest."

Ingwa made a soft sound in her throat and then was no longer there. Tslu left his nest and walked briskly to where the high tide had left its mark before ebbing. Down the long slope ahead of him he could dimly see the sea. He walked slowly down the incline, listening and carefully scrutinizing the muddy floor on both sides of him, a floor which at times was sea bottom and at times not.

What seemed to be a great claw stretched out toward him from his right. Seeing no shape ahead of him he sprang forward. This was not a particularly close encounter. On other occasions he had been touched by the vaguely seen creatures lying on this tilted plane. But he had always escaped their clutches so he continued to advance cautiously until he neared the sea. The tide had already turned and the water was beginning to advance rapidly. In the dusk the waves seemed an ominously dark purple, their crests shedding spume like jets of fiery light.

He began to back up the incline, straining his ears to hear the least sound coming from behind him. Unlike the fish he could not swim. Should he be caught by the waves or perhaps by one of the vague shapes on either side or behind him and held until the waves covered him he would die.

It would be impossible for Ingwa to understand why he played this game, why he found it so fascinating. Certainly no other Rashkiki did. Was it because as a nulu it mattered little whether he lived or died? If so then why did he put every effort into remaining alive? At this moment he felt a snake like form curl around his left leg. He jumped backwards but the thing held him. He fell. Quickly he twisted around and sank the talons of both hands into the dim shape in front of him. The coil on his leg loosened and he tore himself free. Scrambling to his feet he raced to the top of the incline. There he turned and gasped his watch word and war cry, "I am Tslu! Not nulu!" Then he went to his nest to sleep.

It would soon be morning and both red sun and white sun would rise. The combined rays made the earth pink. It would be time to gather the yelt. This must be done by every group of ten crests before it held its mating dance. He had expected to be chosen. Many Rashkiki might be asked to play this particular dangerous game and considering what he did during the red dusk he was certainly a likely candidate.

In the morning, wide awake, Tslu looked out at the wide, blue sea stretching in every direction. He could see the great splotches of white yelt which irregularly dotted its surface near the shore but in reasonably deep water. They would harvest its water spores.

The red moon could now be seen far to the west but only Itu, the old one, could decide when it had reached the point in its passage when the yelt could be gathered.

Tslu went to consult Itu and found him recounting the history of the Rashki to the latest class of six three crests.

"We were once a great people, large, red birds who lived on a chain of islands far to the west. There it was always warm and sweet fruit grew on almost every tree. We were well adapted to pick this fruit for we had talons not only on our feet but on the end of our wings.

"But in some respect we disobeyed the Mighty Ones in the sky and they condemned us to live on this little island. We were forbidden to fly so we could not return home. Since we no longer had use for wings little by little through thousands of moons they disappeared and now we have arms instead. Our projecting sternums, needed to support the wings we once had, also shrank but only partially disappeared. They are still sufficiently large, making it impossible for us to sleep on our stomachs. Of the red feathers that covered our bodies we now only have the crests on our backs.

"Perhaps some day the Mighty Ones in the sky will change their minds and we will have wings again. Then we shall be able to fly back to our original home, the beautiful islands of Rashk. But this is only a dream. For thousands of moons the mighty ones in the sky have given us no sign."

To Tslu this was a very old tale. He had heard it many times. He waited until Itu had finished and after offering him the very deep ceremonial bow appropriate to one who was so much his elder he said, "Caw, old one, I have come to gather the yelt."

"Come then," said Itu and they walked to where the bank of the Green River met the shore of the sea. Here, not far from the sea or the river sat the yelt raft. A new raft was constructed each year of broken disparate lengths of logs of the Mbula trees which grew along the upper reaches of the Green River. These trees were constantly being knocked down and broken up by the strong winds that blew in this area. The pieces of log were then carried down the Green River and could usually be found floating in the pool formed by the river a short distance before it merges with the sea. In the periods between the appearances of the red moon two older Rashkiki delegated by Itu, the old one, came to the river each white morn, gathered these logs and placed them near where the raft was to be built.

In constructing the raft a rough square wide enough to accommodate two ten crests and their baskets was assembled by placing the gathered lengths of logs side by side and end to end. Lengths of the strong but flexible gremli vine were pulled down from the local tutsi trees. These were cut to the needed shorter lengths by sharp edged stones and the resultant pieces were used to firmly latch together the logs of the square. A second but slightly different square was also assembled. On one side of the square the pieces of log butted together were of greater length so that their ends jutted out a short distance from the other logs both to the right and to the left. A similar length of a reasonably straight branch was now cut from a tutsi tree. Since the wood of the tutsi tree is much harder than that of the the mbula tree that was a rather difficult task using only a sharp edge stone but it was finally accomplished. The branch was then placed above the butted length of logs just assembled and they were lashed together with pieces of vine at both ends and in three equally spaced places between the ends. The entire square was latched together in a similar manner as the previous square.

Three longer pieces of vine, each of length equal to three times the width of either square, were placed parallel to each other on the ground. A second group of three was then placed above the first at right angles. The first square of logs was now placed over the vines and the second square of logs on top of the first and also at right angles to it. The ends of the vine were then brought over the top square, stretched and firmly tied. All this was accomplished in such a manner that the logs jutting from the top square were more or less parallel to the shore and that the area between them formed the back of the raft which faced up river.

Itu and Tslu had been joined by Psko and the other ten crests. "Caw," Psko said to Tslu, "we have been chosen to gather the yelt. Are you strong and brave enough to work with me?"

"Strong enough?" asked Tslu, his crests rising. "I am heavier and half a head taller than you and the others. As for bravery would you like to join me in my red dusk game with the sea?"

"Not I," replied Psko, "but what we are about to do is equally dangerous. Nevertheless, I must think of the future of the Rashki. It is my duty to hatch at least one egg."

"I should be glad to relieve you of that duty, Psko. It would be my pleasure to take your place."

"That cannot be," said Itu, the old one, and he went to the raft and examined it carefully. All seemed to be in good order.

After the Green River left the pool it had formed for a short distance before it reached the sea it was quite shallow. A short distance in back of the raft on both sides of the stream were large coils of gremli vine, one free end of both tied to a tutsi tree. These coils were formed by tying many lengths of vine end to end and when uncoiled formed a very long vine line.

At this moment Mua approached with two tightly woven baskets which were to be used to hold the gathered yelt spores. Since she was the elder of almost everyone there she was greeted with a deep ceremonial bow in which the beak touched the ground.

"All is in readiness," said Itu. "The tide is about to go out. Let us begin." He signaled to an older Rashkiki standing on the other side of the stream who then picked up the other free end of the coil lying on his side and waded across the Green River, the coil uncoiling behind him. He firmly attached the free end of the coil to the log jutting out from the right side of the raft and then returned back across the stream accompanied by two ten crests Rashkiki and one ten crest Rashkika. Once across the stream they formed a file with the older Rashkiki as head and picked up the vine line. In the mean time an older Rashkiki on the raft's side of the river had attached the free end of the coil on that side of the river to the log jutting out from the left side of the raft. He was joined by one ten crest Rashkiki and two ten crest Rashkika who formed a similar file and its members also picked up their vine line.

Now a number of older Rashkiki picked up the raft and placed it in the shallow stream between the pool and the sea. The two files on opposite sides of the stream now held their vine lines taut so that the pull of the stream would not carry the raft toward the sea. Mua gave to Tslu and Psko two baskets. They waded out to the raft, and placed the baskets on it then climbed up onto it themselves. When they were settled each waved their right arm and those in the two files on opposite sides of the stream allowed the vine lines to slip through their talons. The raft then moved out to sea where it was caught by the ebb tide and carried further toward the mass of yelt which was their goal.

When it would seem that the raft was moving too far to the left Itu ordered the file across the river to hold. They held fast and the raft veered to the right. Itu cried, "Let go!" and the files again allowed the vine lines to slip through their talons. After two more corrections, in which each vine line was held back in turn, the raft was finally guided to the mass of flowering white yelt. The two on the raft now waved their left arms and the two files on shore kept the vine lines taut so that the yelt could be harvested. This was not too difficult since the raft was buoyant.

They had drawn lots before leaving and Tslu was the first to gather the yelt. He moved to the front center of the raft and placed his basket on his right. He then sat on the front edge of the raft with his legs in the water. The water spores he needed to gather were found a short distance below the flowers attached to the elongated filament-like stems which connected the flowers with the sea bed. To reach the water spores Tslu had to bend forward and there was a chance he might lose his balance and fall into the sea. Since the Rashki could not swim this would prove fatal. As insurance against this Psko stretched himself out with his arms firmly around Tslu's waist and the talons at their ends tightly clasped. The talons on his feet were also tightly clasped to the tutsi branch fastened to the back of the raft.

When Tslu had harvested all the spores he could reach he waved his right arm and the files on shore again allowed the vine lines to slip through their talons so that the raft could be carried further into the yelt. The filament-like stems offered some resistance, bending and stretching as they would in a storm, but finally snapped. When the raft was sufficiently forward Tslu waved his left arm and the two files on shore held fast again. In this manner Tslu was slowly filling his basket.

"How are you doing?" asked Psko.

"Good enough. It's hard on the back but I'll be through soon."

When Tslu's basket was filled they exchanged places. Psko waved his right arm and they moved further into the flowering mass of yelt. Psko worked rapidly and his basket was soon half filled. Suddenly he shrieked, "The bansri! It's got me by a leg!" He raised both arms and threw them into the air. There was a shout from those on shore and the two files began to pull in the vine lines as rapidly as they could. Other Rashki joined in this effort, some wading the stream for this purpose.

As the raft began to move backward Tslu tightened his hold on Psko's waist. As they were being pulled back faster and faster something in the water was trying to pull Psko off the raft and Tslu was exerting all of his strength to hold him in place. In front of the raft a large dark head with a malevolent eye and a cruel, crooked beak emerged from the water.

"The bansri!" sobbed Psko. "Now it's got me by both legs!"

"I've got you," replied Tslu. "We're going in fast." The pressure on his arms became greater and greater. They felt as if they were being pulled out of their sockets. He locked his talons in front of Psko's waist and the talons of his feet around the tough tutsi tree branch which responded with only the slightest of bends to the pressure exerted upon it. Strong as he was Tslu was no match for a bansri. With one mighty tug it pulled Psko out of his grasp and down into the water where he vanished from sight.

The raft shot quickly back through the sea and was pulled onto the muddy slope left by the ebbing tide. Several of the older Rashkiki ran down the slope to the raft. Tslu tried to rise but found himself too weak and fell back. Two of the older Rashkiki picked him up, others grabbed the baskets and all was carried up the slope and deposited on dry ground in front of Itu.

"He should have held on," accused one of the ten crest Rashkiki. "He wanted Psko dead. We all heard him say that he would be glad to take Psko's place in the mating."

"I held on as long as I could," protested Tslu. "My arms were nearly pulled out of their sockets." But he did not expect anybody to believe him.

"Could you have done better?" Ingwa asked angrily of the speaker.

"No quarreling," demanded Itu. "The banshri is strong. No Rashki has ever been able to match the strength of a banshri. Tslu cannot be expected to be the exception. He will take Psko's place in the mating dance. Mua, you and the Rashkika go and prepare the yelt."

"I am nearly as dead as Psko," said Tslu weakly. "I doubt if I will be able to dance."

"With the yelt in you you will dance," said Itu.

Mua and the five Rashkika who were to participate in the mating dance carried the baskets to a large flat ceremonial stone and emptied the yelt upon it. With flat stones small enough to be held in the hand they crushed the yelt spores until their red coats were well mixed with their white centers and a pink paste covered most of the flat top of the ceremonial stone. The two baskets were now lined with leaves. Since the nests in which they slept were similarly lined the baskets now symbolized these nests. With sharp edged stones they picked up pieces of the paste and placed them in the baskets until each basket was three quarters full.

Itu took one basket and Mua the other and they moved to where Tslu was lying next to the sea and the river. Here under the watchful eyes of Itu and Mua the two baskets of yelt paste were placed on the ground. Tslu was now able to sit up. A circle was formed around the baskets in which the Rashkiki, of which Tslu was one, alternated with Rashkika. Of the ten Ingwa, who was the first of all of them to break out of an egg, was seated the farthest to the west. As it turned out, she thus had Tslu as a neighbor.

Beginning with Ingwa, and moving from left to right, each ten crest pressed two talons into the yelt paste and brought out a pinch of it. The free arm was then twirled, the paste placed into the beak and the head moved from one side to the other. When the head had returned to its normal position the yelt was swallowed. This process was repeated until each ten crest had swallowed twice eleven pinches of the yelt paste. As Tslu swallowed pinch after pinch he grew warmer and warmer and felt that his strength was slowly returning.

In the meantime the returning tide had brought the raft, still tied to the trees, back into the shallow channel of the river between the sea and its pool. The two older Rashkiki who had headed the files now twisted the vine lines around the trees in such a manner that the raft was held in place. The red moon, now nearly overhead, caused a new tide. At Mua's bidding two of the older Rashkiki picked up the still partially filled baskets, waded out into the stream and placed the baskets on the raft. Once this was accomplished the two older Rashkiki who had headed the files loosened and untied the vine lines from the trees to which they had been attached.

All watched as the flow of the river and then the ebbing tide produced by the red moon carried the raft with its partially filled baskets out to sea, the vine lines attached to it trailing behind. It was then apparently caught by an outward moving current since it continued to move out to sea. As it went it veered to the left and passed a wide mass of flowered yelt to its right.

They watched the westward journey of the raft until it was a mere speck which finally melted into the horizon.

"I can no longer see the raft," said Itu. "Can you still see it, Mua?"

"No, I can no longer see it."

"Can any of you ten crests see it?" asked Itu.

"No, Itu, old one, we cannot," chorused the ten crests.

"All is well, then," said Itu. "By morning you will all have grown your eleventh crest and you will be ready for the mating dance. Tonight, as you all know, you must sleep in the open, not in your nests. Each of you must sleep flat on your stomach so your entire back will be available to the red moon passing overhead. Otherwise during the night you may not acquire the full eleventh crest on your back. You were all told to dig a short, shallow trench to accommodate your sternum and thus be able to sleep on your stomach. Have you?"

"Caw, Itu. Yes, we have all dug our trench," again chorused the ten crests.

"All is well, then," said Itu. "By morning you will all have grown your eleventh crests and you will be ready for the mating dance."

"I am still very tired," said Tslu to Ingwa. "I did not answer when Itu asked if we all had dug a trench. Since I had never expected to grow an eleventh crest I had not. Now I must go and dig one."

"You had better rest first and recover all your strength," said Ingwa. "Come with me." She gave him her talons and they slowly climbed to the long ledge where all the ten crests but he had been sleeping. Here he settled into the empty nest next to the one occupied by Ingwa. His back and arms hurt but the yelt was warm within him. He laid back with eyes and beak closed and thought of the next day. He, Tslu, was no longer nulu. For this Psko had to die. For that he was sorry but he had tried his best to save him. For him it was not death but a new life. He had been allowed to become an eleven crest and to hatch an egg. It was a wonderful, almost unbelievable thought. And which of the Rashkika would select him in the mating dance? A partner could not be chosen who had been hatched from the same egg. But no Rashkika had come from his egg. Anyone of the five could choose him if they so wished. He hoped it would be Ingwa. Perhaps there was something he could do to make certain that it would be Ingwa. With this thought on his mind he fell asleep.

He was awakened by Ingwa shaking him. "Wake up, Tslu. You have just time to dig your trench before the red dusk comes. Here is my digging stone." She thrust it into his talons. "When you are through with it return to my nest. I shan't be there. I shall be lying flat on my stomach in the open air as you also should be." Before Tslu had a chance to thank her, she was gone.

Although the little island was now enveloped in the red dusk, Gley, he who names, was not asleep. He remained awake during the red dusk on the day before the mating dance occurred since he almost always had a visitor at that time. This red dusk was no exception for he already heard a scratching on his nest. "Who's there?" he called.

"Caw, Gley, he who names, it is I, Ingwa, a ten crest Rashkika who will soon become an eleven crest. I bring you a present."

"Then come in, Ingwa."

Entering, she held out what she was carrying and said, "I bring you a succulent melon just plucked from my own garden."

Gley took the melon but since he could not see it well in the dim light of the red dusk he brought it to his beak and smelled it. "It is, indeed, quite fresh. But why am I being given this?"

"Because tomorrow in the mating dance I wish to be mated to Tslu," Ingwa answered.

"And how do I manage that?" asked Gley.

"By naming names you control the order in which we five Rashkika enter the ring and select a mate. Until today Tslu was nulu and he was not a very pleasant Rashkiki to be around. I do not think any of the other Rashkika will select him. Should I be the last to enter the ring he will be the only Rashkiki there and we will be mated. If this happens you will then receive ten more of my best melons, one during each following white morn."

"He who names cannot be bribed."

"This is not a bribe but a present."

"And if instead of you one of the other Rashkikas should select Tslu will I still receive the other ten melons?"

"No, it is not that kind of present."

"Very well," said Gley, "I shall name you last and we shall see what happens."

At this moment there was another scratching at the nest. "It is Tslu," whispered Ingwa to Gley. "He must not know that I have come here."

"Lie down near the nest wall," Gley whispered back. "In this red dusk he will not know it is you."

Then Tslu's voice was heard, "Caw, Gley, he who names, I, Tslu, the ten crest Rashkiki who is about to become an eleven crest, have a present for you."

"Tslu," said Gley in his natural voice, "you had better go back to your trench while the red moon is above us. Otherwise you might never have an eleventh crest."

"This will not take long," answered Tslu.

"Enter then."

Tslu held out the large, fat fish he was carrying. "Just caught," he told Gley.

Gley took it to his beak and smelled it. "It is, indeed, freshly caught. Are you not afraid to fish during the gloom of the red dusk?"

"Being nulu gave me courage and wishing to mate with Ingwa gives me even greater courage."

"So you want me to arrange for you and Ingwa to mate?"

"Yes."

"And how am I to do this?"

"That is for you to figure out. You are he who names. I shall then give you ten similar fish, one during each of the following white morns."

"He who names does not accept bribes."

"This is a present, not a bribe."

"Will I receive the other ten fish if Ingwa and you are not mated?"

"No, it is not that kind of present."

"Well," Gley said, "I will see what I can do. In the meantime you had better hurry back to your trench. We have used up a good bit of time."

As Tslu left Ingwa rose from the floor. "I did not know that he cared."

"A Rashkika does not easily understand a Rashkiki nor a Rashkiki a Rash-kika. For that reason and others we Rashki prefer that mating be random. Should there be caring between those who wish to be mated this causes ex-pectations that cannot be met. Should the mating be random no such expec-tations are raised. But we do not ban mating by those who care and I will see what I can do for you. Should I be successful I would have quite a harvest, one might say an overabundance of melons and fish."

"Would you prefer to receive only five additional melons and fish rather than ten?" asked Ingwa.

"By no means. You have a reputation as a gardener and Tslu, of course, is our best fisher. Now you had better hurry off also while the red moon is still above us. You have used even more time than Tslu."

In the morning Itu, Mua, Gley and the ten participants with their newly acquired eleventh crests gathered next to the mating dance ring. A number of Rashki who would be only onlookers were also present. The ring was marked by stones embedded into the ground a short distance from each other, their surfaces more or less even with it. Some, however, affected by wind and rain, were raised somewhat and anyone entering or leaving the ring had to be care-ful or they would stumble over these slightly protruding stones. Ingwa was surprised to find Zolda, a Rashkika only a couple of crests older than she was, near the ring. She offered Zolda only the slightest of ceremonial bows before asking, "Caw, Zolda, have you yet been able to hatch a second egg?"

"No, so I shall be in the center of the ring for a second time. Gley believes that the pecking I shall receive from the young rashkiki will improve my fertility."

The Rashki females laid only one egg during each nesting season. Which position in which the body should be held to better warm the egg was an ar-gument which never terminated. Since both mates took turns in warming the egg this argument might occur between Rashki of different genders as well as between those of the same gender. However, the mere mention in public of the laying of an egg was taboo. It was considered altogether too intimate an action to be discussed publicly and only the mates that were involved in the produc-tion of the egg were allowed to mention this phrase and then only between each other in private.

When Ingwa asked Zolda if she had hatched an egg the question was somewhat ambiguous. Since the laying of the egg is required before it can be hatched, and it is taboo to mention this first act, a statement concerning the hatching of the egg is intended by the speaker to include the laying of the egg as well. Nevertheless, there are occasions when it is imperative that the other know, although one does not say so, that what is being referred to is specifically the laying of an egg. Rashki have a rather subtle means of accomplishing this. When the speaker says the equivalent in the Rashki tongue, "hatched a egg," rather than the equivalent of, "hatched an egg" modifying what we term the indefinite article, the first phrase specifically refers to the laying of an egg, the second does not.

The Rashki do not reach puberty until they have acquired their eleventh crest. Before this they are incapable of feeling any sexual sensation whatsoever. When they acquire their eleventh crest they are immediately sexual and they are also immediately mated. In the lifecycle of the Rashki there is no adolescent period with its attendant discomforts and psychological problems. In the Rashki culture there is no prohibition against the mention or description of the sexual act and Rashki who have not as yet reached puberty discuss it freely. Since the discussion of sex by these younger Rashki cannot be based on their own experience it is either speculative or is concerned with the related experiences of older Rashki.

Gley, he who names, was seated on a large, flat stone a short distance from the most eastward curve of the dance ring. In each hand he held a stout stick, each being used to hit one of the two considerably smaller stones which sat before him. Of these two the right was smaller than the left and both had been taken from a lava flow. Far back in the past this little island had been a volcano thrusting up from the sea. The molten lava had contained many gas bubbles. When the lava cooled and hardened the gas left the lava and became part of the atmosphere. Where the gas bubbles had been the hard lava was now pierced with many small holes. When either of the resultant stones was struck with a stick it did not give out a dull thud, as a solid stone would have done, but an almost definite pitch, the smaller stone a higher pitch than the larger stone.

Itu motioned to Gley who then performed his starting signal: three strokes on the smaller stone, two strokes on the larger stone and then simultaneous strokes on both. The ten eleven crests now entered the dance ring and formed a smaller circle within it. Ingwa, who had been the first of the ten to break out of her egg, again positioned herself the farthest to the west. They alternated Rashkika and Rashkiki and each dancer was careful to see that neither of her or his neighbors had been hatched from the same egg she or he had. This was not difficult to accomplish since it had been practiced the previous day. Gley again beat out his starting signal and clasping each others' talons the dancers moved sideways to the right or to the left following the eleven stroke patterns that Gley produced.

In the first eleven beat pattern there were four strokes on a smaller stone, six strokes on the larger stone and finally simultaneous strokes on both. As the pattern of strokes was four plus six plus one making a total of eleven strokes was heard. In dancing this the eleven crests took two steps to the right, two steps back again, three steps to the right, three steps back again and during the double stroke representing the eleventh beat they stood in place while raising their arms as high as possible. Now without losing a beat Gley directed six strokes to the smaller stone, four strokes to the larger, and again ended the eleven beat pattern with simultaneous strokes to both stones. Following Gley's second pattern of eleven beats the eleven crests took three steps to the left, three steps back again, two steps to the left, two steps back again and again stood in place on the eleventh beat of the pattern while raising their arms as high as they could.

These two stroke and dancing patterns alternated until there had been a total of ten. The eleventh pattern was performed the same as the first except that on the concluding eleventh beat the ten crests not only held their arms as high as possible above their heads but also jumped as high as they could. This ended the first dance routine of the four which formed the mating dance as a whole.

The five female dancers now left the ring leaving the five male dancers where they were. Now Zolda came into the ring and faced the most westward of the male dancers. Each male dancer then moved backwards two steps. Now after beating out the start signal Gley beat a different pattern of eleven strokes five times. This pattern consisted of five strokes on the smaller stone, simultaneous strokes on both stones which in the future will be called the double stroke, and five strokes on the larger stone. In dancing this pattern the Rashkiki whom Zolda faced took five steps toward her. This brought him in front of her. On his fifth step he raised his head as high as possible while Zolda bowed deeply. On the sixth stroke of the eleven Zolda raised her head as high as possible while the male stepped forward and pecked her. Both assumed their regular postures while the male stepped back five steps. Zolda then turned to the right and faced a second male. The two of them then repeated the dance pattern. The same was done with the third and forth males.

In executing this dance pattern, however, the fifth male pecked the ground rather than Zolda. Gley halted his strokes and a hissing sound was heard produced by the sharp intake of breath through their narrow beaks by everyone present except Zolda. The male's failure to peck Zolda was a public reprimand of her for having a sexual relationship with a Rashkiki other than her mate. Her face flaming with both shame and anger at Gley for having tricked her, she fled from the ring, jumping over its stone markers without looking to avoid stumbling. A little later she could be seen in the distance running until she disappeared around a hill.

The white morn was now in effect, the white sun having already blotted out the greater part of the red. The five males in the ring remained at ease, waiting for the full eclipse. This soon occurred and the landscape no longer had even a tinge of pink. All was bright and clearly defined. Without waiting for a signal the five males formed a row in the westward part of the ring. Gley called the name of one of the five females and she entered the ring on its eastward side.

Both the dance and beat patterns heard and seen in this third and most important part of the mating dance were similar to those seen and heard in the second of the previous two routines. The beat pattern was again five strokes on the smaller stone, a double stroke and five strokes on the larger stone. In this case, however, the pattern was repeated as often as necessary. In the dance pattern the female danced five steps toward the male raising her head high on the fifth step. The male selected bowed deeply during her fifth step and raised his head high on the next beat which was produced by a double stroke on the stones. During this double stroke the female either pecked the male in front of her or pecked the ground. Should she peck the male this is the indication that she has selected him as her mate. He then dances with her while she moves back five steps and they both leave the ring. Should the female had pecked the ground rather than the male she has indicated in this manner that she has not selected this particular male as her mate. She then dances back five steps and repeats this maneuver with one of the other males in the row. As long as she pecks the ground in front of different male each time she can execute this maneuver as many times as she pleases. However, in her third maneuver this particular female pecks one the males in the row and the two dance out of the ring together.

The Rashki say that the female rather than the male is given the right to choose a mate because the female make the greater effort in the bringing forth of a new life into the community. Such general statements concerning procreation are favored by the Rashki since they avoid the possibility of the unwary speaker coming into conflict with a taboo against mentioning the means by which the egg enters the nest.

A second female is named and soon leaves the ring with her selected mate as does the third female named. Now only two males are left in the ring, one of whom is Tslu, and only two females remained to be named, one of whom was Ingwa. Ingwa knew that she would be the last to be named but she had seen the other female talking with Tslu at least twice and it worried her. Could she count on this female not to choose Tslu?

The female in the ring obviously had difficulty in making up her mind. She had already pecked the ground before Tslu and then before the other male in the ring. Now she was returning to face Tslu a second time. Her head went down and then quickly up again. As Ingwa and Tslu stared in horror she pecked Tslu. Immediately the female's right arm shot up into the air with her talons pointed skyward, a sign of having made an error. Ingwa relaxed somewhat, knowing that she was being teased. But Tslu did not readily understand and kept staring at the female in the ring as she backed up, came forward again and pecked Tslu's neighbor. Then, as the couple danced out of the ring, Tslu's eyes found Ingwa outside of the ring and they smiled at each other.

At last Ingwa's name was called and she went into the ring. Since there were only the two of them left it was obvious that they would become mates but nevertheless they went through the entire maneuver.

It was believed that if this mating dance routine could be completed while the eclipse was still fully in effect the newly formed unions would indeed be very fortunate. However, this desired result had never been achieved in the memory of those present. Each female involved was too anxious to exert her prerogative of dancing up to one or more males and informing them by her casual peck on the ground that she was not in the least interested in having any one of them as a mate. On this occasion since only five couples rather than six were involved it would seem that the routine might have been completed before the red sun peeked from under the white but this did not occur.

Once out of the ring Ingwa and Tslu were congratulated on their union by their friends among the onlookers. Then with some reluctance Ingwa and Tslu joined the other couples in performing the fourth and last dance routine of the morning. The stroke pattern and the dance pattern in the fourth and concluding dance routine were similar to those of the first routine with three exceptions: the first was that the partner to the right of each female was the male she had selected as her mate. The second was that they no longer clasped talons but placed their arms over the shoulders of their neighbors. The third, and the most important, was the tempo or speed at which they danced. This, of course, was controlled by the tempo or speed at which Gley struck the two stones in front of him. In this, the fourth dance routine of the morning, Gley began at a much slower pace than he had in the first routine of the morning. He then very slowly but continuously increased the speed of his performance. By the time the dancers had reached the ninth pattern they were racing back and forth sidewise. Under these circumstances they found it useful to grip their neighbors' shoulders as a means of steadying themselves. This was a very exhausting routine and at the end of the eleventh pattern when they were supposed to jump high they were barely able to raise themselves above the ground. One female Rashki stumbled and fell, bringing her neighbors down with her. Those who were still erect helped the fallen to their feet. It is doubtful that those who had fallen would have made it to their feet on their own power. The Rashki say that newly formed couples are required to go through this exhausting routine as a foretaste of what they will experience when mated. Each couple then dragged itself to the location where they intended to build their connubial nests. After resting several times on the way Ingwa and Tslu arrived at a place where Ingwa had previously drawn a circle on the earth with a stick. The circle marked the limits of the double nest they would build together. Sighing with relief they laid themselves down in the middle of the circle facing each other.

"I was in Gley's nest when you came in yesterday during the red dusk," Ingwa told Tslu. "I never knew that you cared. Why didn't you tell me?"

"It wouldn't have been fair to you. I was nulu and would never be allowed to mate," Tslu replied.

"So, we're mated now," said Ingwa. "I don't know how but I've always known that once I had my eleventh crest I would be sexy and I would want as mate someone who is also sexy. Are you sexy, Tslu?"

"I don't really know. Since I got my eleventh crest I've done nothing but sleep and dance."

"And be mated," added Ingwa. "Since we both have our eleventh crests and we've just been mated I think we should have sex together right now." She waited a moment or two and then spoke again. "When your mate says that you're supposed to get an erection. Did you? You turned away so I can't tell."

"Possibly, I think I turned away in an attempt to get rid of the queer feeling I have. It is apparently caused by my penis being stiff and sticking out right in front of me. Perhaps that's an erection but it's not erect as my body would be were I standing. I'll turn back so you can see it."

"That's definitely an erection," Ingwa informed him, "and I think a rather good one. Of course, this was only a test. I've heard a lot of talk about sex and I wanted to see if you would react the way you are supposed to. You did."

"I'm glad I didn't disappoint you. Does this mean that I'm sexy?"

"I think so."

"Now that I have this erection what do I do with it?"

"You push it into me."

"I push it into you? Wouldn't that hurt you?"

"Probably some the first time but that wouldn't bother me."

"It would certainly bother me."

"That's what I expected you to say."

"When I was nulu I was told that I could never experience sex. To avoid frustration when anybody talked about it I would walk away or, at least, try not to listen. That's why I know so little about how it's done."

"That doesn't matter. I know enough for both of us."

"Then when is this coming down? I'm beginning to feel quite uncomfortable."

"When you stop thinking about having sex with me. When we've had sex it will come down right away. Did you know that we have to have sex together before I can lay an egg?"

"Ingwa!"

"No need to be shocked, Tslu. We are mates and it's alright for us to talk about laying an egg as long as it is done in private."

"I didn't know that."

"Do you at least know that having sex is supposed to be very enjoyable?"

"That I did know. But since we're so tired I don't think we'd fully enjoy sex if we had it now."

"I didn't intend that we should," said Ingwa and they allowed the exhaustion they had been holding back to lull them into a deep sleep.

The UNRELIABLE GENII

Daddy," Cindy said, "you stopped smoking, so could I have your old black pipe? I want to use it to blow bubbles."

"I suppose so," her father said, looking up from his newspaper. "But you'll have to clean it out first or you'll have a terrible taste of tobacco in your mouth."

"How do you do that?"

"Well, first you scrape out the bowl until it seems as clean as possible. You can use my penknife but be careful, don't cut yourself."

"I won't."

"Then you run pipe cleaners through the stem into the bowl." He went to his desk and took his pipe and a package of pipe cleaners out of the drawer, fished in his pocket for his penknife, and gave all three to Cindy. "It wouldn't be a bad idea if you soaked the stem in water for a while."

"Thanks, Daddy." Cindy followed his instructions as carefully as she could. Cleaning out the bowl with the penknife was hard work and took a long time. Finally the bowl was almost but not completely clean, and she decided that that was good enough. She filled the bottom of the bowl with soapy water and went out to sit on the front step and blow her bubbles.

The first bubble she blew came out a dark brown but it remained attached to the bowl. I guess I didn't clean the pipe well enough, she thought. But let's see how big a bubble I can blow. She blew and she blew and the bubble grew and grew, blooming out until it was bigger than she was. It formed a figure with a funny looking head and arms. Cindy put the pipe down, leaned it against the back of a step, and moved back so she could get a good look at the bubble.

"How can I serve you, mistress?" the brown bubble asked.

Cindy was both astonished and a little frightened. No bubble she had ever blown before had spoken to her. Then she realized what it must be. "Are you a genii, like the one in Aladdin's lamp?"

"Same kind of magic servant," the queer-shaped bubble said, "but no relation. I'm a tobacco genii. Tobacco wasn't known until Columbus discovered America. That was a long time after Aladdin."

"I didn't know that geniis knew history. Do you go to school?"

"No. Didn't need to. I know practically everything, that is, I can know practically anything I want to."

"What do you mean?"

"Well, nowadays you might say I'm like a computer attached to a main frame."

"I play games with a computer but I don't know what a main frame is."

"It's like having everything in a hundred libraries at your fingertips."

"Knowing things is nice," Cindy said diplomatically. "But can you do things, also, like Aladdin's genii?"

"Within reason. I'm not as powerful as Aladdin's genii. He was made of oil. I'm only made of soap and water flavored with tobacco."

"Well, I'll start with something simple. Just bring me an ice cream cone of Neapolitan ice cream."

"That's three flavors," the genii objected. "I don't think cones come with Neapolitan ice cream."

"Are you a genii or aren't you?"

"Very well, mistress." The genii disappeared and in a trice reappeared with a cup of ice cream, which he handed to Cindy.

Cindy looked at it. "It's Neapolitan all right, but I asked for a cone, not a cup."

"Sorry, but a cup's better for you. It doesn't have sugar in it like a cone."

"I don't care. Bring me a cone."

"Yes, mistress." The genii disappeared and in no time reappeared with the ice cream in a cone.

Cindy nibbled the ice cream. "Mm, it's good like homemade."

"It's geniimade. That's even better."

Cindy made a face. "Down below it tastes of tobacco. You slipped there."

"Sorry. You're sure it's not the tobacco taste left in your mouth from the pipe?"

"No, it's OK further down and the cone is delicious. I've never eaten one like it before."

"Our special recipe," the genii said modestly. "We use cloud vapor instead of water."

Cindy looked up into the sky. It was half-filled with a fluffy mass of white clouds, gold where they were thin and the sun shone through. She remembered flying over such clouds in an airplane and wishing she could walk on them. Of course, she knew they were just vapor and she would fall through if she tried. "Genii," she said as she finished the last of her cone, "I always wanted to walk on clouds. There's a nice bunch of clouds up there now. Could you arrange it?"

"No problem," the genii said and the next thing Cindy knew she was standing on a cloud, a wide level path between the cloud banks stretching before her.

"Oh!" she said, unnerved by the quickness with which things were happening.

"It's a perfectly fine surface. Don't be afraid to walk."

Cindy took a hesitant step or two and then began to walk with confidence. It was lovely, like walking on a very thick pile carpet. "It's too level," she said. "It's not like walking on clouds. There ought to be a few ups and downs."

"Very well," the genii said, and there were.

As Cindy walked and climbed over clumps of cloud carpet she gazed at the strange shapes made by the clouds rising on either side of her. One looked like her dog, Jason, another like her father smoking his pipe. And ahead to the right was one that looked just like the genii, only about ten times as large and pure white instead of an ugly brown.

"Look, genii," Cindy said pointing to it, "there's you." Suddenly the surface gave beneath her and she fell. She screamed but almost before the scream was out of her mouth she was again standing on the cloud.

"I'm very sorry," the genii said. "But when you drew my attention to that cloud I lost my concentration for a split second."

The tears were streaming from Cindy's eyes. "I'm scared!" she sobbed. "Take me down."

In a trice she was back on her front steps.

"I'm really very sorry," the genii said. "I assure you it won't happen again."

"It sure won't," Cindy sobbed. "I don't want to see your ugly face again. Go away."

"Yes, mistress," and there was a slight hiss of air as the brown bubble poured itself back into the pipe.

Cindy picked up the pipe and spilled its contents onto the sidewalk. It left a thin, wet blotch of light brown. Wiping her eyes, she carried the pipe to the kitchen, picked up the penknife and began desperately to scrape out the bowl. She scraped and she scraped until the inside of the bowl looked like raw wood. Then she filled the bottom of the bowl with soap and water and went out to try again.

This time she got nice, normal soap bubbles. They sailed up and away, rainbow colored and sparkling where the sun touched them until they finally burst. She felt calm. That was the way things were supposed to happen.

She looked up at the clouds, which had moved toward the horizon. Had she really walked on them? She looked at the faint brown stain on the sidewalk where she had emptied the pipe. Had that been the genii? No one would believe that it had happened if she told them. She wasn't sure she believed it herself. Then she felt her fingers. They were still sticky from the ice cream.

So maybe she had met a genii. But she couldn't trust him; he wasn't reliable. And what good was a genii if he wasn't? She was better off without him. She blew another bubble and watched it float up and up until it burst.

$\mathcal{P}$ERSUASION

The Kip's Bay district of New York City's East Side was not Fifth Avenue. The sidewalks were not wide and clean, and there were no expanses of plate glass windows, nor tall, meticulously maintained apartment buildings. Rather, facing the elongated black bridge of the Elevated and down the littered side streets there were mostly rows of tenements. Those who lived behind their dingy brick fronts had rarely been prosperous. And in 1933 their windows were even more frequently glazed with tin or cardboard rather than glass. Some seemed even too poor to afford garbage cans, for they piled their garbage in the street in paper bags that soon disintegrated, their contents providing sustenance for the cats and rats of the neighborhood who were only a little worse off than those who had placed the garbage in the street.

Down one of the side streets just a few steps from the brewery on the corner, in full view of both the East River and Bellevue Hospital, there was a sign above a tenement entrance which read, "Kip's Bay Music School." Within were the quarters of the budding music school that Jerry Reinecke had started a year before with the backing of the Kip's Bay Settlement House. The Settlement House owned this tenement, and the Music School now occupied its first two floors. The ground floor had been renovated to provide room for orchestral rehearsals. Partitions had been removed, paint slapped upon the walls, and the plank floors covered with used battleship linoleum. In the year 1933, that was plenty renovated.

Jerry came to teach music dressed in his cords, a royal blue double breasted jacket and cream colored trousers made of thin waled corduroy, what was then called Vickeroy. It was an outfit appropriate for a denizen of Greenwich Village, which one might say that Jerry was—he called home a small one room apartment overlooking the Italian pushcart market on Bleecker Street—but the neighborhood in which he taught did not take kindly to it. He was forced to overhear many remarks concerning his cords—even from some of the boys in the Settlement House—which were by no means complimentary and at times went so far as to imply that he was a fairy. Jerry was an artist of a kind, a musician and a composer, and he would dress as he felt appropriate and to hell with the consequences. There were members of the opposite sex who could testify to his virility but that was none of the neighborhood's business.

On this Saturday morning, as usual, Jerry, in his full regalia, in the large room on the ground floor was rehearsing the small orchestra he had assembled. The players were not very advanced and the orchestra was not well balanced so he arranged most of what they played. This morning they were again working through the simplified arrangement he had recently made of the "Trepak" from Chaikowsky's *Nutcracker Suite*. Although the piece was beginning to take shape, Jerry was not satisfied with what he had written. He had to make a change in the second clarinet part. For this he needed a desk. Telling his students to relax for a minute or two, he went into his little office back of the stairs. He had just finished rewriting the part when he heard a commotion in the orchestra room and rushed back out again.

Most of the members of his young orchestra were standing and all were looking at Amedio Santomassino, the first trumpeter, who was holding a hand to his eye.

"What happened?" Jerry asked.

He was answered by Mandelbaum, the orchestra's trombonist, who was just coming in from the hall. "A big kid came in from the street and socked Amedio in the eye."

"A big kid?"

"Yeah, even bigger than me." Mandelbaum was twelve but large for his age. He had to be to reach all the way to the seventh position of the trombone. "Ajemian and me went out to look for him but he was gone."

"Let's see the eye," Jerry said to Amedio. "Wow! A real shiner. Has anyone a clean handkerchief we can wet and put on Amedio's eye?"

"Here's mine and I've already wet it," Ajemian, the first clarinetist, said as he came in the hall door. The three boys, Santomassino, Mandelbaum, and Ajemian, were so often together that the other students called them 'the Three Musicateers.' If anything happened to one of them, the other two were sure to know of it.

Jerry took the handkerchief, applied it to Amedio's eye, and told him to hold it in place. "How did this happen?" he asked Ajemian.

"It started outside. Just before we got here a little kid came running down the sidewalk, not watching where he was going, and ran right into Amedio."

Mandelbaum took over. "Amedio pushed him away and told him to watch where he was going."

"The little kid said to Amedio, 'Go to hell, you son of a bitch,'" said Ajemian, taking it back. "So Amedio slapped him one."

"And," concluded Mandelbaum, "the little kid said, 'Yeah! I'll get my big brother after you.' And he ran away."

"Tough kid," Jerry said. "Amedio, do you know the kid who hit you?"

"No," replied Amedio, holding the handkerchief to his eye.

"We live in a nicer neighborhood," Ajemian said. "We don't know any tough kids like they have around here."

"Yeah," Lisa Weiss, who played first violin and was fourteen, said. "You live on Toidy Toid and Toid."

"No, we don't," Mandelbaum retorted. "We live on Thirty Second near Second Avenue and we don't say 'Toid.' We say 'Third.' We go to the same school you do."

"One neighborhood is as good as another," Jerry said. "Does anyone know the kid who came in and hit Amedio?"

"I do," Lisa said. "It was Corny Reilly."

"Corny?"

"That's what everyone calls him. His name is really Cornelius. Angelina knows him better than I do." She pointed her bow at the orchestra's only cellist. "He's sweet on her."

Angelina Maglioni, who was thirteen, accepted this accusation with equanimity. "Yeah, we play a lot of checkers together."

Mandelbaum snickered. Angelina turned and regarded him with her dark eyes. He suddenly felt it necessary to blow the water out of his trombone.

"I know him," volunteered Haratounian, who played percussion. "I play stick ball with him once in a while."

"Anyone else?" Jerry asked. No one answered. "OK, I'd like to see the three of you in my office after rehearsal. I'll stop early so you'll not be late getting home. Now let's get back to Chaikowsky. Amedio, do you think you'll be able to play?"

"Yes," Amedio said.

Jerry picked up his baton and everyone settled into place. "Letter B. Let's take it a little slower and see if we can get everything right. One, two; one, two." Down came his baton and the young musicians bowed and blew to his beat.

After the rehearsal, Jerry and his three students crowded into his little office. There were only three chairs so Haratounian stood. "Armenians are courteous," he affirmed.

"Most of the time," Jerry said. "You shouldn't have to stand, Haratounian. We'll go back into the orchestra room as soon as it's cleared out." Jerry settled back in his swivel chair. "Why," he asked the three, "does Cornelius Reilly go around socking people? Why is he so tough?"

"He's really not so tough," Angelina said. "Tim, his little brother, is always getting him in trouble."

"He's a lot tougher than Angelina thinks he is," Lisa said. "He used to beat up on people who called him Corny. Everyone does, and he can't beat up a whole neighborhood, so he stopped that."

"What's so bad about being called Corny?" Haratounian asked. "I've got a friend we call Stinky. He doesn't seem to mind."

"They're two different things," Lisa said with the wisdom of a fourteen year old. "If you stink, you stink, and everyone knows you're there. But if you're corny, you're out of style and no one wants to have anything to do with you except, of course, Angelina."

"I've tried to get people to call him Nelius," Angelina said. "But that didn't work. Some of the boys turned it into Nellie and then he got into fights with them."

"Why not call him Neil?" Jerry asked. "That's a good boy's name."

"How do you spell it?" Angelina asked.

"N E I L, silly," Lisa said.

"It might work," Angelina said. "I'll try it on him."

Jerry was at the door, beckoning to them. In the orchestra room he sat on the bench of the old upright piano that stood against the wall and his three students moved orchestra chairs so they could sit facing him.

"Good," Jerry said, "now does anyone know if Cornelius can carry a tune?"

"Of course he can," Angelina said. "You ought to hear him sing 'East Side, West Side.'"

"Yeah," Lisa said, "I've heard him."

"We need more bottom to this orchestra," Jerry said. "We need a string bass. I can get one if I had someone big enough and good enough to play it. Do you think we could make this tough guy into a string bass player?"

"What's a string bass?" Haratounian asked.

"Percussion players sure don't know much," Lisa said. "It's like a cello, but about twice as big and you play it standing up."

"That would be as hard on the feet as playing percussion," Haratounian observed.

Jerry had gone into his office and returned with a framed photograph which he handed to Angelina. "That's the Juilliard orchestra when I played in it. The string basses are right back of the cellos."

She examined it for a moment and then looked up, her face bright. "Say, that's a good idea. Will he play the same part as I do?"

"More or less."

"Then I could help him learn."

"Let me see it," Lisa insisted. Haratounian hitched his chair closer to Lisa's so he also could view it.

"Wow!" Lisa said, "That's really an orchestra. There must be a couple of dozen violins."

"And three guys playing percussion," Haratounian said.

"And six playing string bass," Jerry added. "Well, Lisa, what do you think of the idea?"

"I don't know. We could try it. It might work."

"And you, Haratounian?"

"It might work, maybe. Depends upon how we go about it."

"Then," Jerry said, "I appoint you three as a delegation to persuade Cornelius, that is, Neil, to become our new bass player."

"What's a delegation?" Haratounian asked.

"Now hold it, Lisa," Jerry said. "I'll tell them. A delegation is a committee... a group of people who have the responsibility... who are asked to do a particular thing."

Jerry rose and looked down at his three students. "So as director of the orchestra I appoint you three as a delegation to persuade Neil Reilly to be our new string bass player."

"OK," Haratounian said as the three also rose, "we'll do it!"

Jerry shook a warning finger. "Now, Haratounian, no rough stuff."

"Of course not. We Armenians are very nice people. Like you said, we'll persuade him."

As Jerry arrived at the door of the Music School the following Tuesday afternoon, he was met by a boy who asked, "You're Mr. Reinecke, the orchestra director, aren't you?"

"Why, yes, I am. May I ask who you are?"

"I'm Neil Reilly, your new string bass player."

Jerry looked him over. He was a fairly tall, stocky youth with red stubbly hair sprouting over blue eyes set in a liberally freckled face.

"Well, Neil, I'm glad to meet you. Come on in and we'll talk it over."

Cornelius, alias Neil, followed Jerry into the orchestra room. Jerry seated him in an orchestra chair and then sat a few feet away on the piano bench. "How old are you?" Jerry asked.

"Fourteen."

"I don't suppose you've ever seen a string bass."

"No, I haven't," admitted his new string bass player. "But I know what a cello is."

Jerry went to his office and came back with a photograph of the Juilliard orchestra. "Gosh!" Neil said as he compared the cellos and basses. "And Angelina said it was twice as big as the cello but I think it's even bigger."

"And you need big, strong hands to play it. Let's see yours."

Neil handed back the photograph and spread his hands. They were satisfactorily large for a fourteen year old and had straight looking fingers.

"Your hands look like those of a string bass player, and that's a good beginning, but you also need a good ear and a good sense of rhythm to play the string bass. I'll have to test you for those."

Neil slouched back in his chair, both hands in his trousers' pockets. "I don't mind. Go right ahead. I do pretty good on tests."

He certainly doesn't lack assurance, Jerry thought, placing the photograph on top of the piano. That's alright as long he's not too cocksure of himself. "Do you know anything about playing in an orchestra?"

"Sure. Angelina and Lisa explained it to me. It's team play, something like being on the baseball team." He eyed this man who wore cords and made music. "Know anything about baseball?"

Jerry smiled at this city kid. "I sure do, Neil. I was raised in a small town. I played baseball from the time I was in knee pants and in high school, too."

Neil sat up. "With a real bat and a real glove?"

"Sure."

"Where did you play?"

"Oh, mostly in vacant lots. Of course, you don't have any around here. In high school we had a baseball field."

"A real diamond with a backstop?"

"A home plate, a pitcher's mound, and bagged bases. The works."

"Gee!" Neil said, "It must be nice to live in a small town."

"It has its points when you're a kid," Jerry said. "But in what way did the girls say an orchestra was like a baseball team?"

Neil leaned forward as though to launch himself into his explanation. "Like I said, it's team playing. In baseball the pitcher, the catcher, the shortstop, they do different things, like in the orchestra the kids play different instruments. But Lisa said that team play in an orchestra is harder. The different instruments change back and forth in what they do. It's like the shortstop might pitch for a while and the catcher might go and play outfield. So it isn't enough to have a coach who just stays on the sidelines and tells the players what to do once in a while. Instead, they have a conductor who's right in the field all the time and keeps giving signals with a stick. That's probably it over there." Neil pointed to the conductor's stand.

"That's right," Jerry said. "It's called a baton." He went to the conductor's stand, picked up the baton and carried it back to the piano bench. "That's a good comparison the girls made but I'll give you another. Have you ever been to St. Patrick's Cathedral?"

"Once. My folks took me there for High Mass. It's real big and there's so much space up above you."

"Yes," Jerry said, "it is. Now a building that large has to have a very deep and strong foundation to hold up those tall walls, the high roof, to keep them from falling when the wind blows hard. Now the string bass is the foundation of the orchestra. When an orchestra makes a big, beautiful sound it's because there's a string bass deep down there supporting it. Sometimes the string bass plays a melody, usually along with the cello, but most often it's supporting the other instruments, it's acting as the foundation of the orchestra." Jerry paused briefly. "When people go to St. Patrick's they usually don't think about the foundation but there wouldn't be a building there without it. People listening to an orchestra usually don't listen particularly to the string bass but when it's not there they sure know it's not much of an orchestra because it's not supported down below. So," Jerry asked, "do you think you can not only hold up the bass and play it but support the whole orchestra as well?"

"You're saying a lot of things I'm not sure I understand," Neil responded slowly. "But it sounds like a job for a guy like me and I'd sure like to try it."

"OK, then let's get on with the test. I'm told you can sing 'East Side, West Side.' Stand up and sing it for me."

Jerry stood up as Neil sang, "East side, west side, all around the town," and carried the song through until its end. Jerry had trouble keeping his face straight. Neil's voice had not yet changed and his sweet alto was in ludicrous contrast with his robust physique.

"You carry a tune well," Jerry said. "Now come over to the piano." Jerry lifted back the cover and the black and ivory keys grinned up at him. "You look the other way and I'll play some notes, groups of two or three, then you sing them back to me. Sing them on 'oh' or 'ah.'"

Neil oh'd and ah'd until Jerry was satisfied. Then Jerry sat in one of the orchestra chairs and pulled another in front of him, the seat facing him. He told Neil to do the same and gave him a pencil. "I'll tap a rhythm on this chair with my baton and you imitate me, you tap the same rhythm on your chair with the pencil."

"OK."

Jerry began with a simple street beat as played by snare drums when marching in a parade: tap, tap, tap tap tap, and Neil tapped it back. Then Jerry complicated it a bit: tuh tap, tuh tap, tap tap tuh tap and Neil again tapped it back. The rhythms became more and more complex and finally Neil could no longer accurately imitate them.

"OK," Jerry said, "that's certainly good enough. You don't become a musician overnight. You'd probably like to know that you did better than most of the kids in the orchestra when they had the test."

"I passed?" Neil asked.

"You did. I don't have the bass yet but I will by next week. Come around at the same time next Tuesday and I'll get you started. Is that alright?"

"Sure. Could I come around Saturday morning and see what you do?"

"I don't think that's too good an idea," Jerry said. "You'd better give the Three Musicateers time to cool off. That's quite a shiner you gave Santomassino. They might not care for your being present."

"Oh, I don't think they'd mind."

Jerry examined Neil's cool confident face. "Well, I only have a rehearsal once a week. I'm not taking any chances. See you next week." He patted Neil on the shoulder. "I think you'll do well, boy."

Everything went well for a while. Jerry gave Neil two lessons a week, on Tuesdays and Thursdays, to move him forward as rapidly as possible. Angelina helped, too. When Neil came over to her house, instead of playing checkers she would drill him on reading music. She would also have him practice bowing on her cello. He would stand there with the cello propped up on an orange crate and saw away. The cello and the string bass are alike in some ways but very different in others. When he placed his fingers on the cello like he did on the string bass, it didn't sound quite right.

Then it happened. On the fourth Thursday Neil did not show up for his lesson. Following the Saturday rehearsal, Jerry questioned Angelina.

"He's discouraged, Mr. Reinecke. He expected to be in the orchestra by this time."

"It was three months before you were ready to play in the orchestra, wasn't it?"

"Yes. I told him that but it didn't seem to make any difference. He said that playing that big thing was harder than he had thought and he's not having much fun just sawing away. You know what he's like, Mr. Reinecke. He thinks he's just as good as any of the Three Musicateers. If they can be in the orchestra, why can't he?"

"Your Neil is certainly a tough customer. But tell him not to miss his Tuesday lesson. I've written a part for him in the 'Trepak.' I'd like you to play it for him on the cello on Tuesday so the two of you can practice it together a bit on Mondays. Can you make both days?"

"Sure, Mr. Reinecke."

On Tuesday they all sat around the phonograph and listened to an orchestra playing the "Trepak." It's a rapid dance and Neil felt like tapping his foot but didn't. He knew you shouldn't when you play in an orchestra. The last part of the "Trepak" is the most exciting. The music goes faster and faster until it ends with a crash of chords.

Jerry showed Neil the simple part he had written for him and then placed it on a music stand in front of Angelina. A bit of the "Trepak" was played again so Angelina could tune her cello to the pitch of the orchestra. The turntable was running a little fast.

"Now listen and watch," Jerry said to Neil. "Angelina will play the same notes as you will play on the string bass but they won't sound as low as when you play it. Ready, Angelina?"

Jerry dropped the needle and Angelina began to play along with the orchestra in the recording. Her fingers chased each other up and down the strings and her bow shot back and forth across them. As the music moved faster and faster so did her fingers and bow. She ended with the orchestra with a sharp down stroke of her bow and then threw it off the strings with a flourish.

"Wow!" Neil said, "That really sounded like something. All I've been doing is a bunch of sawing."

"First you have to learn to saw," Jerry said. "If you can't bow, you can't play either the cello or the string bass. Now Neil, don't miss any more lessons. When I think you can handle the 'Trepak' I'll try you in the orchestra but not before."

Now Neil really took off. It was only a month later when he stood up for the first time in the orchestra rehearsal. Jerry was surprised at how easily the Three Musicateers in the orchestra accepted him.

"Hello," Ajemian said.

"Hi," Mandelbaum said.

"Nice to have a bass in the orchestra," Amedio said. His eye was now completely healed.

Neil soon learned that playing the "Trepak" at his lessons was one thing but playing it with the orchestra was something else. But by his third rehearsal he was keeping up with the other players. Haratounian, who had memorized where to come in with his thumps on the bass drum and his one cymbal crash, liked to watch Neil wrestle with his string bass, to see how he pushed down those thick strings and scratched out rumbles with his short, heavy bow.

Neil would still flub once in a while. No one would say anything but Angelina would turn and look at him. The next time he was at her house she would have him tap out the rhythm in his part and count out the measures.

"You're really catching on," she said.

"I know. You've really helped a lot. I couldn't have done it without you."

"Not all girls play the cello," was all that she replied.

"That's only part of it," Neil said.

When they were saying goodbye at the living room door, he noticed that there was no one else in the room. He took her by the hand, led her into the hall and closed the door behind them. "Angelina, you're wonderful!" Then he kissed her.

She made no attempt to avoid the kiss and then looked into his face. Even in the dim light of the hall his freckles seemed to have gained color. Suddenly she smiled and her eyes became luminous. "You're a nice boy, Neil, and you're getting nicer." She kissed him briefly and quickly went inside and closed the door behind her. Neil stood for a minute or two watching the door. Then he made his way down the hall to the stairs. He stopped abruptly just before reaching them. He realized he had been skipping. He quickly looked around. Both hall doors were closed and no one coming down from the upper flight of stairs had seen him. Joy rose again within him. He dashed down the stairs and burst out of the front door. Here he forced himself to walk. People might get the wrong idea if they see you running at night.

Some time later Jerry had a preliminary night rehearsal of a few players of an arrangement he had just made of the first movement of Schubert's *Unfinished Symphony*. He had played the work in his school orchestra when he was thirteen and he had liked it very much. It begins with a low solo for cellos and string basses. The violins then play a whispering accompaniment over the plucking of the lower strings and this continues while the oboe and clarinet come in with the principal theme. In Jerry's arrangement the clarinet plays this theme alone. The little orchestra had no oboe.

For this rehearsal Jerry had brought together Neil and Angelina to play the introductory bass solo, Lisa to play the violin accompaniment and Ajemian to play the theme. After they had rehearsed the first few bars until they could coordinate their parts, Jerry asked them how they liked it.

"I naturally like it," Ajemian said. "I have the melody. But everything fits together very nicely."

"We also have the melody at the beginning," Angelina said.

"Even what I play as an accompaniment is really a melody," Lisa said.

"Of course," Jerry said, "if you haven't heard, Schubert was quite a composer. Now rest awhile. I want to talk to you about something."

Neil laid his string bass on its side on the floor and his bow lengthwise on top of it. The two girls placed their bows on the music stands in front of them. Lisa removed her violin from under her chin and propped it upright on her left knee. Angelina was content to let her cello remain resting against her body but leaned one arm on its shoulder. Ajemian put the cap on his clarinet before laying it across his lap. He had finally found a reed he liked and he wasn't taking any chances.

Jerry looked around at his students. "I think it's time you let me in on this. It's three months since Neil met me at the front door and told me he would be the orchestra's string bass player. Well, now he is, without question. I think I know him pretty well and he's not the easiest person to persuade. How was it done?"

Neil looked at Angelina and she looked at Lisa.

"I can tell you about the first part, the part that didn't work," Lisa said. "There were three of us but we girls decided to leave Haratounian out of it. We thought Neil might get his back up if a boy tried to talk him into it. We knew we had to begin with something that boys like and would know about so we decided to compare the orchestra with a baseball team. You know about that?"

Jerry nodded. "A really good idea."

"So I met Neil and Angelina as they were coming back from Mass and we sat on Angelina's front stoop talking about it for about an hour. Neil was nice about it—he's never been rough with girls—but he'd have no part of it. He said he was no sissy and he wasn't going to be seen carrying around a musical instrument in a case. I told him the string bass would be too big for him to take home, that he would have to practice it at the school. But that didn't seem to make any difference. He said he wouldn't have anything to do with a guy who wore cords like a fairy. I'm sorry, Mr. Reinecke, that's what he said."

"That's alright, Lisa," Jerry said, "words can't hurt me."

"We met Haratounian in the afternoon and told him we hadn't got anywhere. He said if we couldn't do it he'd have to, but Angelina would have to help."

"All I did," Angelina said, "was to invite Neil to come over to my house and play checkers. Lisa and I know what happened but we weren't there. Ajemian was. Ask him."

"Well?" Jerry said to Ajemian.

Ajemian looked at Neil. "Go ahead," Neil said. "I don't mind. By this time I'm glad it happened."

"OK," Ajemian said, "I'll spill it. You told Haratounian to persuade Neil but no rough stuff. Right?"

"Right," Jerry said.

"Well, there wasn't any rough stuff. Just persuasion, and I'll tell you how. We were waiting for Neil when he came to see Angelina. It was almost dark so it was easy to hide. Amedio was outside and Haratounian, Mandelbaum, and me were inside the hall. As Neil walked into the hall Amedio called behind him, 'Hey there!' Neil turned to see who it was and the three of us grabbed him and held him with his arms tight behind him. Then Amedio came up to him and said, 'Remember me?' and pointed to his eye. 'Yeah,' Neil said, 'I'm the one who gave you that shiner. So what?' 'I'll tell you what! We need a guy to play string bass in our orchestra and you're elected.' Amedio took brass knucks out of his pocket and put them on his right hand. He rubbed them against Neil's nose and pushed them against his stomach. 'Now,' he said, 'you have your choice. You can play the string bass in our orchestra or you can have two black eyes, a broken nose, and a mighty sore stomach. Of course, I'm on the orchestra's side.' Amedio touched his sore eye. 'But if you decide not to play the string bass it won't hurt my feelings too much.'"

Neil cut in. "I didn't know whether Amedio was bluffing or not. He'd never done anything to me and I'd socked him because of my little brother. He really didn't have any reason to love me and the odds weren't very good. There were at least three guys holding me. If I had stamped on the foot of one of them, that wouldn't have helped much. Anyhow, Angelina was after me to do it. So I said OK. What else can you do in a spot like that?"

"Now I understand why you came to me," Jerry said. "But why did you keep coming? I thought you were going to quit at one point."

"Oh, that," Ajemian said. "There never was any chance of his quitting. We told him there were four of us and more where we came from. If you decided he was good enough to play the string bass he'd learn to play it or else."

"That isn't the whole story," Neil objected. "I could have taken my chances with the boys. But you got me interested, Mr. Reinecke, and Angelina was helping so it got so that I really wanted to learn to play the big thing."

"And you have," Jerry said. He turned to Ajemian. "But I told Haratounian no rough stuff, to use only persuasion."

Ajemian grinned. "That's just what it was, persuasion, nothing but persuasion. Just as we promised Angelina, we didn't hurt him one bit."

"Well, Ajemian," Jerry said, "you might make a good lawyer some day but I still think it was rough stuff. I wanted more bottom to the orchestra and I got it but I really can't approve of the way it was done. I'll forget it this time but let's have no more of it. And I'm only forgetting it because everyone, and this includes Neil, seems to like the end result. OK, let's get back to Schubert."

The three string players picked up their bows and Ajemian removed the cap from his clarinet. Neil hoisted his bass upright, Lisa tucked her violin under her chin, Angelina removed her arm from her cello's shoulder and

Ajemian put his clarinet to his lips. Jerry brought his baton softly down and cello and bass began their introductory passage. Violin and clarinet waited, ready to enter exactly as Schubert had intended over a hundred years before.

NGO and the LITHLA

A Fantasy in the Style of a Folktale

Ngo lay on his side, his sternum resting against the ledge, and stared down into the transparent water of the pool. There it was, the lithla, spiraling up out of the sandy bottom in wider and wider twists and branchings, gold, green, and a strange shining blue, up until it narrowed into a stalk topped by a pure white globe riding just below the surface. Ngo was nervous and the ten red feathery crests on his back were slightly erect. Only the Old Ones with their fifty-five crests came to the lithla pool, not Rashki with only ten crests like Ngo, who since breaking out of his egg had seen only ten red moons arch across the sky.

Why did he have this fierce desire to fly, to soar over the gray and yellow mountains that ribbed the little island, to see the gleam of both red sun and white sun upon the waters of the green river and the pool of the lithla? He had no wings, yet his body ached to be in flight. As a three crest he had thrilled to the stories of Itu, the Old One, stories of how the Rashki had long ago been a mighty people, great red birds circling over a chain of islands far to the west where the weather was always warm and sweet fruit grew on every tree. But the Rashki had disobeyed the Mighty Ones in the Sky and in punishment had been brought to this small island and told to forget how to fly. But Ngo had to learn again how it was done. He must. He could think of little else.

In the Cavern of Learning there were many lithla globes. Before he passed away, each Old One had filled a globe of a lithla with the sounds of his knowledge. Surely sometime in the thousands of moons that had passed some Old One had filled a globe with the sounds of flight; if Ngo could listen to it carefully, he might learn to fly.

Many times he had begged Uma, the doorkeeper, to let him into the Cavern of Learning. "I am not like the other Rashki. They like to lie around, to chatter, and to play kali. I, Ngo, wish to learn to fly. My arms wish to be wings, my beak to breathe high thin air, my lower talons to grasp the branches of the high tsutsi trees."

"No," Uma said, "no Rashki can enter until he has eleven crests."

"But why does one have to wait for the red moon before getting another crest? Why must one have eleven crests to enter the Cavern of Learning?"

"There's no point in asking questions," Uma said. "Things are the way they are and questions won't change them."

"But I am different," Ngo insisted. "I will sit and listen at each lithla globe even if I have to wait until I have fifty-five crests."

Uma laughed. "There may be one globe that contains the sounds of flight but many more that contain the sounds of death. You are young, Ngo, do you not wish to live?"

Ngo extended his feathery crests. "I am not afraid. Let me in."

"No, Ngo, you must wait for the rising of the next red moon."

"But that is a very long time. It is only eleven plus eleven days since the red moon disappeared in the East. The days I must wait for its next coming are eleven plus eleven times eleven plus eleven times eleven. I have tried to count this out with the pebbles near the beach of the Great Sea but no matter how high I pile them, there are never enough."

"Perhaps you forget which eleven you are counting," Uma suggested with a smile.

"That may be," Ngo said with the modesty becoming a ten crest Rashki. "But it is still a very long time. Surely there must be some way I can get in without waiting for the rising of the next red moon."

"Well, there is, or you might say there is. No ten crests who has tried it before has come back alive."

Ngo could not stop the sharp intake of breath through the narrow nostrils of his beak. He hoped Uma had not heard. "Tell me," he said bravely, "what I must do."

"You know what a lithla looks like?"

"Yes, there are drawings of them on the high rocks."

"Yes, they have strong magic. And you know where they live?"

"In the pool formed by the Green River before it drained into the Great Sea."

"Good. To enter the Cavern of Learning before you have eleven crests you must kill a lithla and bring its globe here."

"But the lithla lives in the water and I, of course, cannot swim."

"Very true," Uma said. "So you should wait for the next red moon."

And now Ngo was at the lithla pool looking down at one of its creatures. It seemed to be the only lithla in the pool. Perhaps only one grew at a time, one for each Old One. The Old Ones must know how to kill them or there would be no lithla globes in the Cavern of Learning. He looked at the lithla before him. It was said that it could smell you if you came too near and could kill you with its hiss. It did look very dangerous but he could see no nose nor mouth. How then could it smell and hiss? But Uma had said that it had strong magic so how could one tell?

I, Ngo, he said to himself, am a brave Rashki but to kill a lithla I need to know more than ten crests will tell me. He decided to go and ask advice of the Sacred Orsk of the Gray Mountain. He had been told that the Orsk would help you if you could help it. How he could help an Orsk he had no idea but he would try.

He went to the foot of the Gray Mountain and slowly began to climb. There were many great stones over which he had to climb and they were slippery because they were covered in places with moss. To keep from slipping he clutched with his talons the gnarled branches of the stunted trees that grew between and above the stones, and little by little he pulled himself up the mountain side.

At last he reached the little clearing in front of the cave of the Orsk. He rested for a while and then prostrated himself before the cave. Then raising his head he called, "Caw, Sacred Orsk, I, Ngo, a ten crested Rashki, lie here in the dirt and beg your help."

From in the cave came a high, thin voice. "And what help do you need, oh Ngo?"

"I need to know how to kill a lithla and to carry its globe to the Cavern of Learning."

"How that can be done I can easily tell you but you must do something more difficult for me first."

"And what is that?"

"For a thousand moons my back has itched and I have no hands with which to scratch it. You must scratch it for me."

"Gladly."

"Then rise, I am coming out." Ngo rose and a great blue ball rolled out of the cave and stopped in front of him.

Ngo was just tall enough to see over the top of it. He walked around the ball several times but could see neither hole nor crevice. It was perfectly round. "But where is your back?"

"That is for you to find out."

It talks, Ngo thought, so it must breathe. He scooped up fine dust from the edge of the clearing with his bunched talons. First he threw a bit on the top of the ball but nothing happened. Then he slowly began to walk around the ball, letting the dust sift between his talons down the sides of the Orsk. Suddenly he heard from behind what sounded like a sneeze. He turned quickly and saw two small holes closing at the bottom of the ball. If that was where he breathed, his back must be on the opposite side and higher up. Ngo found the place that he thought must be the back and scratched lightly with one talon.

"Not there," the Orsk said.

Ngo tried further down.

"No," the Orsk said.

Ngo tried further to the right but still there was a negative response from the Orsk. Finally Ngo tried further to the left.

"Wonderful," the Orsk said, "but scratch with all your talons." Ngo scratched with all the talons of his right arm until it became tired and then with all the talons of his left arm.

"More," demanded the Orsk. Again Ngo scratched first with one arm and then with the other, until both became so tired that he could no longer go on. "I am sorry, caw, Sacred Orsk, but I can scratch no more. My arms are worn out."

"One more scratch," ordered the Orsk. Ngo managed to scratch once more and then sat down on the ground to rest.

The Orsk sighed. "After a thousand moons my back no longer itches. Now I will tell you how to kill a lithla. But be sure you do not touch it. If you do you will die. We who live on the land get most of our energy from the red sun but its rays are poisonous to the lithla. Once every eleven days the larger white sun crosses in front of the red sun and blots it out. During these few moments the lithla raises its globe above the water, tilts back its upper half, and drinks in the white rays. That is its nourishment. Then it closes its globe, which again sinks below the surface. It will not rise again until once again the white sun blots out the red. Have you seen the red stones around the lithla pool?"

"Yes," Ngo replied.

"All you need to do is to toss one of these stones into the globe of the lithla while it is open. That will kill the lithla."

"But once I have killed it how will I get the lithla globe to land? I am unable to swim."

"That is your problem," said the Sacred Orsk as the great blue ball slowly rolled back into the cave.

Ngo was tired and found it much more difficult to find his way down the mountain than to climb it. Several times on the way down he slipped on the mossy stones and fell. When he finally reached the bottom he examined himself and found that he had several bruises and had lost two feathers from one of his crests. But this did not bother him nearly as much as the fierce ache of his arms in their desire to fly. He knew that the bruises would heal and the feathers grow back in. But he still had to do something about his arms. The suns were setting and he was tired so it would have to wait for the morrow. He went back to his nest to sleep.

Early in the morning he went to the lithla pool and climbed back onto the ledge. With his eye he measured carefully the distance from the ledge to the globe of the lithla. Then he picked up two of the flat red stones lying near the ledge and made his way up the Green River. There he searched until he found a ledge nearly as high above the water as that at the pool and where there was a boulder showing just above the water the right distance away from the ledge. Standing on the ledge he tried to throw one of his red stones so it would land on top of the boulder. He overthrew and the stone splashed into the river. He tried again. This time his throw was too short and the stone hit the boulder at the water line and again slipped into the river. Ngo went back to the pool and returned with two more red stones. His third throw was a little too far to the left but the fourth landed right on top of the boulder before it slid into the water.

He returned to the lithla pool for more red stones but he could only find one. What a fool he had been but he only had ten crests and could not be expected to have much foresight. He needed more crests but since he could not get them he would have to do the best he could. He got down on all fours and carefully searched the ground all the way around the pool, looking under bushes and moving dead branches to see under them. With joy he found two more red stones but that was all. He hid the three red stones where no one else was likely to find them and returned to his nest to sleep.

The next day he searched along the Green River for stones of the same size and shape and found many that he could use for practice but none was red. Finally, the time came for the suns to cross and he took one of the red stones from its hiding place and went to the ledge next to the lithla pool. As the white sun covered the red, the earth grew white rather than pink. The white globe of the lithla slowly emerged from the water and the upper half opened to the sky as though hinged on the back. Ngo aimed carefully and threw. The red stone hit the forward lip of the lower half of the globe, bounced back, and fell into the water. The globe apparently felt nothing but slowly closed and sank below the surface.

One chance gone, Ngo thought. He had misjudged the distance. He must build the ledge at the Green River higher and practice throwing from further back. This occupied his time for the next eleven days and then he was back on the ledge with his second red stone waiting for the lithla's globe to rise. This time he threw with extreme care. The stone hit the left lip of the upper part of the globe, fell back upon the lower lip, wavered back and forth, and finally slipped into the water. Again the lithla globe did not seem to notice. It closed and slowly sank below the surface.

Now Ngo had only one more chance. He knew he must find some way of getting closer to the globe, so close that he could not miss. He looked around and saw a small log floating in the water. This gave him an idea. Excited, he searched around the banks of the pool until he found three broken pieces of tree trunk, each about the same length. These, he knew, must have come from the mbulu trees that lined the banks further up the Green River, more fragile than the tsutsi trees and more easily blown over and broken by the strong winds that occasionally plagued the island. He laid the pieces of trunk side by side on the bank near the pool and went to pull gremli vines down from nearby tall tsutsi trees. He cut the vines into sections with a sharp stone and used them to bind the logs together. Finding a long, strong vine he tied one end of it to a nearby tree and the other to his group of three logs. Then he searched and found a long straight stick. He pushed the log raft into the water, holding it in place with the vine attached to the tree. Then he stood on the raft, pushed off from the bank with his stick and, after it had floated a short distance, pushed the stick into the bottom in front of the raft to hold it in place. The raft had sunk beneath him and he was in water up to the middle of his sternum. He pulled himself back to the shore with the vine attached to the tree and stepped off his little raft. Dragging the logs ashore, he searched for others of approximately the same length and finding three, placed them next to the old ones. Using additional sections of vines he bound all six together. Then he tried out his raft again. This time it sank only far enough to cover his lower talons with water. Satisfied, he poled out toward the lithla. Two thirds of the way he ran out of vine line and his stick no longer touched the bottom.

This was easily mended. He pulled down another vine and found a longer stick. He tied the two vines together and attached the longer vine line to his raft. Now he was able to pole all the way out to the lithla. Holding his raft in its place with his stick pushed against the bottom he gazed down at the lithla globe just before him under the water. Nothing had happened. Perhaps the lithla could only smell him when its globe was above water. He would soon find out. Either he or the lithla would die.

The next time the suns were near to crossing, Ngo was out on his raft near the lithla globe waiting for it to rise. Soon the white sun blotted out the red and the earth became white. The globe appeared above the water and opened.

Ngo reached over, being careful not to touch the globe, and dropped the red stone into it. Abandoning his stick, he grabbed the vine line and frantically began to pull himself toward shore. The lithla globe turned pink and there was a terrible sound, a cross between a hiss and a scream. The globe closed with a crash. The twists, branchings, and stalk of the lithla began to thrash violently and the water was in turmoil. Ngo's raft came apart and he fell into the pool and went under. He held his breath and still pulled on the vine. When his head finally broke water he spat out and took a great breath of air before he went under again, still pulling on the vine. When he came up the second time he saw before him a mbulu log and grasped it with one set of talons while he held the vine with the other. The log helped him keep his head above water and the concentric waves produced by the thrashing of the lithla slowly washed him toward shore. Finally he touched bottom. Still pulling on the vine, he slowly waded to the shore and sat on the bank soaked and exhausted.

With a mixture of exhilaration and terror he watched the gold and green streaked waves crested with phosphorescent blue come tumbling toward him. Eventually they smoothed and he knew that the lithla had died. The globe had separated from its stalk and was slowly floating toward the opposite bank. Groggily he got up and walked around the pool until he had reached the point at which he thought it would come ashore. When it reached the bank he threw a vine around it and drew it up upon the grass. He touched it gingerly but nothing happened. He lifted it and found it not very heavy but awkward to carry because of its size. Slowly and carefully he carried his prize to the ledge and lying down next to it almost immediately fell asleep.

The next morning he triumphantly carried the globe to the Cavern of Learning, stopping several times on the way, for it was a difficult task.

Uma had been sitting on a stone enjoying the sun. When he saw Ngo coming with the lithla globe he rose and folded his arms. In his eyes there was something like awe.

"Caw, Uma, doorkeeper of the Cavern of Learning, I, Ngo, have killed a lithla and brought you its globe. May I now enter?"

"Enter," Uma said and touched a secret spring, and the great rock that filled the entrance lifted. The way was open.

When Ngo entered he found himself only in a small cave with a little sunlight coming through a hole in the roof and nowhere other globes of the lithla. On a stone seat against the wall sat Itu, the Old One, whose crests of many feathers were almost white.

"Caw, Itu, Old One," Ngo said respectfully. "I bring you the globe of a lithla." He carefully placed the pink globe at the feet of Itu.

"As a three crest you heard the tale of our past," Itu said, "that we were once great red birds living on a chain of islands far, far to the west where the red moon rises from the sea. You were told that the Rashki had done something very wrong and the Mighty Ones in the Sky condemned us to live on this little island for thousands of moons. We were forbidden to fly so we could not return home."

"Two things I do not understand," Ngo said. "What was it that the Rashki did that was wrong, and why can we no longer fly?"

"Good questions from a ten crest Rashki who thinks. The first question is difficult to answer because we, ourselves, are not sure of the answer. We think the Rashki killed a Sacred Orsk. As for the second question, the Mighty Ones in the Sky placed a lithla in a pool of water to watch over us and see that we did not fly. If any Rashki was bold enough to try, there was a hiss from the lithla and the Rashki fell and died. We stopped flying and since we no longer had use for wings, little by little through thousands of moons they disappeared and now we have arms instead. We also lost most of our red feathers. All that are left are those in the crests on our backs."

"And there never has been more than one lithla?"

"Only one. But the Mighty Ones in the Sky are merciful. They told us there would be one means by which we could again fly and return to Rashk. Every thousand moons there would rise a ten crest Rashki who was desperate to fly. He was to be told to kill the lithla and to bring its globe to the Old One. If he succeeded we would again become great red birds and could fly back to Rashk."

"And the Cavern of Learning with lithla globes filled with the sounds of the Old Ones?"

"It never existed," Uma said. "By pretending that it did, we encouraged the ten crest Rashki who wished to fly to attempt to kill the lithla."

"And the others who tried died?" Ngo asked.

"Many," Itu answered. "But you did not and we have waited long enough. Stand and stretch out your arms to your sides."

Ngo stood tall and extended his arms to his sides. Itu held the pink globe of the lithla above Ngo's head. There was a loud hiss, the globe disappeared, and now Ngo had strong wings and was covered from head to lower talons with red feathers like those of his crest. He looked at Itu and Uma. They were also changed and were red birds of the same size and as splendid as himself.

The roof of the cave opened and the three flew up into the open air. Everywhere above the island, transformed Rashki were soaring and swooping with outstretched wings. "Caw, Ngo," they called. "Caw, Ngo, beak of our beaks, lead us to our old home, to the beautiful isles of Rashk."

They arranged themselves into a great flying wedge with Ngo at its point, and with their wings flaming under the red sun they sped westward over the trackless waters, toward that distant point where thousands of times the red moon had risen from the sea.

POEM

CHEMOTHERAPY
1973

We who live between the anvils of ease and despair,

Who in our bravado still till future fields

Of seeds dubious of fruition,

We are the kaleidoscopic changelings,

Writhed by diverse winds within,

Clashing steeled eagle on anguished bowels.

We are actors on a strange and lonely stage

Where we play what we are but might not be.

FOR MY WIFE

One day as my wife returned from gathering our mail from its box she loudly complained, "All we get is junk mail! We hardly ever get any real mail!" While she was out shopping I sat at the typewriter and typed the following, slipped it into an envelope which I had addressed to her and went outside and placed it in the mailbox. When she returned with the mail the following day there was the beginning of a smile on her face which turned into a laugh when she had read what I had written. She then rewarded my effort with a kiss.

DEARTH of MAIL

BY GALACTIC TELEX

Dear Madam:

My genii from the windward side of the galaxy informs me that you receive a dearth of mail, real mail, that is, not junk mail. We all receive that. Due to my combined capacity as Nome of the Greeks, Yahweh of the Hebrews and Isis of the Egyptians—don't worry about my being bisexual—I have an unusually thorough knowledge of history and I thought I would regale you with a few incidents from your most recent transmigrations.

The third one back you were a Natya dancing girl at the Temple of Krishna, sent there in adoration by the Gobi Khan. You wore sandals of sandalwood, a chastity belt of ironwood—which I am afraid was a bit uncomfortable—and your breastplate was ornamented with the finest rubies. Slim, tall and dusky, you danced as lithely as the mist rising from the River Ganges. You were the favorite of the Hindu Gods and no upper caste wife was ever burned alive at the suttee, at the funeral pyre of her husband, without your participating in this most blessed of Hindu rites. Although this career was a most auspicious one, it was rather short since Natya girls once they lose their litheness in dancing are fed to the crocodiles of the Ganges.

In the previous transmigration you had been a tigress living in the jungles just south of Nepal. You were beautifully striped, your eyes blazed and, oh, the lashing of your tail! You raised several litters of cubs, all of whom became great and fierce hunters, scourges of the baboon and patrons of the jackals. Your only enemies were the elephant and the buffalo. Although you never conquered either you left your claw marks on both.

Great was your beauty and great your speed in charge. Simla knew of you and recorded you in his tablets.

But in your last transmigration you were a dolphin, the most sleek, the most beautiful of the cetaceans. I hope you won't mind when I tell you that you were a male dolphin. You mere spirits of the earth do not seem to be able to combine genders as we Gods and the oysters can do. As a dolphin you roamed the great Pacific from Polynesia to Micronesia, from the Hawaiian Islands to the northern tip of New Zealand. You were the most nimble of dolphins. No other could combine two somersaults with a back flip. The beauty of your sonoric poetry excited even the imagination of the sluggish killer whale. Once a sailor fell overboard from his ship and you saved him from drowning. You came up from a dive with your tail under him and flipped him back aboard.

Great have been your transmigrations in the past and great will they be in the future. Worry not then, Madam, at a mere dearth of mail.

Yours most faithfully,

NOME-YAHWEH-ISIS

MUSICAL
PLAYLETS

In the early days of our marriage we occasionally had parties at our apartment. Almost all our guests would be musicians and we might amuse ourselves with what we called "singing opera." I would write a script for this purpose and provide all present with a copy of it. The most skilled improviser among us would sit at the piano and simulate the orchestral accompaniment. Those assigned singing parts would also improvise to the best of their ability. In this case my script was an elaboration of a joke which was going around at the time. "Crazy Over Horses" was a popular song of the day which everyone present would have known.

CRAZY over HORSES

A Horse Opera in Three Improvised Scenes

CHARACTERS

BOSS

SMITH

DOBBIN

DOBBIN'S HINDQUARTERS

MRS. VANDERSNOOT OF THE SPCA
(SOCIETY FOR THE PREVENTION OF CRUELTY TO ANIMALS)

THE COP

Scene One
THE BOSS'S FACTORY. (*Smith enters, leading Dobbin.*)

Smith, recitative: "Well, you weren't overworked today, old boy. Not many deliveries today. Business is rotten."
(*He smacks Dobbin's Hindquarters.*)
"Ow, how bony you're getting."

(*Dobbin puts nose in feedbag and neighs sadly.*)
Dobin: "Less and less oats I find."

Hindquarters:	"And what's refused in front must nourish the behind."
Smith:	"Yes, I know. The boss said we can't afford to feed you like we did in the good old days."

All, HARMONIZED IN CHORUS, REPEATING THE LINE: "The good old days."

Smith, aria:	"Bring back the days of yore, The wages paid before This lousy Depression."
Dobbin:	"When bushels of oats Brought out musical notes."
Hindquarters:	"Excuse the expression."
Smith:	"In the good old days You might get a raise."
Hindquarters:	"But not nowadays."
Smith:	"Woe is me, no dough."
Dobbin:	"Alackaday, no hay."
Hindquarters:	"Neigh, neigh, And no hay. No, no, No hay."

(*The Boss enters. Sadly in minor, very recitative:*)

Boss:	"Smith, I have bad news for you. Business is so bad, It really is too sad, But I have no more use for you."

(*Smith in anguish,* ARIA ALA DONIZETTI:)

Smith:	"Please, please, Boss, have a heart. Must you and I forever part? Forever part?"

Boss, crocodilish:	"I weep for you, I do. I weep, I weep, I weep, I weep But I am afraid it's true."

(*Music, thunderstorm.*)

Boss to Dobbin:	"And you must eat less hay Or keeping you won't pay. Eat less hay, eat less hay."

(*The Boss exits, carrying Dobbin's feedbag.*)

Smith, ARIA WITH LEITMOTIF:

Smith:	"Woe is me, no dough."

Dobbin:	"Alack, there is no hay."

Hindquarters:	"Neigh, neigh, no, no, No hay."

All IN MADRIGAL STYLE A CAPPELLA:

"Woe, woe, no dough.
Alack, alack, no dough, no hay.
Neigh, neigh, no dough, no hay."

MUSIC: POSTLUDE.

———

Scene Two

A PARK, A BENCH AND A CLUMP OF GRASS. (*Smith is sleeping on the bench. He rolls over.*)

MUSIC: INTRODUCTION, SNOW FLURRIES.

| Smith, recitative: | "Brr, brr, brr brr brr brr brr.
It's getting cold." |

(*Smith stretches.*)

| Smith, Aria: | "Being a bum is not much fun
But I would be a better one
If I could grow a plumper ass
To park on bench or clump of grass." |

(*Enter the Cop.*)

| Cop, recitative: | "Hey, you, move on." |

(*Exit Cop. Smith moves to clump of grass.*)

MUSIC, INTRODUCTION. (*Snow flurries as before.*)

(*Enter Dobbin and Hindquarters. Dobbin, very dejected.*)

| Dobbin, aria: | "The wind doth blow and it doth snow
And where shall poor Dobbin go?" |

| Hindquarters: | "Dragging his tail behind him." |

| Smith, recitative: | "Why, Dobbin, old boy.
What are you doing here?" |

(*He embraces Dobbin. Hindquarters wants to be embraced too.*
Smith caresses Hindquarters.)

| Dobbin, bitterly: | "Heartless man, he turned me out, his faithful
servant into a cruel world. Alone, a homeless horse." |

| Hindquarters: | "Remorse, remorse." |

| Dobbin to Smith: | "Have you any oats? Just a wisp of hay?" |

| Smith: | "Sorry, haven't enough cash to buy sinkers and coffee." |

Hindquarters: "Neigh, neigh, no dough, no hay."

Smith: "But for old time's sake I'll stake you to this clump of grass. It hurts me but you can have it."

(*Dobbin begins to graze. Enter Mrs. Vandersnoot.*)

Vander: "Horrors! A homeless horse. Officer."

(*The Cop enters quickly.*)

Cop: "Yes, Madame."

Vander: "I'm Mrs. Vandersnoot of the SPCA. What man of ill repute has mistreated this hardworking, gentle, peaceloving, faithful animal?"

Cop to Smith: "Hey there, you. Whose horse is this?"

Smith: "It belongs to a boss I used to work for."

MUSIC, INTRODUCTION.

Vander, aria: "Sir, take us to him.
I will sue him.
Tell me who's so blind
Treats a horse unkind."

(*She repeats these lines in the aria.*)

Cop: "Let him wail,
Let him quail.
Justice will prevail
Or he will go to jail."

(*All repeat in chorus what the Cop has sung.*)

Scene Three
The Boss's Factory. (*The Boss is counting out his money.*)

Boss, recitative: "Thirty, forty, fifty.
Hm, hm, 'snifty.'"

(*All others enter.*)

Vander: "Are you the heartless man
That a horse can can?
Sir, tell me why
You try to defy
The rules of the SPCA?"

Music, Introduction.

Boss, aria: "I could not a profit make
Off this bony rake.
I must have my ten percent
Or I'll never pay on my rent."

(*Boss repeats these lines.*)

Cop, recitative: "Don't you know it's against the law to kick an
animal out without food and shelter?"

Vander: "Let justice take its course.
Take back the horse."

Hindquarters: "And the end, of course."

Finale

Boss: "If I must, I must,
But I hardly think it's just
To put my business in the red
So a horse will be fed."

Smith to the Cop:	"I have an idear. It seems quite clear That Dobbin and I are in the same boat. Can't you make the boss hire me at a loss?"
Vander:	"Ha, ha."
Boss:	"Ho, ho."
Cop:	"Har, har. What do you think you are, a horse?"

(*The Cop knocks Smith down. All join hands and skip around Smith in a circle singing:*)

All:	"Crazy over horses, horses, horses. Crazy over horses, horses, horses." etc.

The End

I wrote the following script to be performed at a New Year's party at our house in 1951–52. It was based on my witnessing in New York City's Riverside Park during the summers of 1929 and 1930 sailors of the United States Atlantic Fleet anchored in the Hudson River coming ashore to meet the women waiting for them in the Park. It is called a ballad opera since it has the same format as John Gay's "The Beggar's Opera" which was first performed in London in 1728. In this Gay's lyrics are sung to well-known ballad tunes. In that era it was common for hack poets to write ballads concerning events that would interest the populous, a murder, the career of a highway man at his final hanging or a particularly scandalous love affair. These were printed on what were called broadsides with an indication of the tune to which they were to be sung.

In those days, at least, sailors in the United States navy were known as gobs. The part indicated as orchestra was performed by my wife, Eve, on an old parlor pump organ which she preferred to call a harmonium. A piano or even an accordion would do as well.

A Tale of Peace or a Piece of Tail

A Naval Ballad Opera in One Act

I. Overture: ("Anchors Aweigh") *Orchestra*

II. Prologue (recited)

The Sweet and Sour Bard:
> Picture if you please
> (I'm sure you can with ease)
> Riverside Park in the Spring,
> Love is on the wing,
> The fleet—the fleet is in!
>
> The stream's alive with ships
> The park's alive with hips
> Gobs of Gobs in blue,
> Skirts of ev'ry hue,
> Begins our tale of sin!

III. Quartet and Chorus of Gobs and Gals
(To the tune of "Home on the Range")

Orchestra: (Intro—last four bars)

Big Blonde: O give me a gob,
               A well-heeled slob,
               A brute with hair on his chest,
               With a free-wagging stern
               And— money to burn,
               A fall-guy to feather my nest!

Chorus of Gals: Gobs! Gobs on the loose!
                   Gobs hell-bent on romance!
                   With dough in their bow
                   And— fire in their prow (*hold*)
                   We'll clean out their bell-bottomed pants!

Shorty: O give me a broad,
           A high-heeled bawd,
           A babe who'll fall for my jack,
           Who's broad in the beam
           And tight in the seam
           Who'll bother me not when I'm back!

Chorus of Gobs: Gals! Gals on the loose!
                   Gals hell-bent on romance!
                   With a *ci*tified boy
                   They— may— act coy (*hold*)
                   But they fall— for bell-bottomed pants!

Slick Chick: O give me a guy
                Whose fever runs high,
                A Jack with jack in his poke,
                Who'll make it worth while
                To— love him French-style,
                Who'll never come back when he's broke!

Chorus of Gals: Gobs! Gobs on the loose!
                   Gobs hell-bent on romance!
                   With dough in their bow
                   And— fire in their prow (*hold*)
                   We'll clean out their bell-bottomed pants!

Big Boy:	O give me a skirt
	Who knows how to flirt,
	A gal who waits to be made,
	Who puts up a fight
	'Til— ev'rything's tight.
	You lay down the dough and she's laid!

Chorus of Gobs:	Gals! Gals on the loose!
	Gals hell-bent on romance!
	With a *ci*tified boy
	They— may— act coy (*hold*)
	But they fall— for bell-bottomed pants!

| Entire company: | (Repeating chorus in harmony) |

Gals:	Gobs! Gobs on the loose!
	Gobs hell-bent on romance!
	With dough in their bow
	And— fire in their prow (*hold*)
	We'll clean out their bell-bottomed pants!

Gobs:	Gals! Gals on the loose!
	Gals hell-bent on romance!
	With a *ci*tified boy
	They— may— act coy (*hold*)
	But they fall— for bell-bottomed pants!

| Orchestra: | (Postlude-repeat chorus) |

(*Big Blonde and Slick Chick to left of stage. Big Boy and Shorty to right.*)

Spoken Dialogue:

| Shorty: | (*Approaching Big Blonde*) Goin' my way, babe? |

| Big Blonde: | (*Looking him over*) G'wan, beat it, ya shrimp! |

| Shorty: | Aw, c'mon, kid! |

Big Blonde: Beat it, I said— squirt! If I sat on ya, I'd squash ya!

(*Shorty retires in disgust.*)

Big Boy: (*Advancing upon Slick Chick*) Hi, kid!

Slick Chick: (*Looking him over*) Scram, ya big fat slob!

Big Boy: Look, toots, I'm just a comfortable sort of guy—

Slick Chick: (*Interrupting*) Comfortable, phooey! I'd smother!

(*Big Boy retires in disgust*)

IV. Duet— Shorty and Big Boy
(To the tune of "When Johnny Comes Marching Home")

Orchestra: (Intro: last 4 measures)

Shorty: It's hard for a squirt
                To pick up a skirt!
                God damn! God damn!

                They like them six feet
                With plenty of meat!
                God damn! God damn!

                I wish I *were* as big as a whale
                With a *prong* as long as a dolphin's tail!
                Then they'd all come 'round and
                Pay for a lay!
                      God damn!

(Repeat refrain)

Big Boy: Then they'd all come 'round and
                Pay for a lay!

Both:	God damn!
Big Boy:	It's hard when you're fat To pick up a cat! God damn! God damn!
	They like 'em thin With a *single* chin! God damn! God damn!
	I wish I *were* as thin as a rail With a *dick* as thick as a dolphin's tail! Then they'd all come 'round and Pay for a lay! God damn!
(repeat refrain)	
Shorty:	Then they'd all come 'round and Pay for a lay!
Both:	God damn!

Spoken Dialogue:

Slick Chick:	(*In disgust*) What a big fat slob!
Big Blonde:	Who? Him? Gee, I like 'em big! Not like that little shrimp!
Slick Chick:	Oh, he's cute!

V. Duet— Big Blonde and Slick Chick—and Quartet
(To the tune of "When Johnny Comes Marching Home")

Orchestra:	(Intro: last 4 bars)
Big Blonde:	I *don't* like 'em short. It *ain't* too much sport! God damn! God damn!

Slick Chick:	I don't like 'em plump, Except in the rump! God damn! God damn!
Big Blonde:	But I like 'em fat, I like a big brute!
Slick Chick:	And I like 'em short, He really is cute!
Both:	It would be so nice if a Chick had her pick! God damn!

(*Do not repeat refrain*)

Shorty:	It's hard for a squirt To pick up a skirt!
All Four:	God damn! God damn!
Big Blonde:	I don't like 'em short. It ain't too much sport!
All four:	God damn! God damn!
Shorty:	I wish I were as big as a whale!
Big Boy:	I wish I were as thin as a rail!
Both Gobs:	It would *be* a cinch to Pick up a chick!
All four:	God damn!
Big Boy:	It's hard when you're fat To pick up a cat!
All four:	God damn! God damn!

Slick Chick:	I don't like 'em plump Except in the rump!
All four:	God damn! God damn!
Big Blonde:	I like 'em fat. I like a big brute!
Slick Chick:	I like 'em short. he really is cute!
Both gals:	It would *be* so nice if a Chick had her pick!
All four:	God damn!
(Repeat refrain)	
Both Gobs:	It would *be* a cinch to Pick up a chick!
Both Gals:	It would *be* so nice if a Chick had her pick!
Entire company	GOD DAMN!

Spoken Dialogue:

(*Shorty and Big Boy go into a huddle*)

Shorty:	Say, sailor! Let's switch. You take the big gal—I'll take the little chick.
Big Boy:	OK, boy. But me first, this time. (*He approaches Big Blonde.*) Hi, blondie! Goin' my way?
Big Blonde: (*coyly*)	Depends which way you're goin'.
Big Boy	Central Park?

Big Blonde:	(*taking his arm*) That's the way I'm goin'.
Shorty:	(*approaching Slick Chick*) Hi, chicken! Goin' my way?
Slick Chick: (*coyly*)	Might be!
Shorty:	Somewhere lonesome?
Slick Chick:	(*taking his arm*) Won't be lonesome with you!

VI. Quartet
(To the tune of "My Bonnie Lies Over the Ocean")

Orchestra:	(Intro: last 8 measures)
Big Boy:	My baby is big and good lookin'-
Big Blonde:	My sailor is seaman first class-
Big Boy:	My baby sure knows what is cookin'-
Big Blonde:	I sure hope he's cookin' with gas!
All four:	Let's go! Let's go! Let's go over to Central Park! Let's go! Let's go! (*hold*) We'll surely make hay when it's dark!
Shorty:	My baby is cute and slick chicken-
Slick Chick:	My sailor's the best of them all-
Shorty:	By God! I surely can pick 'em-
Slick Chick:	I hope he's got lots on the ball!

All four: Let's go! Let's go!
            Let's go over to Central Park!
            Let's go! Let's go!
            We'll surely make hay when it's dark!

(Repeat chorus in harmony)

Entire company: Let's go! Let's go!
                    etc.

(*The quartet exits*)

VII. Postlogue (recited)

The Sweet and Sour Bard:
                    The gobbs are ready for plucking,
                    The gals are ready for fucking,
                    Bankrolls are sure to be shorn,
                    We hope no bastards are born!

                    So ding, ding dong, derry, down derry,
                    Come one, come all, and let's be merry-
                    And send them on, on their sinful way
                    With a rousing, joyous round-elay!

VIII. Finale
(To the tune of "Anchors Aweigh")

Orchestra: (Intro— last 4 measures)

Entire company: So ends our tale of peace,
                    Come join the song!
                    Gal meets her man and gets him
                    Wish them luck, the night is long!

                    So ends our piece of tail
                    Come join the song!

Entire company: Boy meets his girl and makes her
Let's be merry!
Life's not very
Long——!

The End

NOTE: The dialogue or verse that I have written for the two gobs is an expurgated version of what the sailors might have sung. In what I actually heard in the Park the sailors used "fuck" or "fucking" in almost every second sentence, primarily using these for emphasis as in "I don't give a fuck" or "that fucking bastard." I have made use of the present participle of this evocative English verb in the second speech of the Sweet and Sour Bard. In this case, however, it is used in its proper and pristine meaning, that of coition.

Some readers may possibly not know the meaning of Slick Chick's reference to "love in French style." In the early part of the 20th Century the prostitutes and "women of easy virtue" referred to fellatio, oral sex offered by a woman to a man, as "French." In some circles in the 21st Century deep kissing or tongue kissing is still known as "French kissing." These two Gallic appellations are probably a heritage left by American dough boys who were stationed in France during the First World War and learned that the mademoiselles had a somewhat larger repertoire than the women they had known in these United States.

FOR CHILDREN

When I first came to New York City in 1928 at the age of 17 I lived for the summer with my sister, Gen, and her husband. Gen was a journalist and at that time had a children's column called "The Round-about" which appeared in the English section of the Sunday edition of the Jewish Daily Forward. One day she was tearing her hair because she had no copy for the coming Sunday column and no idea as to where she might secure it. I sat at her typewriter and wrote the following children's poem which was of sufficient length to fill her entire column and which she used for that purpose the coming Sunday. In writing this poem I imitated the style of A.A. Milne who was famous for his books concerning Christopher Robin and Winnie the Pooh.

As a small child I did indeed have a puppy which I named Puppo and which died after I had it only three months. However, it died because it ran out into the street in front of a car. I changed the cause of its death to the eating of fly paper since this produced a more interesting poem.

PUPPO

I had a dog,
A little dog,
And I called him Puppo.
'Cause he
Was a puppy. That's so.
You see,

He was three months when I got him
And six months when he died,
And though I only had him—
Three months; I cried 'n *cried.*

He was dirty
Awf'ly dirty,
Terrible dirty when he came!
And so
We played the wash day game.
You know:

Lots of water
Almost hotter
Than the bad place;

And tar soap,
And flea soap,
All on his face,

And scrubbing,
And rubbing,

(And ki-yi-ing)
Then you're done!

He had a nose,
A warm, pink nose,
And the most pettingist fur.
His ears
Were cute. But he was a cur
It 'pears–
'Cause Pa says so
And Uncle Joe
And Me. But I should think
That such a nose
Most plainly shows
('Specially as it's pink)
Including his fur,
He's not a cur.
And 'cause curs bite
And like to fight;
He *don't.*

But then he died;
And how he died
Was very very bad.
He ate
Some fly-paper and had
Any rate
Of tummy ache,
And stayed awake
Crying all the night,

The Doctor said
He would be dead
Soon if we didn't
Quite hurriedly boil
Some *castor oil*
And things he'd give;
They'd make him live–
But he *died!*

I had a dog,
A little dog,
And I called him Puppo.
'Cause he
Was a puppy. That's so.
You see.

He was three months when I got him
And six months when he died,
And though I only had him--
Three months; I cried 'n *cried.*

When I was a small child a stable was located across the street from my father's shop. The stable attracted many flies and whenever the front door of the shop was open a number of them flew in. To get rid of at least some of them my father hung flypaper from the ceiling by strings.

The sticky stuff spread on the side of the flypaper attracted flies and I would watch as one settled on it. After a while the fly would try to leave but could not. As the fly struggled to free itself it became more and more immersed in the sticky stuff and finally was smothered by it.

At least, that is what I thought happened. I later learned that the sticky stuff was made of sugar or syrup and had arsenic mixed with it. It was the arsenic that killed the flies, not the sticky stuff. In those days we were rather casual in our handling of arsenic. There was some in most kitchens since it was useful for killing rats and other pests. Unfortunately, it also could be used to kill pestiferous human beings.

The LITTLE BLARNEY

There once was a little black kitten named Blarney. He was called Blarney because he talked all the time. His little sisters and brothers mewed when they were hungry and squeaked when they hurt themselves. But Blarney began to MEOW the day he was born and never stopped. He was the noisiest kitten in the world. He said, MEOW! MEOW! in a very loud voice all day long.

You could hear him if you were on the front porch. You could hear him if you were on the back porch. You could hear him if he was in the cellar and you could hear him if he was in the attic! He made so much noise that everyone's ears hurt. His mommy's ears hurt! His daddy's ears hurt! His brothers' and sisters' ears hurt!

One day Blarney's mommy had a headache and she was cross. She just couldn't stand listening to Blarney's loud MEOW another moment. "Blarney," she said, "please, go outside. I can't stand that meow of yours another moment!"

"Meow," Blarney answered and he went out the front door, down the porch steps onto the sidewalk. "I will go for a walk," he decided, "around the corner!" And off he went MEOWING as loud as ever. He had gone only a few steps when he came upon a big, green grasshopper who was chewing on a very tender green blade of grass. The Big Green Grasshopper was so surprised at hearing little Blarney that he dropped the blade of grass out of his mouth. "Dear me," he said to himself, "never in my life have I heard a kitten who made such noise.

Young man," he said to Blarney, "if I were you I would not meow so loudly. A Big White Bulldog lives right around the corner and if he hears you he will come out and bite you!" Blarney said, MEOW and, putting his tail into the air, he walked right on MEOWING as loudly as ever.

Just before Blarney reached the corner he came up to Mr. Nut Brown Squirrel who had just found a nut to put away for the winter. "Dear me," the squirrel said to himself, "never in my life have I heard a kitten who made such noise." He was so surprised that the nut fell out of his mouth.

"Young man," he said to Blarney, "if I were you I would not MEOW so loudly. A Big White Bulldog lives right around the corner and if he hears you he will come out and bite you!"

But Blarney only said, MEOW, and putting his tail high into the air he walked on right around the corner MEOWING as loudly as ever.

As soon as he was around the corner the Big White Bulldog heard him and came rushing out to bite him! "B-r-rf, arf – b-r-rf," barked the Big White Bulldog.

Blarney faced the Big White Bulldog. His eyes became slits. The hair on his back stood up and his tail became big and bushy. "P-s-st, ps-s-st, brar-r-ro, ps-st," said Blarney so loudly you could hear him for blocks around.

"My goodness," said the Big White Bulldog to himself. "What a strange kitten! He makes more noise than five full-grown cats. I must be careful. I might be hurt!"

The big bulldog said, "B-r-rf, arf – b-r-rf," and he circled around Blarney to the left, trying to get behind him.

But Blarney turned around too, facing the Big White Bulldog. "Ps-s-st, brar-r-roops-st, psst," said Blarney, louder than ever.

"B-r-rf, arf, br-r-f, b-r-rf," said the Big White Bulldog, circling Blarney to the right.

"Ps-s-st, brar-r-ro, pst, pst, pst!" said Blarney, still keeping his face to the Big White Bulldog.

"Well," said the Big White Bulldog to himself, "if he is as strong as he is loud he will surely try to hurt me if I try to fight him." So he put his tail between his legs and went back into the house.

Blarney stood silently and looked after him for awhile. His eyes became big again. The fur on his back came down and his tail became silky smooth again. Then he began to MEOW very loudly and began to walk home. He turned the corner and came up to Mr. Nut Brown Squirrel.

"Did the Big White Bulldog bite you?" asked Mr. Nut Brown Squirrel.

"No!" said Blarney, "because I said, 'Ps-s-st, br-ar-ro, ps-st!'" And he walked on 'til he came to the Big Green Grasshopper.

"Didn't the Big White Bulldog bite you?" asked the Big Green Grasshopper.

"No!" said Blarney, "because I said, 'Ps-s-st, br-ar-ro, ps-st!'" and he walked right on home saying, "MEOW, MEOW, MEOW!"

He went into his house and said to his mother, "Mommy, I met a Big White Bulldog but he didn't bite me because I said 'Ps-st, ps-st, br-rar-o, ps-st.'"

And his mommy was very proud of him. His daddy was proud of him. His brothers and sisters were very proud of him. They thought he was the bravest kitten in all the world and no one every minded after that no matter how loudly he said "MEOW, MEOW, MEEOW!"

THE END

NOTE: We found this little story typed on the back of several carbon copies of old letters I had written. However, I have no memory whatsoever of having written this little story. This is unusual since I usually remember whatever I have written. Nor have I been in the habit of copying other writers' work. Nevertheless, there are places in the manuscript where words or phrases are X'ed out and replaced by others. This I was in the habit of doing. On the basis of this evidence I decided that I must have written the little story and I therefore reproduce it here. Should I be mistaken, should the story actually have been written by someone else I offer in advance my apology for cribbing it to whomever he or she might have been.

About the Author

George List at age 96.

GEORGE LIST is best known as an ethnomusicologist and folklorist. However, during a very long life (this book is being published during his 97th year) he occasionally wrote fiction, the bulk of which is being presented in this volume. The diverse items of fiction which it contains were written, and some rewritten, in periods ranging from 1928 through 2008. He has been blind since 1977 and much of what is published here was written after he had lost his sight.

List was born on February 9, 1911, in Tucson, Territory of Arizona a year and five days before Arizona became the forty-eighth state in the union. In 1934 he married Eve Ehrlichman who had just received the Diploma in Piano from the Julliard School of Music. Their marriage lasted until her death during its sixty-seventh year. They had one child, a son, Michael, a practicing veterinarian in Bloomington who died prematurely at age fifty-seven.

List graduated from Tucson High School at age fifteen, the youngest in a class of 155 and the tenth in scholarship. He would have done better as a scholar but at age thirteen he discovered girls. Being delayed by the Great Depression, the Second World War and the necessity of making a living as he went he secured the Diploma in Flute from the Julliard School of Music in 1933, the B.S. and the M.A. in Music Education from Teachers College, Columbia University in 1941 and 1945 respectively, and the Ph.D. in Music Theory and Composition from Indiana University in 1954.

For a generation after he graduated from the Julliard School of Music he was active as an instructor, flutist, conductor and composer of our Western music. During this period he was director for three years of a music school for children in the impoverished Kips Bay region of Manhattan; conducted and taught children's ensembles, two Jewish bands, a Hungarian band, a Croatian tamburitza orchestra and a Lithuanian mandolin orchestra for the International Workers Order, a fraternal organization in New York City; and taught instrumental music and conducted orchestras and bands from the forth grade through high school for four public school districts in the state of New York, mostly part time. After securing his M.A. he was a member of the music faculty of Colorado College for a year, of the University of Wyoming for a summer and of Miami University of Ohio for seven years. In addition to teaching courses at Colorado College he conducted chorus, orchestra and band and at Miami University an a cappella chorus.

He was employed for two years as a flutist by the Federal Music Project, WPA in New York City where he performed in chamber music, theater orchestra, symphony orchestra and at the weekly Composers Forums. While teaching at Colorado College he was also a member of the Denver and Colorado Springs Symphony Orchestras. At Miami University he participated in yearly joint flute and piano recitals with his wife, Eve, who also was a member of the music faculty of Miami University.

He published compositions for piano, flute and piano, women's voices, men's voices, mixed chorus and band. His compositions and manuscript include those for piano, organ, voice and piano, women's voices, mixed chorus, woodwind trio, woodwind quintet, string quartet, band and symphony orchestra. His symphonic satire, Marche O'Malley, was first performed by the Eastman-Rochester Symphony Orchestra under Howard Hanson in 1947 and his string quartet by the Berkshire String Quartet, the faculty quartet of Indiana University, in 1951.

After securing the Ph.D. he joined the staff and faculty of Indiana University and moved into the fields of ethnomusicology and folklore. At IU he was director of the Archives of Traditional Music, an archive of recordings of folk, tribal and oriental art music (1954-76); founded and edited a journal, The Folklore and Folk Music Archivist (1958-68); and taught as lecturer in music, lecturer in anthropology, and Associate Professor and Professor of Folklore. In 1966 he founded the Inter-American program in Ethnomusicology within the Folklore Department and was its director until he retired in 1976. This program offered graduate degrees in folklore with an emphasis on ethnomusicology.

During his tenure at IU he recorded the music and researched the folklore of the Hopi Indians of northern Arizona (1960 and 1963); that of the Coste-ños, the inhabitants of the Caribbean Littoral of Colombia (1964, 1965, 1968 and 1970); and the folk harp music of the Ecuadorian highlands and the songs of the Jíbaro and the Low Land Quechua Indians of the Ecuadorian Amazon (1965). He published three books and sixty articles, the bulk of which were concerned with ethnomusicology and folklore. All three books and eighteen of his articles were published after he had lost his sight. One book and several articles were translated into Spanish and reprinted in South America. He was the recipient of a number of fellowships and grants including a Fulbright-Hays Fellowship and a Senior Fellowship from the National Endowment for the Humanities.

List suffered from glaucoma and for that reason was deferred from service in the Second World War. At age thirty-nine he had an operation on both eyes. He was then only able to read with one slightly damaged eye and his sight slowly deteriorated until he became blind a few months after he retired in 1976.

The Archive of Traditional Music and the Ethnomusicology Program are still flourishing. The latter is now part of the Department of Folklore and Ethnomusicology. Those who studied with him hold or have held positions at the Library of Congress, the Smithsonian Institution, Indiana University, the University of Maryland, the University of Maine, Indiana University of Pennsylvania, the University of Illinois, the University of Missouri at Saint Louis, the University of California at Berkley and the University of California at Los Angeles. At this date (2008) a number of his former students are also retired.

About the Back Cover

The comic picture appearing on the back cover, *Pastorale: Cow Snorting at Daisy*, was one of several I painted for the entertainment of the younger children at a summer camp where I was music counselor in 1933. The next year I married but found that my newly acquired wife was unwilling for me to hang the painting, still unframed, on our also newly acquired living room wall. She eventually relented sufficiently to permit me to hang the painting, still unframed, on the bathroom wall. Finally, two years later, I came home on my birthday and found the painting, now attractively framed, hanging on our living room wall.

Printed in the United States
202838BV00002B/316-348/P